MAN IN THE MIST

CHERIE ROBERSON

For information contact cherieroberson.com

ISBN 979-8-9864506-1-2
e-book ISBN 979-8-9864506-0-5

Cover design by Lena Roberson

Edited by Megan Montgomery

THIS IS FOR RIC.
THE STORY BEGINS AND ENDS WITH YOU.
~ALWAYS~

ONE

Raey camped in front of the television under a fleece blanket, clutching warm chai tea in her *Keep Calm and Teach On* mug. She grabbed the largest of the four oatmeal cookies from the plate on her ottoman. Ten seconds in the microwave had revived the store-bought cookies to a fake freshness. When she hit unmute on the TV remote, carousing flooded the room. Voices readied to ring in another year. A sea of people huddled close to loved ones while she sat alone. Millions of eyes focused on the ball in Times Square as she lowered her eyelids from the crystal kaleidoscope to stare hard at a leather cover on the end table, embossed with *Mr. and Mrs. Davenport*. She relinquished her chai and cookie and cradled her wedding gift from Josh. It crackled upon opening. She read the word "Princess," and Josh's low timbre filtered through her head. Her finger traced his markings, forming large optimistic loops and handwriting strangely neat for a doctor.

Our Wedding Day

Dear Princess,
    Soon you will become my Mrs. Davenport. It's a dream

come true for me, getting married to you today! In this journal, I hope to pen a note to you each day. Hang on to your hat and my hand for this wild ride. See you at the altar for the beginning of our ever after.

I love you always,
Josh

Raey's eyes drifted to the memory framed on the wall in front of her. Her five-foot ten confidence had soared in the elegance of her silk-chiffon trumpet wedding gown. Her blond hair fell in soft, natural waves just below her shoulders, just as she always wore it with Josh. She had felt exquisite, accenting it with a thin silver-beaded, clear-cut rhinestone headband. Sun-kissed highlights glowed along with her glossy smile, beaming across her oval face. The off-the-shoulder, v-neck, lace bodice augmented her small chest the best that padding could. The sleek skirt hugged her small waist and gradually flared from her hip to a short lace trimmed train. Even walking barefoot down her sandy aisle, she had felt like a million bucks.

Josh, clad in a black tuxedo and blue bow tie, hugged her with mischievous eyes and a wide smile, despite the sweat that dripped down his forehead at their beachside wedding six years ago.

A worn photo slipped from the journal to her lap—their first trip to the Fairy Glen in Skye, Scotland. The shutter snapped the moment he engulfed her in his arms and smashed his lips against her rosy cheeks. She gazed upon the stubble outlining his square chin, cheek lifted in a grin, and the brown waves hiding beguiling eyes. Raey's heart skipped a beat when she tucked the photo in the back between the pages Josh penned three years into their marriage.

I have news. Let's talk tonight over wine and pasta.

Raey quickly flipped past that page and landed on a note Josh wrote to her on their first day of living on Skye together.

MESMERIZING—Both You and Skye.

The program host beckoned her back to the screen. "Folks, we have seconds left until we turn the page. You can feel it. You can hear it. People are ready for a new year. Let's get ready to count it down together."

The blanket of smiles snuggled closer for the final ten second descent into a new year full of hopes, dreams, challenges, and changes.

"Here we go folks." At the host's signal, their united voices roared an animated slow-motion countdown.

10

9

8

It's been a year and a half since cancer stole him from me.

7

6

5

I need to stop the blur of trudging through this knee-deep emotional sludge.

4

3

2

1

It's time to get on with life.

"Welcome to a New Year!" The crowd said goodbye to the

passing year, serenading one another with the few words they knew of the yearly resurrected "Auld Lang Syne."

When voices belted "New York, New York," Raey froze wide-eyed, hypnotized by a call for a fresh start that invaded the recesses of her heart like confetti fluttering from the sky. *A new start? How?* The frayed edges of a dare fluttered through her thoughts. *Wake up in a new town.* She forced it into focus. *Can I make it there? Without him?* She clung to the challenge as ethereal as a deal forged with the Fairy Queen.

As kisses, hugs, cheers, and well wishes mingled with Frank Sinatra's baritone crooning, she pulled the photograph from the journal by its crumpled corners. His cheek blurred slightly from the frequent caress of her fingerprints. Drawing it closer, she zoomed in to scrutinize her face. The soft, creamy blues and greens of the faded background enhanced the whites of her wide smile and her beaming eyes. Her crinkled nose and rosy cheeks, taut with glee when he settled his lips on her moments before the shutter closed, clicked the moment back to life.

As the syrupy voice floated over the airwaves, she focused on the Raey from a distant lifetime ago. Her chin, tilted to the sun, boasted a playful grin that captured joy and peace and fearlessness, spilling across expectant, vibrant eyes. Standing tall with one hand on her hip and the other wrapped around Josh's neck, the shroud of mist hovering over the mountains didn't dampen her outlook on the day. The person she admired in that photo sat lost to her now, empty of the energy to dream about tomorrows.

In her world, love invited loss. At seventeen, her parents' death struck her with a pain so severe, a paralysis so crippling, that taking her next breath seemed a grueling choice at times. Losing Josh, the love of her life, dealt her a death blow. But here she breathed, among the living, learning to walk through life all over once again.

Exposure. Adjust my exposure.

She jumped to her feet and grabbed her laptop. She wouldn't be leaving today as Sinatra suggested, but she would follow his lead. Sitting on the edge of her ottoman under the diffused glow of the lamp and TV, she searched round trip flights to Inverness to depart the week after school let out for the summer.

Stalling, her cursor hovered above SUBMIT. Pinching her lips together with her fingers, she sifted through the conflicting voices in her head. Fear of making such a hasty decision shook her insides. Her nervous legs bounced her laptop up and down. Her best friend would throw caution flags at this rash decision, but Brenda's frown would be tomorrow's concern. Gulping through a dry throat despite the tea she'd been sipping, she clasped her hands together to still her trembling fingers and gather her resolve. The clock ticked the seconds away, echoing through the room and mocking her wavering. *The only voice I need to listen to right now is my own. Good or bad, I am going to Skye.*

Her countdown to a decision was a countdown to a life, to breaking free of living trapped in this trance. Blood rapped hard in her ears as doubt wrestled with determination in her chest. She steadied her hands and the strong beat of her heart, and then clicked submit, exhaling a deep breath. *Start spreading the news. I'm leaving….*

* * *

Reluctant to share news of her trip, Raey beelined to the fridge for her coffee creamer without a word or a glance at Brenda.

Still in her pajamas, Brenda chomped an oatmeal cookie at the counter and tilted her head at Raey's lack of greeting. She pulled Raey close for a quick hug and whispered, "Happy New Year." Placing a warning finger across her lips, Brenda pointed in the direction of the living room. Her boyfriend, Brian, crashed on the couch under a throw blanket, fully dressed. Brenda chuckled, "He wanted a little nap before driving home."

"A good night?" Raey asked and turned toward the counter, beginning her morning ritual at the Keurig machine.

"We danced way past the midnight countdown. So fun."

"I'm glad."

"Thank goodness you loaned me your comfy heels."

"Definitely."

"Brian's best friend on the police force and his girlfriend came, too. You've heard me talk about him before, right?"

"Great."

"The music stopped at one o'clock, and then the restaurant offered a bite to eat. I'm glad he bought us tickets to that type of party. Safest way to go, just staying at the restaurant."

"Uh-huh."

"I wish you had come."

"I'm glad I didn't." Coffee gurgled from the Keurig.

"The earth swallowed us up just as the Uber dropped us off."

"Hmm."

"Raey?"

"Yeah."

"Sweetie, what's up?"

Raey rotated to face Brenda. Words welled from deep inside. "I bought a ticket to Skye for the month of June."

Brenda smacked the orange juice container from mid-pour

to the counter. Raccoon eyes from sleeping in mascara fixed on Raey. "You did what?"

"I need a kickstart. Mind, body, and heart." Pulling last night's gumption from her gut, she waited for Brenda's response like a runner listening for a starter pistol to propel her forward.

"But what about your summer vacation?"

"Our summer will be different this year."

"It certainly will."

Raey spread her arms wide and pointed at the beach eight steps off her deck as she said, "An entire month of not competing with the vacationers migrating to the sunny beaches of Wilmington, North Carolina." The positive spin wasn't working on Brenda.

During high school, Raey and Brenda stretched summers as long as possible on Carolina Beach. When they waited tables for tourists on the boardwalk, they reveled in the added benefit that their work had them sun-soaked until sunset. They had unconsciously agreed upon a daily plan to hang out together when they were not scheduled at the diner: sunning on the golden sand and swimming in the sapphire water until phone bells beckoned their retreat to family dinner, unless rare permission allowed them to watch the sun wane behind pink, red, and orange watercolor streaks. They fell asleep expecting to do it all again the next day.

"Hmm. This doesn't sound like you."

"But it is me." Raey tapped her chest.

"You don't want to go across town for a New Year's Eve celebration, but you will fly across the Atlantic?"

"To dance with strangers? I want to go where my heart last danced."

"It's oddly impulsive for you?"

"Impulsive decisions are not my style. But I want to do this. To visit those places that I loved. It's weird to say this–but maybe they'll light a fuse inside."

"Places that maybe you both loved?"

"Well, of course. Josh loved the land as much as me. I'm not chasing after your brother there. I'm chasing after myself."

"Don't you think this trip could cause a bunch of extra pain? It's where you found out he was sick. That's the dream you had to leave, months before he died. I'm worried–"

"And I'm going," Raey interrupted with a reproach in her voice that startled even her.

She swiped away tears flooding her eyes. She couldn't respond. Doubt took hold as her eyes caught Brenda's, holding a suspended challenge. When her throat relaxed, she pounded her fist on the counter, like she was nailing her decision into finality for both Brenda and herself. "This is a fight for my sanity."

"It just might be more like your undoing."

Raey's eyes flared before she cradled her forehead in her palms, exhausted already by the conversation.

"I'm not trying to get you to change your mind. Really, I'm not." Brenda gently tugged Raey's hands from her forehead. "Why there?"

Raey lifted her lashes and confessed, "I've been hanging by a thread inside since Josh died."

"You're doing a great job. You just don't see how far you've come."

"No, I'm not. Even you can't see it, and you're the closest person to me."

"I see you. I do." Brenda rested her hands on top of Raey's in assurance. "I see how hard you've worked to talk about Josh without crying. Now you're back to teaching kiddos with full steam. Your bit of laughter at the television the other night did my heart good. It's been a long time since I've witnessed it."

"From the outside, I look like I've gotten back to normal–work, shopping, walks on the beach."

"You're doing it."

"But no one sees inside. I'm numb. I want my joy and fearlessness back."

"You're working on it. I know you are. You might need to fake it until you make it."

"I'm tired of maintaining a fiction of doing well. I need to find my new life. My life without Josh."

"I'm with you. Some days since my brother died, I get overwhelmed with sadness–not having him to share life with me, with you, with us. Maybe leaning into the pain will help. Maybe more than toughing it out and stuffing it down so that we look like we're doing better."

"Skye was the last place I felt truly alive. I need to find that again."

Brenda tilted her chin, asking Raey to clarify.

"Your support day in and day out, month after month, year after year, helped me cope with my parents' deaths, and now, more than ever, I'm hoping you'll understand."

"This past year and a half has been hard for us. I'm lucky to have you. We don't need to pretend with one another. It's okay to be sad. You've journeyed through this pain of loss before. This deep loss is new to me. I couldn't have found peace without your strength, without you being close. You know what you have to do. I just wish it didn't mean going so far away."

"Thanks for not seeing me as a problem to solve," Raey said.

Brenda edged around the counter and fully wrapped Raey in her arms. "Oh Sweetie, you'll get there. You will."

Between sobs, Raey mumbled, "I want…. No. I need my life back."

"If it gets to be too much, I'm right here. Always."

* * *

Navigating her venture to Skye from the Inverness Airport proved easier than she'd imagined, except for the last hour. She rolled her car window down, the night chill battled her droopy eyes. An hour before midnight, she pulled into the parking lot of Shelter Hill Guest House.

"Well, there ye are, lass! We've been waiting for you," the owner bellowed from the door.

Raey startled, pulling her luggage from the back seat. "Oh, hi there. It took me longer than I expected on those twisty and dipping roads."

A hint of orange swirled with a mixture of thyme and rosemary hit her upon stepping into her home for the next month.

"You're wise to take yer time. I'm glad for ye that the roads weren't misty tonight. For a second, we thought Nessie swallowed ye up."

He laughed at his own joke and took her suitcase, setting it near the steps. Raey couldn't help laughing with him. "My name's Finlay, lass. Let me give ye a quick show around."

"That would be lovely." Raey admired his full head of white hair and matching trim beard in the dim light of the entry.

All was quiet at the late hour. No guests roamed the floor. Sconces lit their way to the dining area adjacent to the lounge.

"This here's the dining room. Breakfast is served early at six, closes at nine." Finlay's eyes locked on her, but he didn't meet her eyes. "Start yer day getting some nourishment on those long bones, lass."

Raey glanced down at her thin form as if it were foreign to her and nodded. She surveyed the set table, complete with white rose bouquets, tartan placemats, red floral china with matching tea pots, and embroidered linen tablecloths.

"Make yerself at home any time of day in the lounge." Finlay guided her into the room. A flickering fire invited her to warm her hands at the smooth and gentle curves of a large river stone fireplace, flanked by dark cherry-stained, floor-to-ceiling bookshelves. A national portfolio of classics lined the shelves with the likes of *Dr. Jekyll and Mr. Hyde, Treasure Island, Rob Roy*, and world-renowned Scots–Sir Walter Scott, Tobias Smollett, and Sir Arthur Conan Doyle. Diana Gabaldon's *Outlander* series spanned an entire shelf. An elaborate red and yellow crest with the surname MacNicol hung above a carved-wood mantelpiece, not the owners' last name.

She meandered under a wide archway into the conservatory that boasted wall to wall uncurtained windows. One deep brown and three beige leather couches, which could comfortably accommodate ten guests, circled a glass coffee table, displaying a tall vase of red and yellow carnations. The lights of Portree twinkled in the distance and the moonlight glinted off the bay. From her vantage point, she counted three patios which allowed guests to enjoy distinct features of the gardens.

Finlay pointed to a terrace in the corner of their property at the edge of the bay. "That patio fills up early this time of year. Best view of the bay if ye ask us."

"It's stunning. It must be fabulous in the light of day with the mountains behind it." Raey hid a yawn when Finlay turned back to the check-in area.

"I bet yer ready for a few winks. Here's a wee dram to help with that." Finlay winked and handed her a small whisky bottle and a key. Picking up her luggage, he said, "Follow me up the stairs."

"Oh, no, I'll carry that," Raey said.

"Oh no, ye don't. My wife says I'm as stubborn as I am strong." Finlay patted his belly. "And ye can see I am strong."

Raey ran her hand along the polished pine paneling as they climbed the thick, scarlet carpeted steps, watching Finlay's shoulders and hips tip from side to side. Mountain photographs lined the entire hallway to her room, probably taken by a local hiking enthusiast.

"Tomorrow, you'll meet my lovely bride, Maisrie. She's the real glint behind the shine of this place." Finlay set her luggage at her door and took a deep breath. "She'll be up early to make ye a braw breakfast."

"Thank you so much," Raey nodded goodnight.

"Sleep well, lass."

Raey plopped her suitcase on the bed of the large en suite room. Peeking inside the mini fridge, she smiled at finding cream and sugar. Turning around the room, taking it all in, her wired excitement faded when she thought of Josh loving this place.

Raey slumped against the window seat wall and gazed at the moonlit mountains across the bay on the Isle of Rasaay. *Mesmerizing.* Reminded of Josh's words and his love for this misty isle, she jumped to unpack his belongings that she couldn't live without, not even for one month. She brushed her fingers over the *Dr. Davenport* engraved in the stone nameplate Josh had kept on his office desk and set it on the nightstand. She carried Josh within her every day, but his keepsakes bolstered her determination to rediscover her joy. Shortly before he died, she lay at his side. He'd tightened his grip on her hand, and through a barely audible, quavering voice, begged her not to lose her sparkle. He'd needed to hear her promise him. She'd agreed, mostly to ease his urgent concern. But on this first night in Skye, the weight of her memories were crushing her. *I'm trying, Josh.*

She set his blue Duke baseball hat over the bedpost, ready for her frequent hikes. Unwrapping his stethoscope from her Patagonia sweater, she secured it on a hook next to the door. It had hung beside their front door since the day they returned to the States upon resigning his residency in Skye. It was the embodiment of the life they built, a life in which he had often sacrificed sleep for the sanity of sharing movies, hikes, baseball games, concerts, and beach visits. Her tired mind and body longed for his tenacity to make this month all she hoped it to be.

Pushing the ruby rosette throw pillows that matched the kettle and lounger to the other side of the bed, she flopped down. After the lonely, draining drive and now facing her first night sleeping alone in Skye, the full strength of reality hit her. She missed Josh. She stretched out on top of the down comforter and let her tired heart and head sink into the thick pillows. Picking up Josh's journal from where she had set it on the nightstand, she opened to the last entry. She had lain at Josh's side as he penned it. ***I love you now and forever. Sparkle through the rest of your life.*** She wasn't living up to his admonition just yet. She'd need to read his words over and over throughout this trip.

Sparkle...She had smiled at him as she read that last

13

sentence over his shoulder, and he gave his last smile and a wink back at her. She told him she loved him. Then she spoke the toughest words she'd ever spoken, telling him it was okay for him to go. He nodded and closed his eyes. His tears flowed as she held him through the night. He never opened his eyes again. Two days later, laying in her arms, he stopped breathing.

Bone weary from the trip and her memories, she closed her eyes and relaxed her shoulders, exhaling the sadness. She said a prayer for strength to conquer her days ahead alone, hoping to set aside the doubt creeping in over coming to Skye.

Raey woke the next morning to dark skies and Josh's journal, still lying at her side. The weather almost deterred her plan to take a quick run, but living on Skye taught her that lower-than-normal morning temperatures would slowly rise and cheat the high winds of their bite. The faint sun fighting through the clouds lured Raey to pull herself from her mental quicksand. Like yanking off a band-aid, she whipped the covers off her body, plunging herself into the cold air and dressing in a hurry.

Her hunger pangs and growling stomach urged Raey to detour to the dining room for sustenance before embarking on her morning run. Surrounded by other guests on the patio overlooking Portree Bay, she nibbled on toast and sipped a warm cup of coffee with heavy cream, while she watched the fog roll off the water like a floating ghost. Birds, banded together on the shore in the mist, scooted frantically toward the water, leery of her intrusion on the edge of the terrace. Waves crashing onto the low tide shore danced across the sand, forcing the skittish birds to retrace their steps through bubbly foam collecting at their feet.

"Can I get ye something more than that wee bit, lass?" A sweet voice startled her. "I'm Maisrie. Finlay told me ye arrived quite late last night. I hope you could rest." A petite woman with short, curly, salt and pepper hair in a blue jean jacket bent to look her in the eye.

"It's nice to meet you, Maisrie," Raey said. "Your place is lovely. And your breakfast is exquisite." Raey glanced at their view of the bay. "I'm going to go for a quick run, and then I'll grab more. It smells so good."

"It'll be here for ye. Enjoy." Maisrie's ringlets bounced as she skipped among the guests in grand style, offering smiles, answering questions, and taking orders.

Leaving her empty mug on the table, Raey climbed the winding staircase to a second story overlook of Loch Portree. Arriving late last night in the dark, she hadn't noticed that the eighteenth-century farmhouse was painted peach or that four flags whipped in the wind–Scottish, American, and French, and one she didn't recognize. Later, she'd explore the impeccable grounds, complete with arches, statues, and a winter garden.

A run would stave off the energy loss that her body suffered from jet lag, but Raey needed to run for much more. She ran for focus–to focus on pounding the sand and rocks of this land that sifted through her heart, to focus on filling her lungs with the cool air rolling across mountains that had once proven her tenacity, to focus on the thrill when an entire flock of shorebirds soar in flight.

Life's twisted turns often propelled her strongest runs, as if she were on a wild race toward a desperate escape, but not today. The drag of her tangled, wet, wind-blown hair, the damp sheen collecting on her jacket, and her running shoes' sand-clogged soles mocked her spirits. Her slow start never picked up the pace. Every sluggish step begat the next down a long stretch until stopping became the next natural move.

Raey sheltered on a sand dune between patchy vegetation, hunkering in the sand like a lost turtle hatchling seeking light for direction. Readjusting her headband against the rushing wind, she wrapped her arms under her thighs and rested her cheek against her knees. Soothed by the rhythm of the waves beating the shore, she closed her eyes to the coast and opened her mind's eye to majestic moments on the Isle.

Twirling her wedding rings on her finger, she contemplated a plan for the days ahead. Guilt rose like bile in her throat at forming a future without Josh, the underlying cause for her morning restlessness. She couldn't exist on memories. They would never coalesce to form the passionate life she came here to regain. No matter how much she craved her life with Josh, he was not part of her present. She'd be alone on Skye. When she planned this trip in North Carolina, she knew that, but she hadn't expected to be overwhelmed by how wrong it felt to explore the Isle without him. Was she mistaken, thinking that Skye could pull her from her numb existence? Angry for allowing confusion to wreck her sensibility, she willed herself to shake her doubt and find her purpose. Slipping her rings from her finger, she traced the remaining vestiges of their love: an engraved promise under the band. *My love lives with you.* She placed the solitary princess cut diamond and band back on her finger, along with five years of memories tethered to a longing for what would never be.

She groaned at her shifting shadow and the persistent goosebumps along her legs and arms which proved she sat longer than intended.

Raey etched the initials R.D. in the sand with her fingertips, drew his J.D. below hers, and surrounded them with a heart, an instinctive act. In the early days of their dating, Raey penned them inside the cover of her notebook like a twenty-year-old junior high school girl. One time, her notebook dropped from the couch to the carpet, open to a page of her doodles, and Josh acted like a knight in shining armor and presented it to her like a bouquet, proclaiming with a grandiose British accent, "For you, my lady." Her breathing stopped as she caught his frozen stare at the page, spying his last name added to the end of her first name. He had briefly wrestled with his response but then winked and said, "It'll be our little secret."

Now, halfway through this second year of seeing his face only in her dreams, people expected her to be beyond this stage of reliving the past, but these moments paralyzed her. Her faraway eyes and forced smile told the world she still longed for him, a need beyond her control. Could Skye's beguiling nature yank her from this wretched state and compel a brash and brave new launch that she couldn't muster on her own?

She scratched two lines in the sand with her heels as she stretched to stand. A deep voice, so reminiscent of Josh's, emitted a half-suppressed laugh. "What are you waiting for?"

Raey startled and her eyes widened. *Coming to Skye may have been your worst move yet. Now you're hearing Josh's voice.* She listened for the voice again, but the wind must have stolen it. At the same time she yearned for it to be possible for him to be with her, she chastised herself for the wish. Her heart pounded in her chest. When her slow glance revealed lyme grass waving in the wind, her shoulders relaxed. *Raey, you need to get a grip.*

Sand kicked up near her foot, and she jolted when she glanced to the other side, spying familiar Keen boots, blue jeans, a gray Henley, and a charcoal skull cap. She stopped breathing. Two feet from her, elbows propped back in the sand, taking in the ocean view, sat the five-o'clock shadow version of the love she lost. The crinkles at the corner of his playful eyes smiled back at her when he turned his head.

"Morning, Princess. You look delightful," Josh said, crossing his long legs stretched out on the sand.

As if struck by lightning, Raey's head jerked back, and she kicked toward the figure in the sand, crab crawling away from him, and then stood. Her muddled mind raced through the possibilities. This couldn't be real. She wasn't delusional. She gaped as his chest rose and fell against his cotton shirt and his Adam's apple moved up and down.

Standing slowly, he inched closer, and the intensity of his gaze transfixed her. He ran his soft fingers along her jaw, along her chin, down her throat to her neck. Locking his eyes on hers, he tugged at her heart necklace he'd given her for their first anniversary, resting his palm over it for a few seconds. Was it his breath that brushed against her neck? To have Josh this close, flesh and blood, overwhelmed her.

If she had fallen into the middle of a very real dream, she wanted to enjoy every minute. She glided her fingers along the prickly edge of his chin and gasped. This certainly didn't feel like a dream. His eyes followed her palm as she dared to caress his thick shoulder and massage the bicep of this lionized bronze statue. His strength, his calm beneath her fingers, comforted her. The desire to stroke his arm again filled her chest.

Her breath hitched in her throat at seeing Josh healthy and vibrant once again, and her words stumbled through a breathy, quavering voice, "So do you. So alive. So healthy. So strong."

Josh slid her palm down his sinewy arm, resting it in his hand. Tugging at her fingers linked with his, he pulled her to his chest. She wrapped her arms around his neck and rested against him, wanting time that could tear him away from her to stop. She tangled her fingers in his wavy locks. Standing on her tiptoes, she locked eyes with him, and they both gave in to the natural consequence of being in one another's world. The tip of his nose sunk into her skin. She closed her eyes to the kiss she'd ached to have one more of. His lips captured hers, and she pressed into his, holding him to her. This was the stuff of her dreams.

Still savoring his lips, she whispered into them, "I love you."

"And I love you. I always have. I always will," Josh breathed into her.

When her hijacked brain returned, she asked, "What are you? Um, I mean, how are you here?"

He held her hand as he led them to sit in the sand.

"Some call me a ghost," he said through measured strains.

"But ghosts aren't real," she said, more a question than a statement.

He shrugged his shoulders and raised his eyebrows.

A tingle rose along the back of her neck and goosebumps layered her arms. Her imagination worked overtime to figure out how Josh could be sitting next to her, speaking to her, touching her. The crawl of fear up her spine she was supposed to have when a ghost presents itself didn't arise, only a wanting of more of him.

This moment in the mist could end as quickly as the fog rose, so she took a deep cleansing breath and then sat still with this gift, wanting to glue the warmth of his touch to her memory.

Moments later, when her breathing relaxed to a consistent rhythm, his first words rewound in her mind. *What are you waiting for? How far gone am I to converse with an imaginary Josh?*

Grateful for this moment with him beside her, she answered, "I'm not sure what I'm waiting for."

"But you are." His careful voice pressed her to interrogate her own thoughts.

She slid her hand from his and crossed her arms to rub her shoulders, suddenly chilled again. *Was she spineless, tolerating push-back from a figment of her imagination?*

"You can't wallow Princess." His glance implored her to regard the initials she just finished outlining with a heart.

"You, a ghost, are accusing me of something you know nothing about. I'm among the living but barely living." Welled frustration flooded from her.

"I know you. Don't ignore what you're scared of." He pulled her hand back into his.

"What do you think you know?"

"Your parents' deaths strengthened you. At your core, you are stronger than you imagine you can be."

"I can't fight through the pain of loss again."

"You can, Babe. I believe in you. It's not easy, but you're a fighter." A tight squeeze of her hand summoned her to believe him.

Her brown eyes pleaded for him to know her struggle. "I can't envision this life without you. And this gift of having you sitting here with me makes no sense, either."

Josh scooted closer. The warmth of his fingers wrapped her hip. She fought against the urge to grab him and seal her lips to his again. How could her hallucination unleash such need? She released a captured breath and sank further in the sand.

"I'm glad you are here. But why is this happening?" *How easily my mind dupes me into believing this is all real.*

"You're in Skye. Tell me what's going on."

"I can't calm the storm inside."

"Babe, I'm so sorry. Talk to me."

"My grief has become a very close friend these last couple of years," she said. His brows lifted in a grimace.

"What do you mean, a friend?"

"Missing you hurts like hell. Holding it close connects me to you."

"Our life together connected us."

"My grief reminds me I loved you deeply, and you loved me back the same. It causes me to miss you and that causes me to remember moments with you. That's what I want. I don't want to forget any part of you, of our life together. Years from now, I don't want to have to look at pictures to remember our love."

"I wish you didn't know this deep pain. I hate being the cause of it. I wanted to live a full life with you, to be healthy for you, travel the world with you, have babies with you, fight with you and make up with you. Give you the full life you deserve."

"There's never a happy ending. You're still gone."

He drew her chin to his, and his lips softly kissed hers. "But you will always hold all my love in your heart."

Josh gazed at the spotty fog encroaching over the waves, crashing at the shoreline. Out of habit, he bit the corner of his bottom lip, not wanting his words to sound like a lecture.

"I may not have all the right words, but I'm here for you," he said, searching her eyes for understanding.

"If you're not real, how can you be here for me?"

Here for me? She clenched her jaw at the unfairness of life taking him from her, wrecking their plans. Rationally, she understood no one was to blame, but her anger rolled like a powerful wave. She dug her fingers under the sand, watching the wind wrap an amber brown curl around his ear. The object of her very longing sat next to her, gorgeous and healthy. Raey acquiesced to his truth wrapped neatly as an interrogation, knowing he's the only one that could understand.

"You asked what I'm waiting for? I'm trying to survive. I have to *survive* without you, but I don't know if I will *live* without you."

"You will. It may take longer than you want it to, but you will get back to a life you love living."

"I can't let go of you."

Her shoulders slumped, and she closed her eyes, waiting for his ardent admonition. When seagulls screeched, as if calling her name, she opened her eyes to face the man she begged to meet each night in her dreams, but he had vanished.

Raey searched the descending fog for his form. She dropped her head between her bent knees, smacking the sand with her palms.

Why did I allow myself to entertain his presence as reality? Trying to get life to imitate heart? I've stepped back onto the slippery slope of despair.

She ran from the sand dune and her loss of sanity, her legs carrying her to the B&B. The speed of her feet mirrored her desperation to remove herself from his loss—this having him by her side, only to lose him once again.

I'm waiting for you to come back to me! That's what I'm waiting for.

TWO

The next day, a forlorn lethargy replaced her traveler's gumption. Raey woke later than she had planned and peered at the empty left side of the bed, a habit that time didn't alter. Josh's absence clung to her like moss on a shady hillside. Her chest ached for the warmth of his touch on her skin and the brush of his brown locks across the bridge of her nose when they kissed. Yesterday's encounter usurped her eagerness to venture out to the places on her list. Today would require two cups of coffee and even more gathering of her will. Stalling under the covers, she lamented losing the best part of the day. Once, her days exploring the Isle of Skye with her husband had begun early with thick misty air, which later burned off to reveal clear blue skies wreathed in rainbows. If only the descending fog in her head would lift like that.

She altered the day's itinerary to include walking to Portree, finding a unique lunch spot, and meandering around the B&B to acquaint herself with her temporary home. Hiking boots secured as if expecting a serious day of trekking through the Highlands, she bemoaned the fact that she woke too late for the extensive buffet breakfast and to feast once again on the Royal Albert Old Country Roses china. The lingering coffee aroma summoned Raey from her room.

As Raey bounded down the carpeted steps, she turned the corner toward the glass sunroom and collided with a tall man about her age. His grip on her hips steadied her. Her palms clung to his muscular chest, and she surveyed the smooth hollow of his throat above his soft, blue, v-neck pullover. His eyes hesitated on her palms, and his lips curled up in a grin. She pushed off his chest, relinquishing the warmth that emanated from him, and rubbed at the heat creeping up her neck and into her face.

"I'm sorry. Are you alright?" the man asked, picking up her coat from the floor.

"Oh, yes, I'm fine." Raey pulled her eyes from his, only to fix them on his long, lean torso. She blushed even more.

"Great," the man said, raising a single thick, dark eyebrow. Whether his short, messy brown hair was intentional or due to speeding through his morning routine, it definitely worked for him.

"Just making my way to grab some coffee." Raey smiled, fiddled with her necklace, and took two steps back.

"Have a good day," the man said as he watched her all but run to the coffee table.

Raey sipped her coffee alone in the conservatory, on the lookout for the hosts, Finlay or Maisrie, to garner a bit of hiking guidance for her afternoon. The sidewalk paved a mile walk to downtown Portree, where she planned to explore the town and grab a bite to eat, but she hoped for a longer, less traveled trail for her return trek to the B&B. Taking in the expansive lawn, landscaped garden, and the bay stilled her nerves after her run-in at the bottom of the steps. Glancing to find no one behind the desk, she settled into a second cup of coffee and studied the birds at the feeders, fighting over food.

Deciding to ask a local in Portree about trails, she left her cup on the table, and set off for the day. Her heartbeat sped up when she spied the same handsome man she had crashed into, now standing behind the counter. She swiped her cheeks to erase the heat that rose once again from her throat. As she approached, his attentive eyes diverted to the paperwork on the desk. A few paces from the desk, she stumbled on the carpet and caught herself against the counter.

"Oh, hi. Thanks for dropping in again," the man chuckled.

Recovering her scattered wits, Raey laughed with him and averted a clumsy conversation by asking, "Oh, hi. Um, is Maisrie around?"

A wee lingering laugh remained hidden behind his smile.

"Gram's in the back clearing up the buffet with Gran'da. I'm Nic. Can I be of help with something?" He leaned his elbows on the wooden counter.

"Sure. I'm Raey Davenport. Do you know a moderate trail into town?"

Readily grabbing a map and highlighter from below the counter, Nic traced the route of a trail.

"I love to walk this route. It's a peaceful, mild hike around the headland overlooking Portree Bay. You'll get splendid views. I'll warn ye, though. It can get a wee bit rough and stony along the shoreline. When you turn inland, there's an ascent which gets steep for a short bit, but it's a good warm up for the legs." Nic leaned across the counter and peered down her legs to her boots. "Your legs look like you can master it." He winced at his awkward comment and averted her eyes by peering down at the map and rubbing the back of his neck. "Anything else I can help ye with?" Nic said, clicking the highlighter cap on and off.

She glued her eyes to the route he mapped but dared to glance at his thick, brown, textured hair which faded to the tan of his cheek and strong jawline.

"Any good lunch spots nearby you'd recommend?" She knew a couple from her years living there, but she sought his recommendations.

"Hmm, well," he gazed at her for a few long seconds, assessing what type of food she might eat, "I love to hang out at Café Ailm. It's a nice bistro that uses locally grown food."

"That sounds like something I'd love."

"Plus, it has a relaxing view to take in the loch. It won't eat up your pocketbook, either." She kept a keen eye on the small movements of his lips as he spoke. "And you get one heck of an espresso, if that's your thing."

"Mmm." She caught his eyes and hesitated to speak, so he would continue talking. His long eyelashes, the envy of every woman, intensified his azure eyes.

"I'm going into town this evening to catch a band. My friend has a gig at one of the pubs. Would you like to hear some local music?"

With him? A date? Nic's invitation caught her off-guard, ruffling her composure, and she couldn't respond.

He didn't give her time to think through a proper response before adding, "Dinna fash." He blew off any formality to his invite as he surveyed her trepidation. "Really, don't worry, but if you decide you might like to go, I'll drive ye. Meet here at the desk at eight. They start their first set at nine, but we're meeting for drinks ahead," he added nonchalantly. He plopped the highlighter into the pen container with a ping, signaling the conclusion of their conversation.

She answered with equally noncommittal cheer as she slid

the map off the counter, "Great. Thanks, Nic, for your help and the invite." With his easy, casual manner, reminiscent of the care Finlay showered on her at check in, he tipped his head and offered a polite smile. She caught herself glancing back once more before exiting the B&B.

As she stepped into the brisk air, a battle in her brain between caution and courage drummed to life. She loved listening to live music. It was something she and Josh had done often, especially when they traveled. The musical ambiance of a place soothed their feet, bodies, and souls at the end of a long day of adventures or struggles. A night of music would be a perfect balm for the start of her adventure.

Stop panicking. It's not a date.

Raey expected the music that evening at the harbor to be the culmination of her serene day. Exploring alone today, she glimpsed herself coming alive on Skye, putting one step in front of the other, the majesty of the terrain helping her heal.

Waiting alone in the foyer, she scanned the parking lot for Nic when quick footsteps tapped from behind. "How are you this evening?" Nic greeted. Raey caught his reflection in the glass door.

She turned around to take in blue jeans, a black leather jacket over a light gray turtleneck, and a crooked smile. "I'm doing well."

"Sorry, I'm late. I picked up a few things for Gram and needed to help Pops move some furniture."

"I just got here, so no worries."

"Well, then I'm glad I was late, so that I didn't miss you."

Raey's face flustered for a second when Nic offered her his arm. Quickly gathering her wits, she accepted the arm-in-arm escort to his Range Rover. Holding the door for her as she settled in, he said, "I'm glad you came."

She rubbed her arm. Being linked to another man disconcerted her. As soon as he settled into his seat and started the engine, she filled the quiet with constant chatter.

"I'm looking forward to the music this evening. Thanks for your lunch recommendation, by the way. They sure serve large portions at Café Ailm. I need to try their pizza next time I go. I ate my fish and chips as I walked the pier. Lots of yachts today. I peeked inside the rainbow of houses. If I stayed in one, I think I'd pick the pink one. The harbor was calm and the pinks and blue of the sky mirrored in the bay. I sat and watched the moored boats with a cup of coffee from the place you suggested. Then, I walked Scorrybreac Road to the trail and trekked the two-mile loop. Have you ever done that?" She glanced to take in his nod. "Of course you have. It was boggy in spots, but I love the pungent smell of damp earth. There's a stone memorial to the Nicolson clan. Well, it's not your clan, but anyway." Her throaty chortle raised the corner of Nic's mouth in a smile. "What a glorious day, but I'm ready to sit after all the walking. I walked the A87 directly back instead of the local trail you mentioned. Maisrie greeted me on the terrace with the most delicious caledonian cream." She squeezed her eyes shut and shook her head. "Yum."

Nic peered at her delight. "Good day, then?"

"Oh, yes. And I'm talking non-stop."

"Nervous?"

"Yeah, must be." Raey clasped her hands in her lap and gazed at her diamond wedding ring. When she glanced at Nic, level honesty caught her eyes.

With a quick tap of his palm to her shoulder, Nic said, "No need to be. My friends are all great."

A couple minutes later, she gathered her wits, fired him a nervous smile, and followed him into the loud, dark pub. His three friends waved them to their table, not surprised by her presence. After a round of handshakes, she sat next to the only other woman in their small group. Trying to disguise the feeling that she was an imposter, spending an evening among friends, she plastered a smile on her face, willed her shoulders to relax into her chair, and ordered a Strongbow when the waitress arrived.

Raey's current circumstances were almost foreign to her. The previous year, she sought solace in oblivion, tolerating only the barest social nourishment, often sitting silent in a room of people, conversing with the little energy she could muster, limping toward normalcy while keeping her eyes fixed on a distant past.

They surfed the menu, the waiter took their food orders, and the woman next to her drew her out with simple questions.

"Where are you from?" Rose asked.

"I'm from the States. I live on the east coast of North Carolina."

"What brings you to Skye?"

"I'm on vacation." She evaded the deeper truth and then turned the table. "Are you from Skye?"

"No, I'm actually from Glasgow. I moved here for a job. I'm a midwife. I see you're married."

"I was married for three years. My husband died of cancer nearly two years ago." Raey unconsciously grabbed her wedding rings.

"I'm sorry." Rose paused and then pointed with her thumb toward the head of the table. "That curly, red-bearded man, jawing away at the end of the table, is my husband. We met at university."

"He's a doctor?"

"He's an accountant for a local distillery. How long are you on holiday in Skye?"

"I'll be here for a month. Time to hike, visit the usual touristy spots and relax."

"How do you know Nic?"

"Well, I don't, really. I'm staying at his grandparents' B&B, and I literally ran into him today. He thought I'd enjoy the local music."

"Brilliant band. Nic's friend is the drummer."

The waiter arrived with their drinks, interrupting her answer. They toasted Slàinte Mhath as the band stepped on stage.

A night of drinks and music with Nic proved to be an easy balm, but the intimacy of sitting shotgun with a man other than Josh on the ride home set her nerves on edge. She listened to the gravel ping against the underbelly of the SUV as it drove out of the parking lot on its short journey back to the B&B. She clasped her hands in her lap, jiggled her foot to the music droning low from the speaker, and checked out the immaculate condition of the inside of his car. She didn't reciprocate his glances and understood from his preliminary inhale that an inquiry loomed.

Nic's slow speech mirrored his careful weighing of her mood. "You seem quiet. Did you enjoy yourself?"

She swallowed hard and quipped, "When wouldn't appetizers, a nice cider, and lively music be a lovely distraction?"

"Honestly, you surprised me, showing up tonight." His

gentle voice and palpable empathy filled the little space between them. "You seemed hesitant when I asked." Nic's warmth nudged her closer to him, like low embers on a cool, moonlit night.

Raey clutched her purse and twisted her wedding band as she stared out the windshield at the painted lane markings ticking by, debating whether to explain why she joined him and his friends. She could finagle her way around the truth in the minutes it took to get back to the B&B, but his sideways glance, like a lighthouse beacon, helped her navigate her way.

"This won't make sense to you, but I came to Skye to find closure and let go of my past," she answered. Hearing herself say that aloud on Skye added a layer of unexpected finality. Her words came out staccato. "My husband..." her breath caught in her throat, "died.... Almost two years ago."

Nic shuffled in his seat and resituated his grasp on the wheel. "Is he buried here in Skye?"

"No, we came here after our wedding, five years ago, for Josh's residency at MacKinnon Memorial Hospital. We returned home to North Carolina when he got sick, but our time here was magical."

"What made 'here' magical?" He peeked her way.

"We came to Skye just after getting married. Here, our lives flowed with a better rhythm. We were able to spend more time together, finally living in the same town under the same roof. And we both loved exploring this rugged land. Even though his schedule got crazy, it wasn't like in the States. Being away from family was difficult, but we flew back as often as possible and for the holidays. I liked that our world here was just us. We concentrated on our work and each other."

"Mmm." Nic inserted.

Cocking her head toward Nic, her voice grew animated. "It's hard to explain, but there was this feeling of pure satisfaction when we sat on the deck together, sometimes early in the morning, sometimes later in the evening. Whether reading a book or magazine or staring into the countryside, I'd prop my feet on him, and he'd rub my feet or leg while we read or talked about our day. Sometimes, we took slow drives through the countryside with no destination, and sometimes with no idea where the roads led, but we didn't care. The drive together was the discovery. Times like those all felt right with the world. They weren't monumental, but during moments like these, we bonded together and became better versions of ourselves. Everything would always be right with the world with him by my side."

"Definitely magical," Nic agreed.

Nic's honed listening skills unmasked her. "We both grew in our professional careers during the three years we lived here. I felt capable and confident. We knew what we wanted and pursued it. Living was easier than it had been in a long time."

Raey closed her eyes and took a deep breath. "But right now, my life...." She rubbed her eyelids. "My life feels like I'm running downhill, and my feet can't keep up with me, like I'm gonna fall, roll into a ball, and keep rolling."

Nic glanced her way and nodded.

"I've lost the ability to find inspiration. I feel the pull of my own expectations, but I can't get the energy. It feels hard, figuring out how to put one foot in front of the other toward new goals."

He didn't interrupt, and her voice ramped up. "I want where I was back. I want who I was back. I want Josh back."

Her voice broke, and she shook her head as she looked at Nic to clarify. "Even though I know that's impossible."

Nic waited.

"When I look at my life, I know I am truly blessed. Family and friends are so supportive. I work hard to make a difference, teaching kids every day. I wake to the sunrise over the ocean. But something is missing. At my core." She tapped her chest with her fingers to the beat of her final four syllables, exhaling a bit more air with each one, "I'm trying to get back the joy…of…liv…ing."

They pulled into a parking spot in front of Shelter Hill Guest House and Nic waited to turn off the engine while Raey continued.

"And it's hard, really hard," she finished.

Facing her with furrowed brows, Nic softly clasped her shoulder and vowed, "You will."

"You're so kind." Raey bowed her head, sorting through the last few minutes of what tumbled from her haze.

Nic smiled.

"Wow," Raey exhaled like a runner gasping for air, "Sorry for all that."

"No, it was real. I'm glad you shared."

His silent steps followed her into the house. *He must want to keep his distance from the raving lunatic.* At the door, she leaned to pull it open, but he reached around her to grab it. With a wave of his hand, he offered for her to enter first. As she released her hold on the door, she stopped and smiled at him and said, "Thanks. I'm sorry. That was a lot."

As she climbed the steps to her room, he said, "Losing your husband is a lot. Don't be sorry for sharing it." Her feet rushed the rest of the steps toward her second-floor room.

The red tartans, red flowers, and red carpet struck a restless chord with her racing heart, sweaty palms, and confused thoughts. She threw her purse on the desk chair and plopped on the bed, expecting to wind and rewind the reel of the evening with Nic—exhausted but unable to sleep.

THREE

"Guid mornin," Finlay greeted her with charismatic cheer at the buffet as she decided between a bagel or croissant. His thick accent instantly drew her in.

"Hi, Finlay. This all looks so delicious."

"Maisrie works her magic in the kitchen. What can we get you?"

"Uh, I'm not sure, yet."

"Well, you'll find today's specials there," he pointed to an extensive list on a sign, "but Maisrie cooks to please."

"This table setting is truly impressive. I'm having trouble making choices. I'll just take both the bacon and ham. Oh my, I'm going to walk out of here a little piggy."

Finlay's smile swelled with each item she added to her plate.

Glancing in the sign's direction, she scanned for Nic. Her heart sank when she didn't see him. Then guilt barged in like the devil, and she jerked her head back to the table and the rose garden created of cut tomatoes.

"I think I will take two eggs over easy."

Finlay leaned into her as if revealing a secret, "Ye know, Maisrie has square sausage and black pudding coming from the kitchen, if you fancy, to go along with yer eggs. Nothing better to get yer insides cranking for the day."

"I think this bannock, potato scone, and oatcake will go with the meat on my plate quite nicely."

"Suit yerself, lass, but when you get a whiff of the black pudding, ye'll be back at this table."

His demeanor reminded her of her father. On days that her mom's nursing shift began before she woke, he started her bleary-eyed mornings with a laugh. As she poured her cereal at the kitchen counter, he would often sneak up behind her, kissing her all over her head and growling as if he were eating her for breakfast. Then he chattered next to her as he made his coffee.

"I'll see if I can find room after this," she said as she raised her plate to him. It would be heartless to dwindle Finlay's enthusiasm by suggesting that black pudding would never appear on her plate and choosing square sausages would be a strong maybe.

Concentrating on her choices, Finlay approved, "Oh, lass, that's a good start. Add a little haggis or square sausage to it. Braw."

When he rubbed his belly, she chucked again and bestowed the same grimace she gave her dad when he encouraged her to add berries to her cereal 'because it is healthier.' She often created grandiose facial gestures to induce his laugh, but when she refused to react at all, he unleashed his funniest shenanigans.

She smiled at Finlay. *What a darling.*

"I'm sure I will. First though, coffee," she insisted.

"Let me set that at a table," he said, taking the plate from her hands.

She scanned the room again and followed him to a table by the window. "Well, lass, enjoy this beauty of a day."

Nourished by a Scottish breakfast and Maisrie and Finlay's warm hospitality, she ventured out into Skye's wild landscape.

During the quiet half-hour drive along a one-lane road leading to her first visit to the Fairy Pools without Josh, she rehashed her conversation with Nic. She felt exposed, sharing so much with him. Was it because he was a man? Had she betrayed Josh? She really hadn't shared that much. Had she? Besides Brenda, she'd not explained her struggles with her grief to anyone. Why had she loosed her emotions? Rehashing it now, the intimacy of it bothered her. How did Nic interpret her? His brief responses seemed odd. She forced herself to lock away her unease over what Nic thought of their conversation.

Distracted, she missed the signs directing her to the Fairy Pools, but after her GPS rerouted her, she finally turned into a small parking lot. After taking two steps on the gravel, she spied a small green marker across the public road pointing toward the trail to Sligachan, a well-known settlement with a magnificent view of the Black Cuillin Mountains.

On her first visit with Josh, excited chatter and hand holding enriched the hike. Today, the early hour's promise of sunshine energized her solo flight of discovery. She concentrated initially on her footing along the steep, wet, gravel path, which soon eased to a smooth downhill trek across the River Brittle.

Large stepping stones, kissed by the morning dew, helped her avoid getting her feet soaked as she crossed streams and ditches that opened to a moor, wild with heather and grasses. She recalled the days she and her mom had played among the stones in the creek behind their house. Jumping together hand in hand, they became dragonflies on turtles' backs, getting free rides. The next minute they were frogs on lily pads, searching for flies. Sometimes, they transformed into trolls on rocks, hunchbacked and menacing.

Raey stopped when a boulder came into view, standing as a reflection of the harsh changes of the Ice Age. If rocks could talk, they could commiserate with the sorrow and loneliness of being left behind.

After carefully maneuvering more stepping stones, the whistling wind abated as the rush and whirl of a thunderous cascade heralded the anticipated magical pools. A torrent of water spilled over a cliff of gray rock carved into a natural oval.

The crystal aqua water rekindled her memory of the intensity of Nic's eyes. He had gazed into her grief with his softly spoken, "You will." Simple, sure words that reverberated like a distant echo in her mind, mingling with Brenda's encouragement, "You're doing it."

His few words drew out her own, and boy, had she let the awkward rant flow. For those moments, it felt like she had thrown the windows open to a fresh spring day until worry about Nic's reaction had her suddenly slamming the curtains shut. Like sunrays streaking through gaps in the clouds, every once in a while she saw glimpses of her blessed life shining through the muddle of her mind–a best friend, a teaching profession, a beachside house, and now this trip to Skye.

Loss clouded her joy. She shook her head at the simplicity of her realization. Stop living exasperated by the dark moments. She had a full life. She was doing it, getting on with her life bit by bit. After all, coming to Skye was her choice to open herself to joy. For a second, her unexpected attraction to Nic confused her view, just like she'd gotten off the healing path so many times before in the last two years of her life since Josh's death. Her insides raced at the challenge she set before herself, to lift the mist suspended over her mind's eye. Today, guided by a new motto–*seize the day and all its joy, not cease the day*–she would get on with it. It's a matter of will, as Nic pointed out last night. At the thought of him, an unguarded flutter spun in her stomach.

Let loss go.

Moving higher up the glen past crags of fern and heather and a few spritely trees covered in white lichen, she balanced at the edge of the crystal turquoise water of the two small falls, separated by a rock buttress and underwater arch. One choppy fall cascaded to the still water, dotted with moss-covered stones and pebbles of every size, contour, and color. Fairy mischief lured sojourners to dive into the sparkling, bone-chilling water and sunbathe on the flat rocks. She smiled at her vision of a fairy flitting among the tourists' secret thoughts and conversations.

Catching her reflection in the darker blue water, the lines of her body etched the surface like rock carved by glaciers, creating jags and jetties. She cared little for keeping herself well nourished. Josh possessed the culinary skills. Her repertoire of cereal and sandwiches sufficed but kept her gaunt.

She climbed the rocks at the final fairy pool and was rewarded with a view of the mist-shrouded valley and vast, jagged Black Cuillin Mountains. The summit, Bruach na Frithe, blanketed by a descending mist, flaunted this land of enchantment, steeped in legends, myths, and magic. Navigating her path forward without Josh seemed as heavily shrouded in mystery.

Fleeing North Carolina like Bonnie Prince Charles, she sought to chart a new course to feed the resistance rising within her. Skye could be her sympathetic Flora MacDonald, helping her to escape defeat in the face of the cancer which had left her husband lifeless on its violent battleground.

Retracing her steps to the carpark, she stopped to linger once more where the gurgling water flowed over pebbles at the shallow water's rocky edge. Reaching into the blue and green glassy surface, she cupped the chilly water in her hands and splashed it on her face.

A snapshot didn't do this kind of coarse beauty justice and a mind couldn't quite hold it well enough to retell with words or paintings. Scotland's visceral beauty soaked deep into her chest, her gut, her bones. No wonder the lines between mayhem and magic, crazy and curious, and fact and fiction blurred here.

This land's transformative effect suffused her veins. Without self-consciousness and with the compulsion of a warrior, she spread her arms wide to the sky in admiration and declaration, like a clansman brandishing a claymore above his head. She squinted fierce eyes at the ray of sun slaying the early mist. Unwilling to let this elusive serenity escape her, she kept her eyes closed and worshipped God's majestic landscape.

"Princess, you look like a fairy trying to take flight."

She jumped at the voice. Josh had called her Princess on their first date, nearly seven years now. For their second anniversary, he gave her a homemade, crown-shaped card with the words *You are my royalty* written inside. On each jewel of the crown, he wrote words describing her: bold, brave, strong, determined. On the back, he added: *You are not a fragile princess. I love that you tread your own path.*

Had her desire conjured him in this magical place? These happenings were not real.

"Or maybe *you* are the reason the fairies dance about. Might you be the Fairy Queen?"

Curiosity could shatter to chaos the moment she opened her eyes. She ached for him to be real, to stand at the pools with her, to wrap her in his arms. The idea of him as a ghost was strangely less frightening than her very foolish longing for him. She'd suffer the same confusion and sorrow as when he vanished from the dunes. Her brain refused to find reason. If he were a ghost or figment, however he appeared, she would suffer the consequences of his departing. This time, she didn't second guess if the voice belonged to Josh. She just couldn't help but lean into it.

"Fairy Queen or not, you bewitch me." At his sentiment, Raey's foot caught on a jutting rock and threw her off balance, but Josh grabbed her, steadying her in his powerful arms. A soft murmur like the wind whispered, "Ahhh, you're safe."

She dared to squint through sunbeams at his stubble-shadowed cheek. Tugging free from under his hold, she wrapped both arms securely around his waist and laid her head on his chest, afraid her ghost might disappear. They swayed to the harmony of the waterfalls and wind, the weight of his hands resting just below her waist and his voice softly humming in her ear.

"If this is a dream, I don't want to wake," she mumbled to herself.

"This is not a dream. I'm here because of you." Josh pulled back to peer into her eyes as if answering a question that she had asked.

"But why? When you leave, I'm more fragile. I don't want to be weak and breakable."

"You say the word fragile as if it's bad. It isn't necessarily bad."

"You see right through me, so I can't hide it, but admitting I feel fragile to anyone but you scares me."

"This trip doesn't seem like a fragile move. To me, it shows you are resilient and bold."

"But then I walk through my days and get sideswiped by missing you."

"Fragile things break, but in the breaking, you can create something new."

"That's a very poetic sentiment, but living my life without you is way harder than I want it to be."

"Difficult things aren't easy, but they're worth it."

"Please don't quote platitudes to me. You're the last person I'd expect to get them from."

"Can we talk about moving through your grief? It's been nearly two years now."

"I don't want to talk anymore about it. I just want to make this moment last," she begged, hugging him tighter and laying her head once again against his heartbeat.

"What are you waiting for?" he forced forward, exhaustion tinting his voice.

That question sat between them again like a dark, gaping chasm.

"I'm always waiting for this…being with you. I don't want to forget your voice, your smile, your face, how you speak to me, how you love me. I could stay here forever."

"This isn't real."

If it's not; it might just be the best substitute.

"I can't stay. You can't keep holding on to me this way." As if he could read her mind, he added, "This isn't a substitute for your life."

"But I don't want to move on from you." *Physically, mentally, or emotionally.*

"But you do," he asserted, as if trying to convince her of her own mind. "There's a better way to live."

"But if getting better means losing you, then I don't want to."

"I want you to carry me with you. I do. But not the sorrow. Find joy for the rest of your life."

"I want that, too."

"Remember that stained glass you hung in the kitchen window of our cottage? Broken pieces of purple, green and yellow patterned into thistle."

"I snatched the last one at the Plockton craft fair. It was so beautiful."

"You saw the beauty created from broken pieces."

"After you vanished from the dunes, missing you was nearly unbearable. I ached to keep you."

"Letting go of grief won't change who I am to you." She surveyed his pleading eyes.

"I'm afraid of letting go of the heartache. It feels like letting go of you."

"But do you want my memory always mingled with misery? I don't mean this to sound harsh, Babe. I just want you to be happy."

Raey thought for a second about what he had said. "You're like water through my fingers. I can't grab hold and keep you and I want to. When you touch me like this, the gumption to risk letting go of grief spills through me, but then it subsides at your leaving."

"It doesn't have to."

"Every once in a while, clarity peeks through my gloom. I laugh at the tv screen, sleep through an entire night without waking, find awe in a sunset, sing along with the music on the radio, and truly relax and enjoy dinner out with a friend."

"That's the life I want you to fight for. Don't give up. I want that for you."

"I'm better in those moments, but then the sadness is back. And the worst is that I know it's not logical. I want to let go, but I'm scared you will disappear."

"I'm your reminder not to let your grief eclipse your joy. When your pain diminishes, it doesn't mean your love for me disappears. You can let it go, and I will stay right here." He rested his palm above her heart, and his warmth felt safe.

She laid her palm on top of his and interlocked their fingers.

"When you refuse to stare into the anguish, you find space to keep me alive in your memory. I hope you look at my picture and smile instead of cry. Hold my stethoscope and remember my dedication, not cancer. Wear my cap at a Hornets game and cheer like crazy. Watch a sunset and wish you had one more of the kind we shared at Neist Point."

"This is you changing me, isn't it?"

Josh caressed her cheek and responded with a manly chortle, "Girl, it's you that changes everyone you touch."

He pulled her hands from around his neck to clasp between them like on the day they vowed to live as husband and wife. When she looked into his blue eyes, he said, "I promise it won't always be like this."

"The torture of losing you or this finding you?" Raey panicked at his words that hinted at finality.

"Honey, let the pain go. You won't lose my love."

Tears rimmed her eyes, and she looked at him through blurry rainbows. He swiped at the teardrop that landed on her cheek. "Life didn't leave you behind. There's so much more for you," Josh whispered, once again pleading with her. "It's time for you to get on with loving your life again." She cupped her hand over his as he wiped away another tear.

She let go of his hand and turned around to take in the sparkling turquoise fairy pool. Wiping away a tear, she gained some composure along with a vow. Either she was holding her breath, or he was holding his, but everything stilled except the falling water. She spun back around and pledged, "I'll try. With your help–" but Josh was gone.

She needed a little more time, a little more of him. Like her shallow-breathing life, she needed more oxygen crashing into her lungs, forcing her to inhale deeper. Her body melted at the edge of the pool until her tears ran dry.

I miss you.

FOUR

Entering Shelter Hill Guest House, a sweet aroma triggered her taste buds, igniting her hunger. She followed her nose to the placard and snagged some sticky toffee pudding and read the announcement of a bonfire on the patio with fixings of her favorites: shortbread, crisps, cheese, and tattie scones paired with an Irn Bru, a pint, or whisky. After a day of long jaunts and an exhausting encounter, she needed to add some more fuel to her belly and headed outside to the patio. Raey offered guests quick smiles and kept her eyes busy on the food table.

A young lady, who Raey presumed to be about her age, initiated a conversation. "It was a gorgeous day today. How are your travels going?"

Raey placated her inquiry. "The Fairy Pools were enchanting."

"I'm excited to go tomorrow." As her husband approached, she reached her arm toward him. "We're hoping for pleasant weather." Her eyes darted in search of Raey's partner.

Her resolve to mingle dissipated with the billowing smoke from the fire. Raey balanced shortbread, grapes, and cheese on her plate, leaving no room for the handful of chips she piled on top of her food. Politely ending their conversation, she said, "Have a great time."

The woman pulled her husband closer and asked, "Are you on your honeymoon, too?"

"Eh, not this time. We honeymooned here years ago. I'm just revisiting."

"It's all so fabulous. The second time around must be just as magical."

"Uh, definitely magical." Raey contemplated her last word and the pain of seeing and losing Josh once again before continuing, "Well, congratulations on your marriage." With attempted cheer mingled with finality, Raey offered, "I hope you and your husband have an amazing time on Skye."

The couple retreated from the food table. She overheard other guests discussing their trek to the Fairy Pools, remarking that the magnificence of the pools' colors emerged from the blessing of an early clearing of mist to such a perfect sun-filled day.

Having lost her appetite, Raey set her food behind her as she sat on the edge of the lounger. Resting her elbows on her knees, she propped her chin on her fists and concentrated on the crackling from the substantial fire Finlay stoked. Guests charmed one another with traveling tales, eager to give suggestions for places to experience: "If you do nothing else while here, you have to go. Make it happen!"

Those words floated through her mind, thickening into her previous challenge to herself to embrace enjoying her life and be intentional about reveling in it. But after seeing Josh again, "make it happen" spun like hogwash through her head.

Summoning every ounce of her energy, she had willed Josh to beat his cancer, but his life had still drained from him before her eyes.

Now, she summoned every ounce of her energy to mold a life without him. But moving forward meant letting go, and she couldn't muster the strength when his visits in the mist kept hacking her desire.

Carrying her Irn Bru to the edge of the lawn to watch the moon sitting on the mountain summit, she stood guard over the bay.

They're gone. I am not. I will go on. Raey lamented the familiar refrain she repeated to herself after she lost her parents. Surviving the agony of their deaths should have been enough of a challenge for one lifetime, but molding a new beginning without Josh required a warrior's courage. *Could the ashes of my heart be transformed into a diamond?*

"Fabulous full moon tonight, aye?"

Raey jolted. "Oh, hi, Maisrie." She hummed a strong, "Mm-hmm."

"Can I pull up a chair for ye?"

"Oh, no thank you. That's sweet of you, though," Raey responded, "I'll just sit on the lawn if that's ok?"

"You ken the sun will set in thirty minutes or so," she offered.

"Oh, I *do know*," she raved. "Seeing it never gets old."

"I'll be back to check on ye." Maisrie lightly patted her back and meandered toward the next guest.

"Maisrie?"

"Yes, dear?" Maisrie turned to search Raey's face.

"Can I ask you a question?" Raey picked at the hem of her jacket.

"Sure, darling, anything."

"Um, well," Raey dug her nails into her palms. "I was wondering about ghosts on Skye."

Maisrie stepped closer to Raey. "Well, there's a long

history of ghosts on this misty island. I suppose many of the stories surround Dunvegan Castle. Softer and gentler ghosts haunt it compared to other old castles in Scotland. The ruins of Duntulm Castle…"

Setting her hand to Maisrie's wrist, Raey whispered, "What about you, personally? Have you ever encountered a ghost?"

"Um, well. I've had my moments, I suppose," Maisrie cringed as if in pain. Raey's silence prodded Maisrie to continue. "When my daughter, Nic's mom, died," Maisrie hesitated before interjecting, "I'm not sure if he shared that with ye."

"Oh, I didn't know. I'm so sorry for your loss." Caught off-guard, Raey regretted the faraway look of pain her question caused Maisrie.

Maisrie looked at the bay as she spoke, "Well, I wasn't sure if it was my need to see her again or a ghost. I was afraid asking would make her vanish in the mist."

"What did you do?"

"I looked straight at her and told her I believed in her, of course. It was soothing to my soul to take in her beauty and feel her tenacious energy again."

"What did she do?"

Just for a second, Maisrie traveled in her mind to a past world. "She pulled up a chair in the kitchen like she did when she was a teen and set to telling me all her woes about dying."

"Oh, my. That must have been difficult." Raey exhaled and took Maisrie's hands, stilling her wringing of a dishcloth.

"I miss seeing her face," Maisrie eventually took a deep breath and continued, "and hearing her laughter, even in the face of sorrow." Tears pooled at the rim of her eyelids as she looked up at the sky, and then at Raey. Locking eyes, the women connected at the edge of their deep pain. At Maisrie's half-sigh of indrawn breath, Raey captured her in her arms and held her until courage was restored to both.

"Do you suppose your mind can play tricks on you?" Raey dared to ask.

"I suppose it can, but ghost or grief, I thank God for the gift of seeing her." Maisrie squeezed both of Raey's hands before releasing them and swiped a tear from her cheek. Strength renewed, Maisrie forged a path ahead for them as she joked, "If ye encounter a ghost, be sure to believe it. I hear mad ghosts are no fun."

"Thanks for the wise words of caution," Raey said, but was deeply thankful for much more. The gift of Maisrie's vulnerability reignited her bravery, and she asked, "Did you see her just once?"

Mairie hesitated for a moment, and gandered toward the nearby guests before she responded, "We had three lovely visits."

Raey gasped and then quickly covered her mouth, wondering how many more visits she'd have with Josh.

"It's been a very long time since the last." She hugged the empty serving tray to her chest.

"Why?" Raey asked.

"Why what, dear?"

"Why don't you see her anymore?"

"I don't rightly ken, but my heart is full with the blessing of them." Maisrie's faraway eyes chased the memory.

"That's a lot to take in."

"Oh, and ye ken if ye encounter fairies, refuse their drinks. They will seduce ye to fall into time holes and ye will remain forever on the island. But then, would that really be so bad?" Maisrie chuckled again and squeezed Raey's hand affectionately before walking away.

Raey pulled her jacket tight and stretched her five foot ten inch frame out on the lawn. She was determined to enjoy the tranquil magic of the descending sun over the bay, scattered with fishing boats and pleasure craft.

Minutes later, Nic joined her seascape contemplations. He balanced his whisky glass on the lawn near hers, plopped down closer than comfortable, extended his legs, imitating her, and leaned back on his elbows. "Man, what a peaceful night."

"Sure is," Raey said. She followed the rise and fall of the blue cashmere sweater as Nic released a deep breath.

"You are thoroughly interrogating the moon."

"If I could only hold all these lovely surroundings prisoner."

"And I'd gladly let you." Nic winked as he caught Raey's glance.

"Would you now?" Raey said, thankful now for the connection and energy she derived from his playfulness.

"Mm-hmm." Nic smiled a boyish smile and held her gaze as he lifted his tumbler to his lips.

Her banter with Nic lifted the weight of encountering Josh as a ghost. "Rough day?" Raey asked.

"Let's just say, being your prisoner sounds nice compared to the last few days," Nic said. "How did your day go?"

"I went early to the Fairy Pools. You know how the mist hovers. But it ended up lifting earlier than I guessed it might, and everything was just magical." She couldn't explain the true magic of that morning, as even she didn't understand Josh's appearance.

"The mist can be tricky. All kinds of things are hidden until suddenly they are not," he quipped with an amused glimmer in his eyes, as if unveiling a truth.

"What sort of things are hidden?" She wanted to ask him

what the rising mist unveiled for him, but she dared not go that deep. He could turn the tables and her pain would be exposed again, so she redirected the conversation.

"Just keep looking, and they'll magically appear, lass."

Oh, my, if he only knew how right he is.

She found sure footing. "My first experience with the magical nature of the mist was our first visit to Neist Point. We went for the lighthouse but stayed for the sunset. Since there were so many people at the lighthouse, we headed toward the cliffs."

"Always lots of tourists." Nic rolled his eyes as if feigning disgust but switched to delight with the raise of his whisky salute, "Can't live with them; can't live without them. Slàinte."

"Very funny." Raey raised her glass in a toast, allowing herself to be the butt of his joke for a second. "But then the clouds rolled in, and we were bummed."

"Can't live with or without those, either." They both laughed.

"Josh still wanted to head out to the cliffs." She animated Josh's optimistic manner as she said, "'...just in case the clouds cleared.' I had my doubts, but I humored him. The weather here is fickle."

"Fickle?"

"Yeah, fickle, meaning it changes. It changes its loyalties. One minute you think all is well and then weeping weather descends."

"I know what fickle means," he teased. "I just like hearing you say the word. It comes out funny when you say it," he grinned.

"Oh, really?" she challenged. "Well, I'll be on the lookout for something you say funny." She pretended to cough and uttered under her breath, "Everything."

Midway to a sip, Nic paused and countered with a raised brow, "Ha, well, as long as you are looking, I'm good with that."

"And now back to our regularly scheduled program," Raey commented, re-routing him to a safe conversation zone with a hard stare. "I'll just finish the story I was telling, if you don't mind."

"I don't mind. It's fun watching you talk. You do a lot with your hands."

Raey kept to casual banter and held her bottle, scratching at the Irn-Bru label to keep her hand motions and Nic's attention to a minimum. More guests milled around, as hopeful as Raey and Nic to witness the moment the heavens kiss earth.

"We determined to stick it out, but I couldn't take the cold wind. Luckily, Josh found this concrete lookout a little way along the cliff, which helped shelter us, but we ended up deciding to head back to the car anyway."

"Well, that's a bummer. I imagined this to be the best sunset ever, happy kind of story."

"Wait now." She turned toward him and set her drink on the lawn as her excitement ramped up. "We trudged back to our car, disappointed that we didn't get to experience an epic sunset, but when I glanced back over my shoulder, stunning rays of light peeked through heavy clouds." She waved her hands in the sky, making the shape of the orb, and then slapped the lawn. "We almost missed it. I shouted, jumped up and down, pointed, and both of us raced back to the cliff edge, the blowing gales be damned. The clouds didn't totally clear, but the rolling pinks and purples in the sky blended with the blues below, creating a striking watercolor painting."

Nic smiled and kept watching her.

"We loved that sunset the best because we worked so hard

for it. It was magic. Like you said—what wasn't there suddenly was. After that day, on mild weather days when we weren't too tired or busy, we'd say, 'Let's go see the best,' and we'd jump in the car toward that same vantage point."

"Okay, so there's the best sunset ever, happy kind of story I thought you would tell."

"See!" Her hands jutted out toward him.

"On a gusty day, I took a group of teens up there, but not for the sunset. You can imagine trying to keep them back from those cliffs."

"A group of teens?"

"Yeah, I volunteer with Highland Hope. It's a charity that promotes opportunities for youth, well, people of all ages really, but I enjoy working with the teens to college age."

"How often do you do that?"

"I try as often as I can, but it ends up being about once a month."

"What do you do for Highland Hope?"

"The organization creates opportunities in just about any interest you can think of. But I offer group hikes, since that's my hobby."

"Gets them out and moving?"

"Yeah, it helps build some confidence and resilience in, hopefully, a safe space. Plus, I hope being outdoors promotes a positive effect on their mental wellbeing."

"Unless you're getting poured on," Raey teased.

"Well, finding shelter strengthens problem solving skills," he jested.

"Why did you join that charity?" Raey asked.

An air of solemnity pervaded his response. "When I was young, my parents were killed in a car crash."

Raey gasped at learning Nic has lost both parents. Shocked

by his misty eyes, she didn't know where to look, but she helped carry his burden and settled her gaze on him. In the silence that floated between them, they carried each other's pain. She discovered a kindred spirit. She wanted to erase his sorrow and mend the deep wound she knew his parents' death created, but life had taught her that was nearly impossible. She understood the crushing pain that makes it hard to breathe.

Her voice shook as she said, "I'm so sorry for your pain, Nic. That must have been extremely difficult."

He nodded, speechless. A familiar intensity washed over his face. He swallowed hard and then squinted at the bay, as if the sun were far too bright. But he didn't turn away from it.

She touched his arm as if to steady them both. "I'm very sorry for your loss," she whispered, imagining him as a child, feeling alone in the world.

"Gram and Pops did an excellent job of trying to help me and my brother recover from losing Mom and Dad. Many days, I'm sure we wore them out."

"I bet you did," Raey said with a grin, exaggerating the word *bet*.

"They tried any outlet for my energy and found hiking helped ease my angst and build confidence." He took a sip, concentrating on the golden-brown whisky he was swirling. "I want to give that to kids. This charity helps me do that."

With a heavy sigh, she said, "I understand that pain."

Lifting his chin in a questioning manner, he encouraged her to continue.

She spoke to the bay as she relayed, "A drunk driver killed my parents when I was seventeen. Everything changed in that instant. I watched my life like it was an out-of-body experience. I couldn't see how my world could go on." Raey caught his earnest eyes. "Thinking of myself as an orphan made it hard to breathe at times. So many changes. Suddenly, I had no family. I didn't belong to anyone. I wanted to tell those buying Mother's Day and Father's Day cards not to take their parents for granted. My parents left me everything, but I had never truly been in charge of my own life until that moment. Every decision became mine, and I didn't want to make any of them."

Nic gently placed his hand on top of hers. "I'm so sorry you've experienced such deep pain–twice."

A comfortable silence hung between them until Raey asked, "Now you look like you're the one interrogating the moon. Your thoughts are far away."

"Well, I'm thinking, 'let's go see the best' sometime."

She stiffened at the idea of sharing that sunset spot with him. Picking up her drink filled her awkward pause. Attempting a natural tone, she answered, "Maybe we could do that."

"Great. I'll wait to hear from you, then." Nic stood with his empty whisky glass and challenged, "Come find me when you're ready."

"Wait. Where?"

"Uh," Nic's eyes widened as he cocked his head and nodded at the B&B, "ye ken."

She stuck her tongue out at his teasing.

He raised his tumbler in a toast. "Sweet dreams, Raey."

FIVE

After a long, hot shower, Raey combed through thick, sun-kissed blond locks, as difficult to control as her emotions after seeing Josh twice. She wiped the fog from the bathroom mirror and leaned in close. Running her hand down her pale, freckled cheek, she didn't see the Princess that Josh tagged her as.

When her phone chimed Brenda's ringtone and interrupted her reflections, she stiffened in shock. It had to be four o'clock in the morning for Brenda. Raey had promised to call when she settled in, but she kept putting it off. Her episodes with Josh hijacked her thoughts. *Should I test my sanity and disclose Josh's manifestations? Will he vanish if I expose him?* What stirred her quandary even more was that Nic captured her attention and stole her composure.

Raey and Brenda's friendship formed at the beginning of their junior year in high school when giggling at passed notes made Algebra II bearable. They scheduled their senior year classes together and worked the same shift at the hot dog joint on the boardwalk.

When Raey's parents died at the beginning of her freshman year of college, her simple life had dissolved. Brenda steadied her through her tough remolding when Raey struggled with an introspective rage that periodically invaded her mind. She depended upon Brenda for clarity, confidence boosts, and frequently, a good dose of unadulterated truth. But as her sister-in-law, Brenda also struggled with losing Josh, her only sibling. After he died, Brenda moved into Raey's beachside cottage, and they witnessed each other's pain from a front row seat.

Before answering her phone to face Brenda's inquisitions, Raey sat on the edge of the bed, took a deep breath, and said a silent prayer. "Hello, favorite sister-in-law."

"Yes, your one and only amazing sister-in-law. Who else would wake this early to catch you before you head out into the wilderness?" asked Brenda in her chipper morning voice, so much like Josh's. "I miss you already."

So much of Brenda was like Josh. Their brown wavy hair, their dark olive skin, and their optimism. Raey marveled that her in-laws, who transitioned to surrogate parents after hers died, produced two children that persevered with hope against all odds.

"Somehow, I doubt that you'll miss me for long. Brian will keep you busy."

"Oh, yes, ma'am, he does. The man never sits still. We're heading out for a bike ride this afternoon, but I may need a nap after getting up this early."

"I'm sorry I didn't call you yesterday, but I'm battling jet lag. On a better note, this B&B is charming, and the view of the bay is heaven." Raey peered out the window, finding Maisrie in her garden with Nic. She leaned closer to the window to watch Nic as he rested his arm on Maisrie's shoulder and then kissed her goodbye.

"I'm so glad for you. What did you do your first few days?"

When Raey didn't answer, Brenda said, "Hello? You there?"

"Oh, sorry, got distracted for a second." Raey paced the room. "Um, I trekked through Portree and hiked to the Fairy Pools."

"Oh, you love the Fairy Pools!" Brenda's cheer deflated to caution as she asked, "How was it?"

"Strange but magical." Raey answered honestly, forgetting herself.

"What happened?"

"Oh, um, just something unexpected." Raey paced around the room, finally settling on the edge of the bed.

"You're not telling me something."

"It was all so different when I experienced it with Josh." Raey intended the double entendre.

After a pause, Brenda asked, "In a good way or bad way?"

Raey hesitated. "Maybe both?"

"I'm sure," Brenda said, her measured speech not completely disguising her disapproval of the trip. "It will be a challenge to walk those same paths."

"It's like he's with me, challenging me to see it all in a new way."

"Even in death, he's pushy," Brenda chuckled.

"Certainly is." Raey joined in with Brenda's jest.

"Call me anytime if you need to talk to someone."

"It really is a never-ending ache." Raey released a sigh that Brenda copied.

"It's great that you're pushing toward what you want. I'll trust that you know the reason Skye is where you need to be."

"In just the few days I've been gone," the strength in Raey's voice faltered as she continued, "I can see this may be more difficult than I thought."

"Can I confess right here that the first time you left to live in Skye I was selfishly unsupportive of my best friend and brother moving so far away from me?" Brenda paused and her tone grew more serious, "But Raey, my reservations about this trip aren't that you might not come back. I am worried about you facing the tough stuff alone."

"I'll only be gone one month, and you'll be just a phone call away," Raey reassured herself and Brenda.

"Just don't dig yourself into a deeper pit of pain. You've been zombie-walking for over a year and a half."

Heaven hadn't given her a voice in Josh's stage four pancreatic cancer diagnosis. The oncologist's account of "rare" befit her life circumstances. Revisiting that now spilled a wave of heated blood throughout her body, like a stab to her gut's soft tissue. Guilt penetrated her head when she hadn't been able to differentiate his fatigue, lack of appetite, and weight loss from his routine work as a resident doctor. Like the shredded coastline exposed to turbulent waves, the trauma of living without him tore her asunder. She had begged on her knees for a do-over with a different ending. If she was playing God, she would have gifted Josh the miracle of life.

"I know the counselor in you worries about me, but I'm where I need to be to find some clarity." *Coming to Skye may not be logical, but the decision is entirely mine.*

Brenda fell silent before continuing, "I want to say something else."

At Brenda's ominous introduction, Raey turned her eyes to the peaceful view out the window of boats dotting the bay. "Yes?"

"I need you to know that I am proud of you and..."

"Aw, thanks," Raey interrupted, not expecting her comment.

"And I realize I let my concern show over your decision, but I am proud of your bravery."

"I promise to keep you posted on how things are going."

"What do you have planned for the week ahead?"

"Well, I need to finalize my plans with a friend."

"Wow, already making new friends. Do tell," Brenda teased in a husky voice tinged with winking humor.

"It's with an old friend. You remember, Isobel, my co-teacher?"

"Oh, bummer. I was hoping to hear that you made a new friend. Ahem." Even thousands of miles apart, Brenda dispensed with stealth in her predictable push for Raey's love life. As subtle as the eddies invading the coastline, Brenda proceeded with her tactics. "See anyone interesting?"

Out of habit, Raey pursed her lips and glared daggers at her phone, and then chose a different tactic to serve Brenda right. "Oh, my. There are just too many to count." Raey huffed. "I just can't fit everyone in. I've already promised Finlay and Nic that I'd go somewhere with them. That's why I'm having such difficulty getting my plans set."

"Really?" Brenda buzzed. "No, wait. You're joking, aren't you?"

"Hmm. Am I?" Raey enjoyed her non-committal reply, thinking of Nic's invitation to the pub and his offer to visit Neist Point.

"That's not nice!"

"Touché!"

"Okay, okay, I'm pushing. I know." Brenda jumped into the silence. "It's just that dating Brian reminds me of when you dated my brother. I want that for you again."

"Someday, but right now…"

When Raey paused just a bit too long, Brenda rushed in

again. "Maybe Skye is a safe place to begin again. Or, at least, consider a date."

Raey pantomimed beckoning the heavens and slapped her arms back down far too hard on her thighs, her phone falling to the ground. "Why does everyone keep saying that?"

"Everyone? What?" Brenda inquired.

"That's what a guy at the beach implied." As soon as the words left her mouth, she regretted blurting the word *guy*, but she couldn't admit to conjuring her husband and hearing him talk to her. Brenda would appear at her doorstep in a flash and drag her back home to the States.

"Oh, do tell! Which of those that you named might that be?" Brenda voiced with a mix of enthusiasm and difficulty.

"Give up. There's nothing to share," Raey warned.

"I won't say anything. I'm all ears. Just tell me something, anything, about him. What's his name? I'll even take something easy like his hair color or if he's cute."

"Not going there." Raey ambled back to the mirror, smoothing the deep frown lines between her eyes.

"Wait, one thing," Brenda begged, knowing Raey's tone conveyed a brush off. "I have to know he's worthy of you!"

A long exhale broke Raey's silence, and she feigned a breezy tone. "Brenda, I know thinking of me with someone other than Josh is hard for both of us. You don't have to project that it's not by encouraging me to be with another man."

Brenda's voice broke when she added, "And you know that you have my brother's approval to move on, don't you?"

"I do." Raey recalled the most difficult conversation she had ever had with Josh. One she had refused to participate in.

Brenda said, "It's hard, but I'm glad you are trying."

Too weak for a reality check, Raey said, "Thanks for checking on me. I'll call you later. Love ya."

Choosing jeans and a Duke sweatshirt for the day, her usual comforts, she laced her hiking boots and finished applying her makeup. Zipping her cosmetic bag closed, she leaned both palms on the basin for balance, still frustrated by her heart's pleading for Josh's physical presence. She stared into the mirror and said to herself, "Was I conjuring him?"

Her stomach churned from her chaotic thinking, or perhaps from not eating. She pulled her damp hair into a tight ponytail, grabbed Josh's baseball cap, and avoided the former by pursuing the latter.

SIX

Raey lingered over her coffee in the lounge until Maisrie asked, "Can I get you anything else before we clear everything, dear?"

Yeah, I'm wondering where Nic's been hiding.

Nic had not passed through for a couple days. She couldn't muster the gumption to accept a hike to that hallowed sunset at Neist Point, a memory she shared with Josh. She thought she might welcome his company on another late-night hike, but now his absence shot down her hopes. She could get ahead of herself with this step, so she let the idea fall, but not without some residual disappointment.

"Oh, I'm stalling here with the peace of the bay, but I should get a move on. Thank you for everything, though. It was delicious."

Isobel would not overlook today's dallying. Raey was late, and Isobel was early. Her baby's birth, three weeks earlier than expected, solidified Raey's plans for the day. A herd of blackface sheep refusing to budge at her honking and a quick side trip for two chai lattes delayed her timely arrival at the hospital. Isobel, so often teased at staff meetings that time could be told by her fashionable lateness, would certainly rib her about her tardiness, especially since Raey considered *on time* as arriving fifteen minutes early.

The energy she had mustered to pick up the phone and plan this visit to the hospital where Josh had worked had exhausted her. Isobel's warm voice still worked its charm at soothing rough edges. It was just as effective in the classroom as it was today, at Raey's reluctance to visit the hospital. Reconnecting with her good friend shouldn't feel this monumental, but it did.

Raey pulled into the hospital parking lot and her heart rate spiked. She turned off the engine and her eyes froze on the hospital doors, opening and closing to promises and pain. She imagined Josh's feet, tapping across the pavement to those doors, settling into each day's quick pace. Blowing out a cleansing sigh, she glanced at herself in the rearview mirror, wrapped her scarf around her neck a couple times, shaped her locks, and practiced her smile. Clinging to the steering wheel, she steeled her mind to tackle the visit. She grabbed the lattes, the warmth melting the melancholy tightening in her chest.

I can do this. And I'll do it with all the warmth and grace my friend deserves.

A man in an open white lab coat, holding flowers and zigzagging between cars, caught her eye. She grinned at the irony of a doctor running away from the hospital, not to it. Dark hair complemented by a five o'clock shadow, a strong jaw, and a tall, slim build enhanced his smooth stride. Her body and cheeks suffused with warmth when she imagined him looking a little like Nic. He grasped his keys and phone from his pocket and smiled at an obviously recognized caller. He set the flowers on top of his black Range Rover and leaned his back against the driver's door, shedding his lab coat while calming into a brief conversation.

Black Range Rover? Nic?! He's a doctor at the same hospital where Josh worked? Why hadn't he said so?

When the shock of this realization subsided, she studied his smooth moves. Once finished with the call, he carefully placed the flowers on the back seat, along with his lab coat. When he sat in the driver's seat, he checked his phone screen again. He ran his hand through his hair and then wasted no time driving off the lot.

The low simmer of attraction caught her by surprise. A twinge of jealousy passed through her, even though she had no right to feel it.

He wasn't her Nic any more than Josh had been her Josh that long-ago Sunday afternoon. A familiar flutter in her belly swept the cobwebs off that day. Brenda had invited her to lunch only days after her parents died. When she first laid eyes on Josh, her face suffused with heat and her skin tingled all over. Home from his medical studies at Duke, she had met him for the first time when he threw open his parents' front door and yelled for her to hurry inside, rescuing her from waiting for an answer to her knock in the pelting rain.

When he smiled, her body came alive. She averted her vulnerable eyes from his dangerously transparent smile, but they skirted to the opening in his button-down shirt, pulled tightly across his chest. Her flushing fever rose higher and her face glowed brighter. Her eyes darted back to his. Exposed under his intense gaze, her need to be rescued mirrored in his eyes.

His casually-rolled white sleeves rested against his tanned forearms as he fanned the door wide open. She never regretted her boldness when she reached for his helping hand. Her heart sped as, one by one, his fingers wrapped around her hand and coiled around her heart, lifting her into the house. She stood toe to toe and eye to eye with him, dazed by his dashing good looks. Her heightened focus on his body surprised her more than Brenda not greeting her at the door. Seeing him had been a defibrillation, a shock to her heart.

"Now what to do with this?" he asked rhetorically as his hands cupped her shoulders and twirled her around to remove her soaked jacket, dropping it onto the entryway rug. His subtly woody, orchid scent propositioned her senses.

"Um," she stumbled, imagining all kinds of things she would like to do with him: slow swaying to soft background music, walking through a garden of white daisies holding hands, sipping sweet tea under a beach umbrella, and mapping stars under a moonless sky.

Hugging her to his steely side, he said, "It's good to have you here," as if he had known her his whole life.

"It's good to have you here, too," she responded, immediately blushing with her mistake. The twirl discombobulated her. Her pulse raced, pounding like a wrecking ball through her emotional stability.

Her eyes didn't leave him as he found a place for her jacket, not hearing Brenda enter until she giggled and said, "Oh, I see you have met my brother."

"Um, oh yes," she stumbled as she fought to switch her attention to Brenda.

Just then, Josh grasped Raey's hand delicately within his and said, "It's a pleasure to have met you. I hope it's not too long before we meet again."

"Yes, too long," she answered, still sensing the warmth of his skin gently wrapping hers and then wincing upon realizing she had blundered in her response again. Josh gave a good-hearted, knowing laugh as he tapped the top of her hand to settle her nerves and headed out the front door and back to his studies, while Raey prayed her first fumbled moment would soon be followed by a second chance.

Brenda chortled as she grabbed her arm to pull her into the dining room, "Smitten much?"

Her drenched jacket had been an apt metaphor for the sorrow-soaked soul her parents' death had created and that she had hidden from Josh that day. She was grateful he had so tenderly cared for her heart all their days together.

A car door slammed shut beside her, jarring Raey's thoughts back to Nic and the present. She wanted answers to her questions. Nic neglected to tell her he was a doctor at the same hospital where Josh had worked. Did he know Josh? Why hadn't he mentioned it? Resolutely deciding to seek answers to her questions, she put the matter aside and set off for the hospital doors and Isobel.

Peeking through door #304, Raey glimpsed Isobel's long, coal-black hair falling across her chest. She cuddled and caressed the cheek of her nursing baby. Tiny fingers wrapped around Isobel's forefinger, a sacred, tender bond. Gratitude welled up inside her that God had blessed Isobel, who naturally cared for so many children, with her very own child.

She knocked on the door and walked in, greeting Isobel as she leaned to peek at the baby bundled in covers. "Hello, sweet mama and baby."

"I'm so glad you came to meet Isla. She's perfection," Isobel cooed and cupped her baby's full head of hair, the same color as hers.

"She certainly is. I love her name."

"It means *devoted to God*," she voiced with a spirit as soothing as the meaning.

"I love that. I can't believe how good you look after labor. You're still as tiny as ever, even after having a baby." Raey hugged Isobel and placed a small gift bag on her lap and a chai latte on her side table. "Just a little something for you and your little one."

"Well, when you're only five foot four, you have to be careful about gaining baby weight. Teaching my entire pregnancy and hiking with Dad probably helped keep me trim." Isobel kissed Isla's forehead. "I'm trying to keep her awake to nurse, but she's not nearly as excited about eating as I am." Isobel massaged her baby's toes and chest. "Would you like to hold her?" Isobel offered.

"Most definitely." Raey sat in the nearby chair and cuddled Isla against her body, gently caressing her dark hair, her forehead, her cheeks, and the bridge of her nose. *I wish I could have held Josh's baby in my arms.* "I love babies' toes. Hers are gorgeously long. And she smells divine."

"It's great to have you here, but it's too bad you were late." Isobel winked and grinned at her like the Cheshire-cat.

Raey laughed and nodded at the chai latte. "I just knew you would notice, so I brought you that peace offering."

"Well, that definitely works! You're buttering me up, huh?" Isobel gazed at her baby. "This sweet girl halted our get-away weekend."

"No worries."

"Yes, but I was looking forward to our time alone together. Free from fifth graders and lesson plans."

They had weathered the difficulties of being first-time teachers, new to a school and new to fifth grade in the same year. Baptism by fire had made them fast friends, which naturally extended outside of work to exercising, hiking, and shopping. Isobel's enthusiasm for teaching and the way she presented complex ideas in a simple manner for her students impressed Raey. They had dreamed together of babies, strollers, and sharing holidays.

Isobel tossed pink tissue paper in her lap and then pulled two books from the pink and blue polka-dot bag. Gripping *Love You Forever* to her chest, Isobel emitted a heartfelt croon, "Aww, this is my favorite."

"I wrote a little note to you inside the cover of that one."

After reading, Isobel said, "Your words are precious to me. Now, going back to you being late—"

Raey interrupted, "But you said my peace offering worked."

"You missed the doctor. He left shortly before you arrived."

Raey's forehead wrinkled as she tilted her head and shrugged. "Um, I missed the doctor?"

"You missed out. I could have set you up," Isobel chortled.

"Well, he would have to be dang good-looking to sweep me off my feet right now," Raey played along with her light-hearted teasing.

"I'd marry him myself if I wasn't already married."

"On looks alone? Shame on you!" Raey held her hand over her mouth and feigned shock at such a scandal.

"We all have our standards," Isobel joked, aware that her husband possessed the complete package–sincerity, humility, humor, and looks.

"Well, you know my standards have always been higher than yours," Raey poked back, enjoying their easy banter.

"They wouldn't be if you met him. When he talks, he gets cuter with every word. He drips with charm while examining Isla."

"Shame, shame, girl." Raey rubbed the back of her

forefinger over the other. "By the way, where is your hunk of a husband?"

"He escaped to get a shower at home. He'll be back soon. He's very protective of us. This will definitely be a test of patience for my independent nature."

Isobel grabbed Raey's hand and studied her without saying a word. Raey smiled and searched her face.

"It's good to see you. I know being reminded of Josh around every corner and seeing glimpses of your life here must be tough. I'm selfishly proud of you for coming all the way here to Skye because now you have met Isla." She lowered her voice and gently added, "Coming into the hospital must be difficult. Are you doing okay with that?"

Sudden tears welled up in Raey's eyes at Isobel's soft words. "Just strong enough to get in here today to see this beauty." Raey clenched her jaw and whispered in her ear, "Thanks for standing by and being someone that I can lean on."

"Always." Isobel hugged her tight, and a weight lifted from Raey's chest.

Their conversation strolled down comfortable paths, and that made all the difference to Raey at the start of her days in Skye. Reveling in Isobel's wonder and tender joy at Isla's birth provided a catharsis from her grief.

"Well, I don't want to wear you out by visiting too long. I'll come visit when you get settled in at home," Raey said. She kissed Isla on the forehead and returned the newborn blessing back to Isobel's arms.

"I'll look forward to that."

Two steps into the hall and Raey's thoughts swarmed back to Nic and the questions she needed answered.

SEVEN

As Raey turned off the engine and stepped from her car parked next to Nic's, she saw him hastily exit the B&B with disheveled, wet hair and an untucked shirt. Leaning against her car door, with the contemplative patience of a fisherman waiting for the quiver of a bobber, she waited for him to notice her. Scrambling to hold his keys and phone in one hand while pocketing a piece of paper in his wallet, Nic jolted at Raey's greeting. "Why didn't you tell me?" she charged.

"Tell ye what?" He spun toward her as he unlocked his car. He studied her eyes and then offered, "If you want to know something, Raey, just ask away."

"I saw you hurrying out of the hospital today," Raey posited with an accusatory tone.

"Yep, guilty! That's not a question," he replied, adding a lopsided grin to lighten the effect of his voice.

"Why didn't you say you worked at the hospital or that you were a doctor?" she asked, securing her hands in her jacket pockets.

Holding her gaze, he took slow, easy steps toward Raey. "I didn't want my job to be the first impression you gathered of me."

"Why not?"

When Nic stepped close, he wrapped his hands around her elbows. "Does it change your impression of me?" he defended, waiting for her response.

Raey focused on the blacktop as she admitted, "Well, no, just adds to it."

"In a good way?" Nic bent low to find the answer in her eyes.

Raey lifted her head and broke into a satisfied smirk. "Yeah, now I know you must be really smart."

He lightly squeezed her arms and then released his hands, stuffing them into his pockets. "Oh, ouch. And, by the way, you never asked about my job."

Trying to sidestep any further inquiry about her expectations of him, she flubbed her response. "I guess, um, it just seems like something you would tell someone."

His mouth twisted into a smile. "Careful there, you're wanting to know more about me, aren't you?"

"But it seems like you purposefully omitted that. Why?"

"Cause that place comes with a lot of history for you. I wanted you to know me on my terms," Nic answered, concern dripping from his pinched brows as he ran his fingers through his wet hair. "Something else bothering you?"

"Well, I don't want your girlfriend to get the wrong idea about you hanging out with me." She wrenched her eyes from his, mortified at sounding like a jealous teen.

"My girlfriend?" Nic cocked his head and mumbled, barely audible. "Oh, my girlfriend," his voice piped up in understanding. "I think my girlfriend will be fine with me spending time together as long as I also spend this evening with her. Come have dinner with us this evening?"

Wide-eyed, Raey started, "Oh, thanks, but…."

"Especially since I already delivered those flowers to my girlfriend for her birthday today," he interrupted.

"Aww, well, you are very sweet."

"Your dimples truly show when you are flustered." His challenge threw her further off kilter.

"Oh, bother!" Her hands shot to the blush climbing her cheeks.

Nic brushed the back of his knuckle softly across her cheek and said, "Two small good luck charms on your cheeks."

"Good luck charms?" she echoed.

"Well then, will you join us for dinner?"

"Oh, um, thanks for the offer, but I don't think I can do that," she stumbled, chiding herself for poorly exiting this awkward conversation.

Nic smiled at her answer and then began laughing. "Oh, Dimples, come on. It'll be a fun evening," he coaxed her. "We'll probably play a couple hands of Scrimish after dinner. Do you know it?"

"No, I don't, and that's probably not a good idea," she retorted, as this conversation quickly escalated to an unwanted skirmish.

"You don't think it's a good idea to play Scrimish?" he jested with a serious face.

Raey kicked a pebble and then hit his shoulder. "You know what I mean."

"I know my girlfriend would be delighted for you to join her seventieth birthday celebration," Nic drawled *seventieth* and added a wink. "It will just be the birthday girl, Pops, me, and hopefully my brother and his wife, and now you, Dimples, if you accept. I'm cooking, so I can add one to the reservation. I'm headed just now to grab a few things at the store."

Raey laughed in relief, realizing Nic good-naturedly

tricked her. "Well, I can't intrude on a family event." She fumbled for a polite exit to what might amount to an awkward evening, but she couldn't find one.

"Would you really be so cruel as to make me the odd man out tonight?" he pleaded with his best rendition of puppy dog eyes.

Placing her hands on her hips, she surrendered, "Okay, I'll come," and continued with an ultimatum, "But only if you stop calling me Dimples."

"Deal." Nic shook her hand and then stepped toward his car, but quickly turned and added, "For now."

"Very funny. But after playing me, I do hope you lose miserably." She smirked and waved goodbye.

"Game on at 7, Dim–" he stopped mid-word when Raey emitted a death stare, chortling instead at her antics.

Every ounce of her wanted to look back as she crossed the parking lot, but she didn't dare. When she pulled the door of the B&B open, his car door slammed shut, and she knew he had watched her cross the entire length of the parking lot. The tires hummed and the engine revved louder as he rolled on the asphalt closer to her. She gave in and connected with his eyes. He didn't look away but smiled and waited for her to enter before pulling off the lot.

* * *

Raey sat stiff in her chair until Nic entered the dining room with the finished burgers bathed in whisky sauce. She listened attentively as they each toasted Maisrie. Maisrie was the glue for her clan. Finlay stood at the head of the table and grabbed their attention with a boisterous clearing of his throat. Suddenly, Maisrie seemed shy, staring at her empty plate.

Finlay, usually jocular in Raey's presence, praised her with heartfelt solemnity. "Mo chridle, tha do ghaol dhomhsa fad nam bliadhnaichean air a bhith mar thonnan an uisge–seasmhach agus gun chrìoch. Every day with ye is another blessing from the good Lord." Maisrie raised her lips to his.

Nic leaned against Raey's shoulder and offered her a quiet translation, "My dear, your love for me over the years has been like the waves of the water–enduring and endless."

"How sweet," Raey whispered back.

Nic's sister-in-law, Laurel, stood next. Raey stared at her long, sleek red hair which intensified the green of her eyes. When they first met, Laurel's inviting demeanor drew her in with a hug instead of a handshake. Her devotion to Maisrie and Finlay endeared her to Raey even more. "Maisrie, I love all the ways you lavish love on us and how you see the best in all of us. It makes us want to achieve the good that you see. I love you for growing men that care for and defend others. I wish you all the happiness in this next year, which is nothing short of what you deserve."

Her husband, Alasdair, concisely crafted his words. "Gram, you filled our lives with love and wonderful memories. Cheers to creating more memories we will cherish. Happy birthday and may you be blessed with many more."

Nic, seated between Maisrie and Raey, stood to face his grandma with his whisky in hand. "Gram, thanks for always being there. I've learned many lessons from you over the years." Amazed, he shook his head and paused for a sip of his whisky. He lowered his eyes to the floor and then confidently raised them to hers. "Most of all, Gram, you taught us that pain and strength are a mere perspective apart. I will ever be thankful to you and Pops for bringing the light back to our hearts and guiding us through especially dark times." Maisrie stood to wrap her arms around his waist and kissed his cheek. "Wait, I'm not done here, young lady. Second, I'm thankful you taught us that when we're weary, we need to learn to rest, not quit." He smiled, kissed her gray head, and raised his glass, "And last, if God had not chosen you for my Gram, I'd choose you as my best friend every time."

They all repeated Nic's call, "Slàinte Mhath" with a raise of their glasses, and Nic kissed her cheek.

When Nic returned from the kitchen with the cranachan cheesecake, they sang "Happy Birthday" to Finlay's bellowing lead.

Raey caught the attention of the entire table when she squealed in delight, "I love cranachan cheesecake."

Nic ribbed her, "Wow, I think the cake got a better greeting than me tonight."

"Well, I see why. It's a helluva lot sweeter," Alasdair added, punching his brother's arm.

Raey's face matched the raspberries, and Maisrie came to her aid. "Oh, dear, it's my favorite, too! Wait until ye taste this one. Laurel makes the best!"

Nic hugged Maisrie's shoulder and agreed, "Gram's and Laurel's are both supreme. In fact, I think it's worth taking my chances on eating yours." He pretended to steal her plate, but Raey slapped the top of his hand. The table erupted in laughter as Nic rubbed the sting from his withdrawn hand.

Laurel asked Maisrie what she hoped the years ahead held in store for her. She studied each person at the table. "I ask the good Lord for health and a little retreading of the B&B so we can travel and see our great grandchild more." Turning to Nic, she said, "Oh, and we'd like to be part of a wedding."

Nic quickly steered the conversation in another direction. "A retreading?"

"Well, get some more help in here to cover for us when we're gone."

"We'd love to have you two anytime, Gram," Alasdair said. "Come and stay as long as you want. You know we have plenty of room. I'm glad I worked in Inverness today, so we could be closer for your birthday. Unfortunately, we need to set out now, though, to get back for some early meetings tomorrow."

After prolonged goodbyes, they left, and Nic pulled out the cards to play Maisrie's favorite game, Scrimish. "A couple rounds, Gram?"

"I'm ready."

Nic clarified for Raey, "Gram swears this game soothes her before bed, but I think she just likes it because she's usually the winner."

"I like it because it doesn't require much thinking, so we can chat and play."

Raey grabbed the box after Nic emptied it of the cards, and read aloud, "An epic ten-minute battle of strategy, memory, and misdirection."

"How about the loser of the most games wears a kilt?" Finlay seriously wagered.

An incredulous snort came from Raey as she asked Nic, "You wear a kilt?"

"They're very fetching, you ken? You're hoping I lose now, aren't you?" Nic teased.

At Raey's blush, Finlay cautioned, "Don't let him get yer goat."

Maisrie rescued Raey when she offered, "I'll go fetch Iain's."

Raey shot a confused look toward Nic at Maisrie

addressing him as Iain, but Nic curbed the direction of the festivities. "No, that's okay, Gram. Maybe later," Nic urged.

When Nic lost the first three out of five games, Maisrie encouraged, "It's a lang road that's no goat a turnin."

Confusion settled across Raey's face as she caught Nic's shocked glance at Maisrie before turning to her to explain, "Um, she's telling me not to lose heart." Nic blushed and quickly added, "She means things can't keep going in the same direction forever. You know, my losses." He leaned closer for only Raey to hear, and his cologne shot through her senses, sending hormones surging through her body. "But don't take that as kindness. She's being facetious."

When Finlay inserted that he was heading to bed, Maisrie's concern showed in her uplifted brows. "You're lookin' peely wally," she noted.

"I'm going to sleep like a log," he said, and tilted her chin up for a goodnight kiss.

Maisrie consented to Finlay, "We'll let ye go Scot free on this game. A loue ye." In that moment, Raey saw the cherishing love lavished on Nic as he grew up.

Two games later, Nic still couldn't reclaim his kilt-wearing losses, and Maisrie assented, "Well, it was truly a lovely evening. Thank ye for all yer work, Nic." She yawned as she gathered the cards to place in the boxes. "I'd better head to bed so I can greet the early risers tomorrow. Nic, ye be sure to square up when ye'll be wearing that kilt for the lass."

Nic hugged his grandma goodnight as he said, "Night, Gram. I love ye. Glad we all could be together to celebrate your birthday."

Together, Raey and Nic cleared the table and cleaned the kitchen.

"Can I walk you to your room?"

"That'd be fine." They both knew it wasn't necessary, but she welcomed the couple extra minutes with him. They exchanged smiles and crossed the tiled foyer to the steps. Nic stepped ahead. The posture of his tall body oozed confidence, but not arrogance. He tucked a gray polo shirt, tight at the biceps, in Levi's that hugged his thighs. Raey changed the direction of her thoughts and gaze.

"So, Iain?" Raey slowly pronounced each syllable of his birth name.

He smiled and shook his head, expecting that she wouldn't let that new information slide by unmentioned. "Since junior high, my buddies have called me Nic. With a last name like MacNicol, I guess it's just easier to yell on the football field. Plus, Dr. Nic sounds friendly; don't you think?"

"Well, it is quite easy and catchy. It suits."

At the top of the landing, he turned to her and feigned offense. "So, I'm an easy catch? Or might you be implying I'm catchy like a wee cold?"

"Oh, bother." Raey shook her head and grabbed at his bicep to pull him down the hallway. At her door, she grabbed hold of the doorknob, but then hesitated and looked back at him, sucking in her lower lip and trying to restrain from blurting her question.

Nic noted her struggle. "Just ask it, Raey."

From their conversation earlier in the evening, Raey anticipated his answer to her question but asked anyway, "Did you know my husband, Josh Davenport?"

"Yeah, Raey, I did," he gently whispered, moving closer into her space. He leaned against the wall, ready for further inquiry. "He was a colleague admired by everyone in our small hospital. Our professional paths crossed several times."

"I figured. I guess I just didn't put everything together until

I realized you worked at the hospital. Now," she conceded, fumbling with the key in her hand, "I guess I understand better why you didn't tell me you are a doctor."

"You ken, he was well-respected as a man and a doctor. I'd want him on my team anytime," Nic complimented, but then groaned with a grimace. "But courtside, I didn't mess around with him. I should have learned that sooner." Nic unwittingly covered his nose, recalling Josh's flying elbow that knocked him to the floor. "I did my damndest to get in his way as often as I could until he gave me a bloody nose."

Talking with Nic about Josh's foibles comforted her. Josh arrived home from his pickup games always later than he promised, soaked in sweat, with wild excitement in his eyes as he restaged his win.

Raey came out of her reverie. "I'm so sorry. That sounds like a story I'd like to hear."

"No need to apologize. A guy's got to do what a guy's got to do on the court. If I could have won by giving him a bloody nose, I just might have. We were neck and neck down to the last minutes, and those wins were bragging rights."

"What specialty are you in?" she asked, settling against the doorjamb.

"I'm a pediatrician," Nic answered.

Raey hid her surprise when she suddenly realized that Nic could be baby Isla's "charming" doctor. She redirected her focus by asking the other thought running through her mind, "Why did you decide to become a doctor?"

Nic held her gaze for a second before responding, "I thought I went into medicine because of the frustration of not being able to save my parents. But I chose pediatrics after treating one withdrawn boy. I recognized my frightened and angry self in him. I worked very hard to get him to smile and help him through his fears. I knew then that I wanted to help hurting kids." Nic stopped and his gaze dropped to the floor. "I realized my choice may also have been about healing myself."

Without hesitation, Raey offered, "I totally understand. I guess that's why I became an elementary teacher." She gazed into his faraway eyes. "I wanted to keep kids' dreams alive, if that makes sense?"

"Definitely does."

The key slipped from Raey's hand. When they both reached for it, she breathed in fresh eucalyptus. Picking up her key, she placed it in her back pocket, and then locked eyes with him.

"Why didn't you tell me you knew my husband?"

"I wanted to get to know you, but I feared triggering your grief would get in the way." His eyes searched her face for understanding.

She nodded her head and freely admitted, "Most days, my grief gets in the way, but I'm working through that."

He didn't counsel her, nor did he reassure her. Grasping her hand, he shook it with certainty and offered, "You will."

He held her gaze without words, just understanding between them. When he slowly leaned in and asked with his eyes, time stood still. Waiting to feel the brush of his breath, she breathed him in. He lightly cradled her cheek, and she closed her eyes. Her heart floated in her chest.

"Stay still," he whispered.

A soft press of his lips to her forehead, and the warmth of his body drew her to him. He faintly brushed the tip of her nose. She opened her eyes and stared into his, answering his question once again and pleading for him to find her. And then his lips gently caressed hers for a few, short, paralyzing seconds. His touch flowed to every nerve in her body. Her lips released him or his released her. She didn't know.

"That felt right," Nic whispered.

Her stomach churned, her heartbeat raced, and her throat tightened at the fear of navigating uncharted waters with Nic. Despite her growing panic, she nodded her head in agreement.

"Mmm. It did," she murmured and finally opened her eyes, regaining some balance.

He stood still, surveying her response. Ping-ponging thoughts confused her as she settled her body. Would she run from him or lean into his offering? She might be unclear about her feelings, but she was shockingly clear about what she didn't feel. No guilt, shame, or regret. It felt odd to be void of these kindred spirits, a wall that she leaned against for a strange sense of balance. If she owed them further loyalty, her heart failed to remind her of that. She might be able to live with this new kind of heart failure, this threat to her emotional comfort zone that left her oddly energized with curiosity.

She jolted when he slipped the key from her back pocket. He opened her door, guiding her to enter with the slightest touch to the small of her back. A puzzling calm washed over her. She longed for his touch, the softness of his skin against hers.

"Thank you," she followed with a soft smile, opening her hand for the key.

He raised his eyebrows and returned her smile and key. Propping against the doorframe again, he added, "I'm off Monday. I'm hosting a hiking tour to a cool spot on the island. I think you'd like it. Meet at the desk at nine?"

She poked the center of his chest and drawled his rarely used name, "Sure, *Dr. Iain.*"

Her familiarity encouraged his antics. He stared at her with a dare in his eyes and raised his hands. Thinking he might take the chance to cup her face in a kiss again, she held still, but sudden disappointment permeated her body when instead his hands imitated a knife being stuck in his heart. "Oh Dimples, you're killing me."

"Touché," she giggled, arousing his own light-hearted laughter. She added, "You owe me a kilt."

"You owe me a trail to Neist Point."

"You wear the kilt and I'm game," she challenged.

"Deal, pick a day," he reeled her in.

"Deal, find a day," she responded, throwing his schedule back on him. A sudden spasm of panic mixed with regret gripped her.

"Touché," he conceded.

For the next few seconds, his gaze met hers, as if a stare could evolve into a revelation of what the other might be thinking. Nic broke the spell by pushing off the wall and knocking twice on the door jamb to her room, signaling the end of their time together.

Before he turned to leave, he nudged her shoulder with his, directing her inside her room and warned, "See ye in a couple days. Close the door before you get yourself into a whole lot more trouble, young lady. Sleep well." She watched him stroll down the hall.

Turning inside her room, she glimpsed Josh's stethoscope on the desk and guilt nudged her nerves.

Oh, Josh, I'm sorry.

EIGHT

S he dreamed of hiking the Red Cuillins under a warm sun with Nic in his kilt and kilt hose. She followed the steps of his ghillie brogues through the rocks and the sway of his red and black MacNicol plaid, her imagined colors for him. His tartan plaid wrapped around his bare chest and under his right arm, pulled firmly to his tan body and tucked into his waist belt.

Despite that stirring dream and her easy exchange with Nic the night before, today she faced an uphill climb, physically and mentally. With Nic's group hike still a couple of days away, Raey would relish a long day of hiking to the Old Man of Storr, a favorite of Josh and hers. Often, the Old Man of Storr had transformed their rough work week into a calm ending. Sometimes, their quiet traipse faded the entire world until just the two of them shared what words could not express. Josh had always joked that while some couples had a song, they had the Old Man.

Skye's unpredictable weather presented a certain obstacle, but she and Josh had always risked venturing out with a hope for more idyllic weather. Today, alone, she would face that challenge with a similar optimism. Stepping out of the car in warm Gore-tex gear, wool socks, and sweater, Raey entertained the notion that she might just be a glutton for punishment, trading the warmth of a North Carolina June for Skye's brisk temperatures. A light overnight rain muddied the gravel trail she followed through a recently harvested pine woodland.

Two trails diverged, and her heart beat faster. Stopping to adjust the weight of her rucksack's load, she considered her paths, taking a reprieve from the guilt ebbing into her conscience over Nic's kiss. Either path would place her eye to eye with the Old Man of Storr. Determined to meet the challenge of conquering her deeply etched memories of this rugged terrain and her inability, at times, to make a simple decision, she quickly stepped to the right, zig-zagging the steeper route up the hillside.

The longer and higher she climbed, the more majestic the landscape grew, and those same views she thought she'd cemented in her memory inspired her as if for the first time. Closing a third wooden gate she passed through, designed to keep deer out, she trudged along the rough and rocky slope. Her footing slipped in areas, forcing her to concentrate with slow and steady steps. She stopped at the uneven rock steps to catch her breath and faced the famous pinnacle of rock, resembling the profile of an old man, set against rolling green hills.

The winds whipped harder around the rocky path as she gained elevation. Strands of her blond hair, freed from under her hood, slapped her eyes. Finagling her phone from her thigh pocket, she snapped a proof-of-life selfie. Proof that perseverance still pumped through her veins.

Just beyond a rock formation, she spied the white of a sheep's rump. She sneaked closer and hunched down, creeping around a grassy mound. When she stood and snapped quickly, the sheep, stunned by her sudden appearance there, stared directly into her camera.

Looming rain clouds broke loose, and she passed unprepared tourists hightailing it back to the carpark, their hopes washed away by the rain. Josh had coached her to be prepared and undeterred by a downpour during their treks. On their adventures together, she quickly learned the greater prize was won when they didn't let the rain chase them from the land.

The mist hung thick and low, creating a clinging, claustrophobic cloud to plow through, much like the other days Josh visited her. Maisrie's daughter had visited multiple times. *Oh, to see him one more time.*

She sheltered under a massive rock, the best shield she could find against the pelting rain in this green arena. Setting her pack to the side, she hunkered against the slick moss formation, hugging her knees to her chest. As she sat, reveling in the fortune of having the Old Man to herself, a traveler also seeking refuge sat too close and bumped her off balance. She toppled over, catching herself on her backpack, annoyed at possibly crushing her sandwich.

"Great choice, Princess. Nothing like a deluge to help you decide quickly!"

Josh huddled leg to leg and loosened the drawstring of his hoodie, releasing his curls to the wind. A mischievous smile played on his lips. Alarm raced through her veins. Not at his presence, but at her lack of surprise at it.

Josh wrapped his arm around her knees, pulling her next to him, and set his temple next to hers to whisper, "I didn't mean to scare you."

She launched a quizzical look at him. "I'm not scared by

you. I'm more frightened by how much I hope for these moments. My first thought is a prayer that this visit isn't your last. That scares me." She spread her hand across his jaw and traced her finger across the crinkles at his eyes that his smile created. "I want this, always." She tugged a loosed auburn curl that had fallen across his forehead and then pulled his hand to her lap. "But it can't be."

"Seeing me this way must be hard. Being with you in the majesty of this place again is a gift."

"Mmm. Such a gift," she murmured and smiled into his eyes. "But if I'm being honest, it's really hard. This having you right now and knowing any day soon I'll be losing you forever —again." Steadying the quiver in her voice, she continued with just a fair bit more control, "I'll never get this chance again. I'd never expected this in a million years. I'll return to my memories of you that have sustained me for nearly two years. I know how to spend my days that way. Nothing is the same without you, and I can't envision moving on. I'm stuck in space and time."

Josh wrapped his arm around her shoulder. "It's hard when nothing feels comfortable or sure. It seems trite to say that it will get better. But it will." The reminiscent smile in his voice and the strength of his hand wrapped in hers offered her assurance.

"People are getting on with their lives. Brenda is dating a police officer named Brian, nine months now. You'd like him. He's a great guy and treats her really well. He's athletic and tall and would probably beat you at basketball. Both your parents retired this year."

At the mention of Brenda's dating, Josh smiled. "He must be a good guy. She's got some high standards, and I'm happy she found a man that meets them."

"I wonder if he's the one because she's never been this serious or invested this much in a guy. It's nice to see her this way." Brenda recently posted their initials within a heart etched in sand on Instagram.

"In time, you'll look forward to the future again. Look at you. You're chasing a dream–getting your best life back. Don't overlook the little steps that you take to find your way."

"Today is monumental, proving to myself I can conquer my memories of this hike and maybe even enjoy it at the same time. I don't want to be broken by this kind of pain again. It leaves permanent scars." She stared at the distant undulating terrain forged by an ancient landslide and at the mud path made more difficult by the pummeling rain.

"It definitely changes a person. Don't you think it is natural to feel scarred by losing love and to be scared of making your way forward through pain?"

"Scarred or scared–they both feel like pain to me—a drowning kind of pain. It may be natural to feel that way, but I'm not sure I'm healing. Do you think I'm scarred for life?" Raey asked.

"Scars aren't all bad. They signify healing." He rubbed her hand with his thumb.

"Is that another platitude?"

"No, it's another truth. You know it. You've lived through grief after your parents' deaths. Right now, your heart still hurts. Maybe it's scary that on most days, there is more sorrow than joy. But one day, you will find more joy than sorrow. You came to Skye to find that, to push through to find your strength. You expected something more out of your days in coming here. That's a significant step, proving to yourself you are healing. It's rough, but you're on the journey."

"My heart and mind might not make it through this grief. I hope coming here wasn't too big of a step."

He leaned against her shoulder. "This is my gentle nudge to help you make it through the grief to better days. It wasn't a bad step."

"I hope so," she said in disbelief. "Seeing you like this and hearing you cheer me on are a balm to my soul."

"Something else to think about, Raey. Don't place a timetable on walking through grief. Healing stalls. You can't always feel the progress you are making, but that doesn't mean it isn't happening. Trying to hide your pain from others keeps you hiding away. The pain will subside."

"When?"

"It's a journey through. I can't say when. You'll know when the pain lessens. Give yourself some time, though. If it were in my power to bear your pain, I would, in a heartbeat."

"It's hard to talk about with others, except Brenda. Most people don't understand it, so I fake a smile and avoid talking about it by telling them I'm fine. It's like they assume I am past losing you. How can I ever be past it? It's a weird pressure to want to keep you front and center of my life and to learn to live with you in the background. Thank God your sister and I have had each other for this madness."

"Don't hide your pain from people, hoping to protect yourself. All of what's beautiful in life has the potential for pain."

"That sounds like a dangerous supposition."

"A safe supposition."

"That clearly doesn't sound safe at all to me."

"There's beauty in the fragile finding their strength. And that strength is a thing of beauty. Like you."

"Are you saying that I'm the fragile? It certainly feels close to that."

"From my vantage point, you are strong. You need to remember that. Heartache won't hang around. What's left when it's gone? I hope what you find is the beauty in life. A life worth living and enjoying."

"I can't see that far. Heck, I can't see through this crazy burst of rain this rock is sheltering us from."

"It will clear, you know."

"Is that why you keep showing up in the mist? To help me see past the clouds?"

"Ah, we've experienced countless times when rain didn't ruin a hike. Your time of grieving is hard and lonely. Much of it is a solo soul trek, it's true. You're doing it. Beyond the clouds, there will be healing. You'll be strong and ready to share your love."

"Wait." Raey stood up, pointed an accusing finger at him, the rain pelting the hood of her rain jacket. "This isn't your push to pass me off to someone else, is it?"

"Hold on for a second," he said, tugging her hand for her to sit back down next to him.

Her hand remained in his hold. "Giving me permission to be with someone else? Is this your way of letting me go?"

"Raey, I'm not…" he started, but she forged ahead.

"Cause you've already done that. Gone and left me here." Slogging through her breaking voice, every word a slow-motion release of raw emotion, she found urgency in her desperation. "Alone. Without you. No permission needed."

He reached her with his soft, southern cadence when he stood. "Raey, you chose our song, Old Man of Storr, as one of your treks to branch out on your own."

"I came to this island for you." She cringed at hearing herself hurl those inaccurate words at him.

"This trip is about you," Josh's deep voice contested. He never let things go when she lied to herself. He softened and placed his hand on her heart, adding, "I'm here, always."

"Why are you here? Are you haunting me?" Raey weakened. Her tears teetered on the ledges of her eyelids.

The weeping sky plopped raindrops on his jacket and the silence hanging between them created a cacophony of noise. Before breaking the lingering stillness that her question brought on, Josh cleared his throat and proceeded with caution, "Raey, nothing you've done is a mistake."

Confused by his utterance, she panicked at his possible reference to her hidden guilt over kissing Nic. Tears quelled, but not before one leaked over her lashes. "How do you know it wasn't a mistake?"

"It's your guilt and regret that is the mistake. It's okay," he said, searching her eyes. He grabbed her hands, laid a soft kiss on her knuckles, and then rubbed them warm.

"But when I close my eyes, I picture us. I don't want to lose those memories by making more with someone else."

"I'll never be just a fleeting memory. And no man will ever compete with me unless you make him," he implored, his voice saturated with empathy.

She absorbed his words as she concentrated on the warmth emanating from their cupped hands. The sky's floodgates closed to a drizzle as the sun broke through the blanket of clouds.

"Walk with me?" she begged, to prolong his presence and evade the inevitable.

As the silver trickle of rain sopped the soil, Josh comforted her, "I'll be right here with you." A frail mist slipped from her eyes, caressing her cheeks, but it was a strangely cleansing renewal, like nourishment to dry topsoil. They strolled along the soggy trail, saturated in the satisfaction of being together before the Old Man of Storr once again.

"Our timing couldn't have been better!" She elbowed him with pride and rubbed her eyes with her sleeve.

"You are so right," he mused, his deep, cavernous voice reminding her of the richness of the life they had shared.

"Look, Josh." She pointed at a couple climbing up the hillside through the mist to the ultimate vantage point. "We took fabulous photos of the coastline and mountains from that plateau."

She turned to join Josh's reverence, but he was gone. She squeezed her eyes shut, fearing those might have been the last words she ever spoke to him. The light drizzle mingled with a single, free-flowing tear.

Standing amidst the rock formations at the summit, the light emerging through the thinning veil painted a watercolor rainbow across the landscape, and she snapped a selfie.

Alone again.

* * *

She lay in bed that night wondering if Josh's presence had been synchronicity or the power of the Old Man. Her phone pinged with a text, interrupting her reflections. She stared at her phone, not recognizing the number, until she read the message.

Nic: Did you have a good day? Are you still on for
Monday at 9 a.m.?

Raey: Yes, looking forward to hanging in the back.

She stepped from the bed, pulling a blanket around her. Opening the curtain, she sat before the windowpanes and waited for Nic's reply. The moon's reflection lay wide over the bay.

Nic: Hanging back is not allowed. Eat a nutritious breakfast.
Come ready for a challenge.

She fired off a quick response.

Raey: No worries about getting a solid breakfast from the
B&B. My worry is eating so much that I can't move.
I don't need another hiking challenge after today.

Nic: I can't wait to hear about your day on the hike.

What would she tell Nic about Josh's visits? She hoped he would forget her comment. Texting with him felt pleasantly familiar.

Raey: Sleep well.

Nic: We'll see. I'm on call.

She laid her phone on her lap. A slight whistle, unnoticeable from the bed, stole her attention from the puffs of mist rolling in the distance. Finding the space between—the space between frame and pane—she set her fingertip over the gap in the seal. A cool breeze penetrated the insulation and floated across her skin. She cupped her hand above the opening, allowing the fresh flow of life to breathe on her palm.

Oh, the cool wind of change. Blow cool wind, blow over me.

NINE

Raey jumped when Nic entered the foyer and called, "Ready?"

"Didn't you say you were hosting a group?" She spun around, searching the foyer for the others, catching Maisrie's smile and wave from the atrium where she cleared dishes from a table.

"Well, we-e," he elongated the word 'we' into two syllables and pointed at the two of them, "do constitute a group. You know, you and me." He pointed at her and held up one finger and then pointed at his chest and held up two fingers in a sign of peace. "And whoever else comes along."

"Very feisty, Iain."

"I've packed our food and water," Nic said, patting his rucksack. "Let's get a move on, Dimples." Adjusting his loaded pack on his back, he tugged at her elbow and guided her toward the door.

"Boy, am I gullible." She pulled her elbow free and squinted her eyes at him. "Why didn't you just ask me on a hike?"

"Did you fret the last few days over this invite?"

"Well, no."

"Not gullible. Worry free."

He perused the length of her body and then nodded his head in agreement. "You look good, so let's go."

Momentarily taken aback by his scrutiny, Raey couldn't recall what she wore. Glancing down at her attire, she stumbled into her response, "Uh, oh, thanks."

"On second thought—" he checked her out once again, "Did you bring sunglasses? The sun is already causing those pretty brown eyes to look fiercer."

Raey teased, "Are they shooting daggers your way, maybe?"

With coy charm, he explained, "I meant you appear to be dressed appropriately for this hike, for warmth, and with rain gear and boots."

"Uh-huh. I'm sure that's what you meant," she facetiously called out his fib and unzipped her jacket. His flirting added degrees of heat to her layers.

"Everything else we need is in here," he said, and pointed to the rucksack on his back. "Except maybe something to take the heat out of your face." He held the door for her with a knowing grin as she headed out.

When she reached his car, he grabbed her hand and clarified, "By the way, just to be clear, *if* I were checking you out, I'd describe you as beautiful."

She composed herself against the flush rising on her face again with a casual lean against the car door. Crossing her arms, she peered at her toes and waited until her heart rate steadied. Darn if he didn't throw her off balance.

What is good for the goose....

Her eyes captured his and then traced his lips, spread across his shoulders, and lingered on his torso. "Well," she said as a shiver rolled through her body, "I'd say you look cute, too, then."

Alarmed by his fingers softly tapping her thigh, she didn't register that he nudged her to move so he could open the door for her. "You didn't plan for anyone else on this tour today, did you?" she accused to distract him from her awkwardness.

He gazed at her blushed cheeks. "Before we leave, I think you're definitely going to need sunscreen." She punched his shoulder in response to his playful mockery. He added a nimble defense to her accusation. "I do give group hiking tours at the height of the tourist season when my schedule allows."

"Just not today, right?" She jumped into his car. "I prepared to be a tag-a-long at the back of a paid tour."

He leaned close to her ear. "Nope, I'm offering you my undivided tour expertise today. And I'll share a secret with you. The tour goes a lot better if you tell the guide he's *handsome,* not cute." He shut her door and smirked through the front windshield as he crossed the car. He explained as he hopped in, "And the best part for lucky you is that I'm feeling charitable today, so I'll let that one mistake slide. And keep in mind that tips are more than acceptable."

"Lucky me. I'll keep those tips in mind," she responded in contemplative monotone. "Where are we headed today?"

"We'll do part of the Skye Trail and the Bad Step. It's beautiful, but parts are boggy and rocky. It may be slippery in spots, so watch your footing. At the Bad Step, we'll shimmy across a large boulder. It's a wee bit sketchy, but lock your footing in the crack, lean forward, and shimmy along. If it goes pear shape, you'll get a refreshing dip in the sea."

"What?"

"That was a wee joke."

"A bad one, for sure," she teased. "The Bad Step. How apropos. I hope this hike isn't an omen."

Nic cast a confounded glance, questioning her comment.

"You tricked me into a solo hike with you."

"I'm sorry I overstepped–"

"Lighten up," Raey slapped his shoulder and chortled, regaining their lighthearted banter. "At least this overstep won't have you taking a 'refreshing dip in the sea.'"

Nic hesitated but soon joined her jest.

"Have you done any of the Skye Trail?" he asked.

"We did small parts of the eighty miles. Such fabulous, rugged coast and cliffs. We didn't do the Bad Step, though." Raey grimaced at including Josh.

Their banter and the intimacy of a solo hike with Nic felt like a date, and she was whisked back to the time Josh asked her on their first date. Her next words might be a bad step or jarring at this juncture for Nic, but she braved sharing a piece of their life together and blurted out, "I remember when Josh asked me out on our first date."

Without a hitch in the conversation, he encouraged her, "How'd that go?"

"He had this love for those Valentine conversation hearts with different sayings." Nic shook his head, but she continued anyway. "He bought bags by the dozen to last the entire year. Either that or he got a lot of rejections and needed that many," she joked.

Nic laughed. "Now that's just cruel. We guys have it tough. Give us some slack, will ye?"

"Oh, the poor male species."

"Valentine hearts? Your story?"

"Well, my friend Brenda, Josh's sister, had invited me to a Sunday game night at Josh's apartment. This huge bowl of those conversation hearts sat in the middle of the table. This wide!" She created a big circle with her hands. "He'd grab a big handful to keep at his side to pop in his mouth while playing. He slid four from his pile under my elbow on the table, inconspicuously, one by one throughout the evening. The first one said *U R Cute*. I rested my face on my hand so nobody could see how flustered I was."

"I can definitely picture that color in your cheeks. Josh has good taste."

Raey held up two fingers. "A second one came during the ruckus of bathroom breaks and grabbing snacks. People were milling about, so, as he left the table to get something to drink, he slid another candy over to me that said *wink, wink*. When I glanced at him, he winked and walked away. I laughed out loud which, of course, piqued everyone's curiosity. At the beginning of our final game, he slid the third and fourth hearts to me at the same time, *You & Me* followed by *Date Me?* What was I supposed to do with that?"

"That's easy. You say, 'Yes,'" Nic answered, and he started the ignition.

"Do men always stick together?"

"Other than seeing him occasionally in passing when I visited Brenda and he was home from college, I had known him for precisely two hours of Cards Against Humanity. It would have been totally out of character for me to say yes." She didn't share with Nic the part of the story about being so elated with Josh asking her out that she headed to the restroom for a silent cheer and to curb her excitement.

"But you said yes, right?"

"Well, I made him wait for an answer."

"So, you're a 'play hard to get' kind of girl? I'd say that's playing a cruel Humanity card on him."

She pitched him an exasperated glare.

"Listening. This is me just listening." He raised both hands off the steering wheel, yielding to her.

"When we left, I graciously thanked him for the game night and left a heart in his palm as I shook his hand goodbye that said *text me*."

"That's a great memory."

Reay reciprocated his genuine smile.

"How would you rate my finesse?" Nic asked.

"So, this was you asking me on a first date, huh?" She waited for an answer.

Nic slid his phone from his coat pocket and studied it. His head bent to send a quick response.

Just then, Raey's pocket vibrated with a text. She sneaked a peek while he was preoccupied. Her eyes jolted to Nic who waited for her response to his text, his phone still in his hands. She wrestled with her response, starting and stopping, texting and deleting. Finally, his phone buzzed. They locked eyes for a second before a glance at his screen told him all he wanted to know.

Nic: Will you go on a Not-a-Date with me?

Raey: Yes

He returned his phone to his pocket and his intense eyes to her. "And 'No' to your previous question. This is our second Not-a-Date." He winked.

Raey forgot what she asked him and then coyly slapped his arm in denial. "No, the band wasn't a date."

"That's what I just said. Is dinner acceptable on a Not-a-Date?"

"Most definitely. No denying a girl food," she quipped.

"See, we men have it bad. Dinner even on Not-a-Dates."

She mocked him with a pout.

"Deal, dinner it is." He combed his fingers through her hair, pushing it behind her ear, and then nestled a light kiss to her neck.

With his breath still warm on her skin, Raey offered a simple, small smile and bowed her head as she confessed, "I liked that."

They quieted into a locked gaze, understanding the attraction growing between them.

"I'm glad. Me, too," Nic finally said and put his car in reverse to back out of the B&B's lot.

As they drove toward Camasunary Bay, their light banter quieted down to the low hum of the heater warming the SUV. She released her hands from warming them under her legs on the heated seats. The rhythm of the windshield wipers against the light mist mimicked the steady calm that had been growing inside her.

The early cool rain cleared to sunny skies and crisp but pleasant temperatures, and the strong morning wind softened to a gentle breeze. Splashes of reds and pinks ignited the skyscape, hovering over a quilt of yellow primroses and celandine.

Spotting a herd of Highland cows, Raey called, "Oh, Nic, look. Pull over for a second."

He heeded her giddy bidding as cars whizzed by.

"They're so cute. Don't you just love their just-jumped-out-of-bed hairstyles?" Raey absorbed every part of the culture that beckoned her to Skye.

"Definitely looks easy. That's it. I'm switching to that shaggy style."

Raey laughed. "Might take yours a while to grow out, but you can see what you would look like. Check out that black one over there."

"And bonus–you'd never know where my eyes were wandering."

The day's journey created its own sublime revelations. The easily distinguishable trail started out simple and straightforward past several houses to the moorland and meandered to the cliff top above the shore and on to Glen Scaladal. She thanked the fairies for waterproof boots when she forded the river at the far end of the Camasunary Bay. In a whimsical mood, she thought about just taking them off and wading across the slow-moving water, but common sense came to her aid.

Along the shoreline at the foot of the small mountain, Sgurr na Stri, seals sunned themselves on the beach, giving a slight glance their way. Once over the shoulder of the hill, their course dropped to the shore where they faced the Bad Step and its fall into Loch Coruisk. Raey's calm whimsy sobered as she tracked this daunting traverse above the loch, and she dug deep into self-talk to find the place where resolve kicks in.

When he looked back and saw her stuck, still surveying the rock, Nic called, "You didn't come this far to let this obstacle deter you, lass."

"I'm with you. Just figuring it out." She steadied herself with both hands flat against the rock. Turning back offered no sense of security, only defeat. Going forward required the same effort. She pressed through her hesitation. Buoyed by the idea that Nic considered her capable of this jaunt, she edged along like a tightrope walker, mustering her nerve with each step.

She placed her feet into a deep crevice which grew narrower as they traversed a zig-zag path over the rock. She edged her feet along while Nic led steadily onward. With fewer places for good holdings, her courage wavered. Slowing to a near halt, Raey sought balance with each step, wary of slipping into the calm, clear loch and ending up as amusement for the passing boats. That thought caught in her throat and paralyzed her feet in the crevice.

Nic's call broke through her brooding. "Raey, it's not a bad step, really." She stared wide-eyed at him and then concentrated on her feet. He stepped back to reach her. "Take my hand, Raey." The reassurance and strength in his voice comforted her, while her newfound reliance upon him unsteadied her.

She clasped his outstretched hand and shimmied her way over the rock. Nic didn't utter a word and let her set the pace. She stopped a couple of times to find her footing and her gumption, lifting her head occasionally to take in the view.

Once across the Bad Step, they exchanged a sigh of relief. Her glowing smile matched the glistening diamond path the sun shed across the water. Raey set her hands to her hips and scanned the rock that she'd scaled. Raising her fist to the sky in salute, she victoriously hailed, "We conquered it!"

Staring at her courageous stance, Nic gave her a high five. "You did it."

"I made it through that epic Bad Step, thanks to you."

"Thanks to your spunk and grace, I think."

"And some of that," Raey jokingly agreed.

"We hiked the Bad Step together. That sounds like a t-shirt! I could make some money off those," he teased.

They ambled along the water's edge to the head of the loch and caught a boat back to Elgol.

They sipped hot tea while standing shoulder to shoulder at the taffrail. Raey nearly spilled Nic's tea in her excitement, grabbing his arm to point out a sea eagle. "Oh, Nic, look there."

"Such a valiant bird of prey."

"There's such power in an eagle's flight. It's majestic."

"Seeing them never gets old," Nic said. "Their comeback from near extinction is miraculous."

"Look at it soar so freely over the loch and the Cuillins. It makes me want to fly." The eagle's struggle was akin to hers, this land a proving ground for her stamina and motivation.

Perhaps the sacred poetry of the mountains reflecting in the blue water provoked her contemplative mood to descend like fog across the bay. *He promised me he would stay as long as I wanted. And now he is gone.* Like a prayer that arises in solitude, she wished away the consuming heaviness that pressed for her attention and threatened her enjoyment of the present moment.

Leaning on the rail, shoulder to shoulder, Nic turned his head to her fixed gaze on the water. No tears fell from her face. No furrowed brow. No grimace flattened her lips. With her cup clutched in both hands and shoulders slumped forward, she stared across the water into the hills.

She closed her eyes and said the first thing that came to her mind, "I'm sorry, Nic." She wanted to explain her change of mood. "I'm trying to let go, but I'm afraid Josh's memory will fade. I want to let go, but then I hold on tighter. What if I never get over him?"

Nic softly lifted her chin and read her expression. "I don't know what to say. I just know I want to hold you right now." He tucked her against him, gently folding her head into his chest, and firmly wrapped his arms around her, letting his warmth soak into her.

He held her beside him as he pointed her attention to a pair of dolphins swimming alongside the boat. The dolphins, lovers of life, played hide and seek as they dove under water and reemerged. Swimming with them was still on Raey's bucket list.

She tugged at his side and smiled as tears washed over her face, an overflow of Nic's compassion and the dolphins' harmony in motion. "Dolphins are symbols of healing and rebirth."

Nic shook his head in understanding and pulled her close.

* * *

On the drive back toward the B&B, Nic interrupted Raey's private musing about the challenges she'd faced that day. "I owe you dinner. What will it be?"

"Got any suggestions?"

"How about Pizza Palace? It's just a food truck and only takeaway, but it's good. It's quite a drive before we make it there. Can you survive that, or do you want to go somewhere closer?"

"Oh, that would hit the spot. Did you hear my stomach growling?"

"The beast is trying to break out. I fear we better get food in you quickly." He cringed as he grabbed the steering wheel tight with both hands and accelerated.

Raey hit him on the shoulder.

"You should be scared," she responded, but spoiled her growl with a giggle.

"Ask the beast if it can wait about three minutes after we pick up the pizza? There's a wonderful place to eat overlooking the bay." He winked and added, "I'm very close with the owners."

"I'll keep her at bay."

"Ah, good one."

"Well, my beast boasts brawn *and* brains," she corrected.

"Believe me. I noticed." He grinned at her.

Parking the Range Rover in the B&B's lot, they ate pizza and watched the sun glimmer over the bay.

She edged closer to asking the question that nagged at the back of her mind for the last few days. It rattled around in her head, knocking into every thought. Even though his answer might perplex her, she needed to hear it. She took a deep breath to steady her nerves.

He broke his trance, "You alright? That was quite an exhale."

Her words shot out of her mouth like a bullet. "Why did you want me to be still the night you kissed me?"

Confusion swept across Nic's face, and he adjusted to sit up straighter in his seat. Seconds invaded the space between them.

"I'm sorry. I should have asked you first," Nic apologized.

"I was confused by your cryptic, 'Be still.'"

"I didn't mean to be cryptic. I wanted the kiss to be all from me," he answered. He rubbed the steering wheel as if soothing it. "I didn't, I didn't want—"

Raey caught his eyes as he glanced her way for help and offered a small smile.

He ran his fingers through his hair and exhaled. "I didn't want you to doubt or regret the kiss. I wanted to kiss you without you feeling you had to kiss me back. I offered you that kiss with no expectations."

"No expectations?"

"I have growing feelings for you. I'm not certain where you are, but I suspect it's not where I am in this, and that's okay."

He squeezed her hand. "That kiss was me giving you a bit

of me. I wanted you to just be still and know." He squeezed her hand again.

"Know what?" she asked.

"Know me. When you played things through in your head, I didn't want you to feel any shame for the kiss or even for enjoying it. I wanted you to take your own time to realize you're ready to take a chance with another man."

Nic's confession stilled her frenzied thoughts. He was right. His tender kiss captured his gentle nature in a manner that words couldn't. He sincerely offered himself without a commitment of her feelings. He understood her struggle, and let her choose her path, allowing her the time to move toward him on her terms.

Nic collected the trash and pizza boxes in his lap during her introspection. When Raey reached for her purse, his soft voice cradled her nerves. "Before we say goodnight, I apologize if I overstepped with that kiss." He studied her face before continuing. "I'm glad you asked about it. I will always be straight with you about my feelings. That night, I didn't know how to tell you. Kissing you seemed the best way to show you my feelings."

Smiling broadly at his honesty, her insides melted at the memory. "You're right. Your kiss was the best way." She giggled to let him in on the thought that flashed through her mind. "And being still helped me feel all of it."

Shocked by her directness, he recovered quickly. "You felt all of it? Lucky!"

Raey forged forward through the disguised longing in his response. "But seriously, thanks for not pushing me."

She sought his hand that rested on her thigh and wove her fingers with his. They captured more moments of the moon resting over the bay. The jostling of keys in his lap broke their separate reflections.

She grabbed his arm to stop him from leaving the car and breaking the cocoon that wrapped them together. "I'm glad I asked. And thanks for sharing the kiss, too." She pitched him a wide smile as she pushed the car door open.

She didn't want their day together to end.

* * *

Raey lay atop the comforter that night, staring at the ceiling, reliving the day. She picked up her phone and called Brenda, needing to sort her emotions.

"Hi there. How's it going? It's good to hear from you."

"Today was tiring but a fantastic day." Raey couldn't hide her cheer.

"You sound good."

"I hiked today and saw eagles and dolphins."

"Oh wow, that sounds wonderful."

When Raey didn't offer a response, Brenda said, "You went all quiet on me. What's up?"

"Today's hike was a date," Raey blurted, ready for a barrage of questions from Brenda.

The composed counselor in Brenda restrained her response. "And?"

"And I have all these thoughts swirling through my head." Agitated, Raey turned on her belly and kicked her feet against the mattress.

"Such as?"

Raey needed Brenda's straight talk. "Such as, I don't like that I'm steadier around him. His vulnerability makes me courageous, somehow. His patience pushes me to change."

"That sounds like you have quite a connection with this man."

"Nic."

"All that from a first date with Nic?"

"Well, we've actually spent a little time together before today." Raey explained the story of listening to music at the pub with him and his friends.

"Dates?" Brenda asked.

"I think he sees them that way, but I told him they're not dates." Raey assured Brenda.

"Time together, meeting, appointment, gig, rendezvous, tryst...whatever you want to call it."

"Tryst? Oh my gosh, Brenda!" Raey yelped in mocked horror.

"I'm trying to get a clearer picture here."

"He's quite unnerving." Raey struggled to express herself.

"In a good way?" Brenda prompted.

"In a–he throws me off balance and, at the same time, helps me find my balance–kind of way."

"So, is this a–days are better–kind of way?" Brenda asked.

"If I'm honest, yes, in a–he makes everything better–kind of way. It's terrifying."

"What are you afraid of?"

"He picks up on my feelings before I share them."

"He gets you, then?"

"Each step with him feels..." Raey paused, gathering her breath, "dangerous but critical. In a way, it's agonizing but healing. I'm sorry this makes no sense."

"It doesn't have to. You just need to say it and hear yourself."

"I just needed to bounce my thoughts off you after today."

"Are you moving too quickly here?"

"Honestly, I'm not looking for this."

"Raey, listen to me. It's okay to go on dates. It's okay to feel again. You don't have to fear it. Melting is messy."

"Huh?"

"Don't fear your emotions thawing."

Before the conversation ended, Brenda inserted her wisdom and reshaped the entire conversation. "Sounds like you're gaining some of the clarity you hoped to find."

"Hmm." Raey doubted, "Confusion and clarity are apparently sisters."

TEN

The morning greeted her with the antithesis of the previous few days' glory. Rain pelted the window in sheets and the clouds lay like a thick, gray blanket, lowering the temperature. Back home, she stayed warm under the covers on days like these, but her days in Skye dwindled away. Peeking out her window, sideways gusts and horizontal rain beat against travelers' legs and sneaked into the crevices of their jackets. They wrestled with the relentless wind like they were dancing a jig all the way to their cars. Raey dressed in rain gear and extra layers to venture out, hoping to find enchanting waterfalls and otters tumbling in the swell and roll of the shallows.

But first, a hot drink from her favorite slow Sunday spot, Wistful Moor Café, would help her tackle the challenging weather and some emails. She and Josh discovered the gem their first week living on Skye and frequented it for a respite from the busyness of the week's schedule.

As their visits occurred with more regularity, the owners, Ainsley and Rowan, became less like acquaintances and more like friends. Rowan explained to them how he hand-sanded the counters and wood flooring, evidence of the passion he put into the café and gallery. Ainsley's photographs hanging on the walls captured the essence of the isle's colors. Raey could travel the island through Ainsley's magical lens while resting in their usual seat, framed by the view of the spectacular Trotternish Ridge and Loch Mealt.

When Raey walked in, Ainsley was waiting on a tourist having trouble choosing between a scone, muffin, or cake. Recognizing Raey in line, she bounced from behind the counter, just as her husband emerged from the back room. Ainsley and Rowan both welcomed her with a long hug. After catching up, Raey relaxed into the corner table with the best view.

She settled into the fireside seat to lift the chill from her bones and opened her laptop. Quiet music, bold coffee, and, most especially, their cranachan cake made tending to emails and tasks for the upcoming school year more pleasant.

Ainsley brought her coffee and cranachan cake, and Raey savored every bite. Her attempts to emulate creating this traditional Scottish delicacy at home in the States had failed. She took home most of the ingredients–her favorite Scottish whisky, pinhead oats, and even some heather honey. But nothing came close to the cream Scottish cows produced. Neither could she replicate the coveted in-season Scottish raspberries. Any she had found in the States were more sour and less flavorful.

Ainsley came to refill her coffee and caught her lost in nibbling the last bite of cake. With a hip bump to her arm, Ainsley gained Raey's attention. "There's an opening at Portree Primary School. You could eat this every Sunday."

"Oh wow, what a delight that would be!" Raey smiled, but her chest heaved at the mental mountains she would need to traverse to belong here without Josh. His spirit surrounded her here. This land filled her heart with the life she and Josh had pursued here together. She couldn't possibly make Skye her own without Josh haunting every place.

Ainsley tapped the table and proposed, "Give it consideration. I would even throw in an occasional, free cranachan cake."

"Now, that certainly gives me reason to consider." Raey spied a crumb left on her plate and snatched it to her mouth.

Raey returned to studying her emails as Ainsley headed to attend to another customer's coffee. Perusing the subject lines, she stopped at one from her principal–*Welcome Back Week*. It had arrived–the annual letter that eclipsed the summer fun–weeks earlier than usual. Raey shook her head in frustration, not expecting to be jolted toward the needs of school seven weeks early. Grateful to read that one new teacher and a couple of paraprofessionals would be the only major changes for the upcoming school year, she scanned the agenda organizing those exhausting days of constant meetings before the kids arrived in the third week of August. She promised herself not to occupy her mind any further with the demands of the new school year but to dedicate late July to preparing her classroom and her curriculum.

She clicked the tab to do a quick social media check, but only Brenda's Instagram posts piqued her interest. For someone who swore off consistently posting to social media, she had quite a constant stream of pictures with a *he's mine* smile on her face, detailing her life with Brian.

Raey hadn't checked her Facebook account in weeks, but she unabashedly read Josh's Facebook page. In the months after his death, she quelled the ache to talk to him about her life without him by writing private posts visible only to his account. Besides talking to him on her beach walks, bike rides, and drives, writing her thoughts to him provided a cathartic release, allowing her an outlet to freely express the running dialogue in her head.

A week after his death, she had tagged him in a picture of her funeral clothes still crumpled at the foot of her bed. *Bet you never thought you'd see this mess? I've quite fallen apart without you.*

Two months after his death, the check engine light on their jeep had lit up on the dash. She had written to ask him a question. *This is all too maddening. Where should I take the jeep to get fixed?*

On his birthday in August, four months after his death, she had decorated a red velvet cupcake and posted a birthday note to his wall. The picture caption read: *Happy birthday, Love. Cheers to you up there in Heaven. Can you let me know how you are somehow?*

On an early October evening when the sun splashed vibrant across the sea, she had written a wish. *It's so very, very, very lonely without you. Eating one of your perfectly grilled steaks on the deck in the sunset with you sounds lovely right now.*

After the first year without Josh, she had posted messages to him much less frequently, usually to update on her life.

She flipped her laptop closed, took a couple final gulps of her coffee, and stepped over to the counter to hug Ainsley and Rowan goodbye.

Ainsley didn't let go right away. She spoke in Raey's ear, "Think about the offer."

Rowan looked quizzically at Ainsley as he embraced Raey. "Whatever she's offering you, I will double it."

Raey winked at Ainsley and teased, "Her offer was something like free cranachan cake for life if I'd move back."

"Och, aye! We could make it so," Rowan whooped in delight, startling the seated customers who all turned to look.

All three laughed as Raey waved goodbye and headed for her car.

With Kilt Rock and Mealt Falls' viewpoints within an easy eight-minute walking distance, she dropped her laptop in the trunk and strolled to the site, trying to push what Ainsley proposed out of her head. The pelting rain lessened to a light drizzle as she walked from the café to the overlook she had last explored with Josh.

She braced herself for a crowded path to the fence, which offered the best unobstructed view of Kilt Rock. Despite the weather, cars dotted the parking spaces. Mingling among the families along the short path from the parking lot, she eavesdropped on their eager conversations. Two boys raced ahead to the fence to get a first glimpse, waving their parents over and yelling, "Hurry, Mum! Hurry, Dad!"

On their last visit to Kilt Rock, a kilted piper captured their attention. A tour bus driver had explained that the piper played the traditional Skye Boat Song, written in memory of Flora MacDonald's heroic acts during the Jacobite Uprising in 1745. Flora had helped Bonnie Prince Charles escape from Scotland and the claws of the British after the massacre of the Jacobites at the Battle of Culloden. She and other clanswomen had created a woman's costume for Prince Charles. Disguised as her maid, Betty Burke, Flora smuggled him through the Highlands and across the sea to the Isle of Skye. After the Uprising, emboldened Highland chieftains employed pipers in a revolt against the ban on bagpipes, which the loyalist government considered an instrument of war.

The thunderous roar of Mealt Falls beckoned, and she hurried her steps, dodging puddles. Without the tour buses dropping off loads of people for a quick view, she secured a great vantage point from the white-washed metal railing surrounding the lookout point.

At the edge of the cliff, the whip of the cool sea wind against her face gave her a slight adrenaline rush. The wind tugged her hair from her hood and flapped it against her face. Looking down, she held tighter to the railing as her heartbeat revved to match the thunder of the waterfall plunging from the sea cliffs onto Raasay Sound's pebbled shore, creating a little rainbow where the water hit the sea. Vertical basalt columns scratched into the cliff resembled pleats in a kilt, completing the coastal backdrop.

Standing there longer than most observers, she listened to the power of the sea spreading out before her. The beating against the rocks below sounded like the heavy rumbling of a timpani. The wind howling through the railings piped a haunting tune.

When Raey MacLaren became Raey Davenport, their decision to begin Josh's career in Scotland connected her to her roots. At the wail of the wind in the fence, she conjured the courage of the bagpipe's shrill cry in the hands of her clansmen's piper, clad in a green and navy tartan, signaling clansmen and their broadswords from Balquidder to Culloden.

Speckled white dotting on the hillside caught her attention and dissuaded her from returning to her car. Following the paved path along the cliff, she spotted newly born lambs cuddling on the hill, guarded by their mothers. Twin blackface lambs, cradled cliffside from the torrents, lifted their heads from the turf, trusting her quiet, solo encroachment.

Josh's death had birthed her into the turmoil of loss–alone and unprotected in the fight to regain the courage to search beyond the clouds for the light of hope. She supported herself against the fence like she'd leaned on loneliness as her certain companion. An unexpected wave of sadness left Raey weak-kneed. She grabbed the fence, swallowed hard, and lowered her head to steady her body.

She turned her gaze back to the hills for solace. At first, they appeared sparse, but as she stilled her eyes to the landscape, she discovered they teemed with life. Warblers, buntings, and wheatears tweeted and flitted about wild grasses in search of insects. Quieting her mind and tuning into her breathing dissipated her dizziness, and the blurry came into focus. Bleating sheep dotted the hillside, resembling large white rocks. When she slowed to being present, things came to life again.

"Mo lúcháir." She smiled upon hearing the Gaelic expression Josh had learned and bestowed upon her in the morning when he wrapped her in his arms, cradled her head, and greeted her as "my joy."

"Nice cap." He tapped the bill of his royal blue cap, embroidered with a large white D. "I'll walk you to your car." The tension in her body eased at the voice she thought had become only a memory.

"It'll be a slow, windy walk back uphill," she answered, grasping for an excuse to prolong his presence. Joy suffused her body at his return.

"Are you trying to talk me out of it?" He put his arm around her shoulders and fell in step with her.

"No, just stalling for more time with you," she confessed.

"Good, because you know what they say, 'Third times a charm!'"

"Third time?" His reference puzzled her.

"You know, for a date with Nic," he nonchalantly answered.

Raey's eyes bulleted Josh. Deflated by his train of thought, she retorted, "Well, aren't you the charmer? Coming back into my life to push me away."

"I'm not trying to push you away," he explained and reached for her hand as they walked to the café parking lot.

He snaked his arm around her shoulder as he said, "I'm trying to help you see that it's okay to be happy with another man."

She carefully withdrew from his arm and strode to her car door, rebuffing his inclination. His words rejected her. When his footfall halted, she pivoted to him, glared wide-eyed into his eyes, and poked him in the chest. The words she readied to throw at him stuck in her throat. She squeezed her eyes closed and lowered her head and her shoulders in defeat.

"What you say makes complete sense to you, and probably the rest of the world, but in my heart, it's utter torture to hear them coming from your mouth. It hurts. It feels like you can so easily let me go."

"Causing you pain is the last thing I want to do. This isn't letting you go or rejecting you. I want what makes you happy. Take a chance. Go on a third date with Nic."

Josh cushioned his cheek beside hers, and she snuggled close. His breath stroked her neck, and the wind buffeted her body at will.

"Nothing about letting you go was easy. From the moment I realized my diagnosis meant I'd lose you, until my last breath, it was a living hell. Saying *I love you* for the last time wasn't easy then, and it isn't easy now." His hand trembled and his head slowly shook hers back and forth. "Whatever you want."

Sensing his struggle to help her understand, she laid her face between clenched fists on his chest.

"Whatever you want," he murmured again.

The familiar warmth of the home where she once belonged bolstered her resolve to respond gently, "I know you keep showing up to let me go. To get me to let you go. But it makes my heart ache all the more," she said, searching his eyes.

"It does," he agreed and shivered as he caressed her cheek.

"I don't know how not to think about you," she confessed.

"You don't have to know that. You just need to know it's okay to think about others like you think about me. It's okay to be held in another's arms like you fall into mine. It's okay to be happy like we were."

"And Nic? Are you somehow mysteriously behind him being around?"

"That's all your doing, Babe. It brings me peace to see you with someone that makes you smile again, though." His voice quivered as he added the last part. "Mo lúcháir, having your heart was my life's joy. That's why I called you that. Forever, you will feel my heartbeat. There will be a tug, right here." He laid his hand on her heart with a gentle stillness. "It's my hope that there will be another pull for you here, too." He lifted her chin to meet his eyes. "It's torture to know it won't be for me, but I need you to be loved. You deserve to be loved."

"Thank you for loving me," she said, hating the finality she voiced from her own lips.

Josh kissed the top of her head as if bestowing a blessing and said, "Make that third date, Raey, but only if it's what you want. But if part of you wants it, be daring." His hands released her to open the car door, and she mourned the loss of her hold on him. When he gestured for her to climb in, she reluctantly took her gaze from him to grab the steering wheel, certain when she looked back, he would be gone.

And he was.

Unsettled by Josh's prompting, she couldn't return just yet

to Shelter Hill and Nic. She trekked back up the hill to the landscape and the black-faced lambs.

With Josh's words, *I need you to be loved*, replaying in her head, she neglected to concentrate on her footing and slipped on the mud. Instinctively, she flailed her arms to grab for the fence to break her fall, but her hand didn't catch the painted wood rail. She stumbled forward, and her forearm scraped down the barbed wire fence. Her knees landed hard on the slick rocks.

A man called from behind her, "Are ye all right, lass?"

"It's wet! It's freakin' all mud!" she yelled back. Blood oozed down her arm. The pain intensified.

The man barking from behind caught up to her. He quickly took charge without her permission and steadied her with a light hold on her arm, turning it over to reveal bloody mud. "Yeah, she's got a right good bleeder," he confirmed to a woman that now stood beside him. "We'll get this cleaned out for ye," he directed to her. "Babe, pass yer water?"

The woman came around to meet Raey's eyes, setting her bag on the ground to grab a bottle of water and a shirt.

The man gently assured her, "Dinnae worry, lass, we'll fix ye up. Whit's yer name?" He flushed the wound of dirt, clearing the mud until the water flowed red.

"It's Raey. Thanks for your help." She let them take charge.

Ripping the shirt, the woman wrapped it around Raey's arm and applied firm pressure. "Hold that in place. We need to stop the bleeding," she instructed to Raey. "Gled tae meet ye."

"We cannae let ye go alone. Ye need stitches. Can someone drive ye to the hospital?" the man asked.

"No, but I'll be okay."

"Ye need to keep the pressure on that. My girlfriend and I can take ye to the hospital," the hiker instructed her.

"I have my car."

"I'll drive yer car. That way, ye can be sure to keep the pressure on that wound. If it soaks through, put this on it." She handed over another piece of her shirt. The woman's explanation settled her nerves.

* * *

The couple protectively accompanied Raey into the hospital, and she relayed the incident to a nurse, who led them to an examining room.

"Thanks. I really appreciate all your help. I'm sorry to interrupt your hike," her voice quivered with vulnerability.

The man corrected her, "Ach, never be sorry for getting yerself taken care of, lass. We are happy tae help, ye ken."

The woman stepped closer to check her hand and noted seriously, "Someone will take ye home, aye?"

Just then, a familiar upbeat voice bounded around the corner into her room. "Well, the nurse tells me...." As the woman moved out of the way, Nic glimpsed Raey. Taking in her tear-stained cheeks, pale complexion, mud-covered body, and the blood-soaked shirt she held to her arm, he stopped short.

His cheer deflated as concern riddled his face. "Raey? What happened?" The hikers moved to stand against the wall to let the doctor care for Raey.

When Nic caught sight of a slight tremble in her hands, urgency invaded his pensive calm. "Oh, I think we need to get you warm." He leaned his head out into the hall and called, "Jan, can we please get a blanket in here?"

"I'm okay," Raey reassured.

His facial muscles subtly tensed as he asked the hikers, "And who are you?"

"Nic, what are you doing in the emergency area?" Raey interrupted, more relief than query.

He tucked his face in front of hers and asked, "Are you really okay? Anything else that hurts?"

"Yes, really," she comforted his worry, "Thanks to these two hikers, I'm going to be fine. You get to mend the rest." Nic's jaw relaxed as he nodded at the hikers.

As the hikers exited, the woman said, "Enjoy the rest of yer trip, lass. Maybe we'll meet ye again on the trail. Slàinte Mhath!"

"Slàinte!" Raey smiled at her rescuers as they left.

"Well, I'm glad to be the only doctor available to tend to you right now." Worry lined his brows as he unwound the cloth to reveal the serrations in her arm. He treated her wound, covering it temporarily with a sterile cloth.

"Here is the blanket, Dr. MacNicol," offered the nurse.

Nic quickly retrieved it from her. "Thanks, Jan," he said, granting her a small smile. He enveloped Raey in the white cotton, tucked her injured arm carefully to his chest, and pressed soft lips to the center of her forehead. Before Raey's eyes closed to everything but Nic's tenderness, she caught Jan's knowing smile.

"Ahem, I'm free now," said a voice, barely stepping into the room. "Ahem, Dr. MacNicol. I'll take over now," pushed the voice with an edge of adamance.

With his lips still fixed on her forehead, Nic mumbled, "No, I got this, Dr. Robertson."

"Maybe you shouldn't," he formally instructed.

Raey pulled back and Nic spoke with his eyes before turning to address the situation.

"Oh, this is my girlfriend, Raey," he replied immediately. "I just found out she came in with an emergency."

"I am really—" Raey started to say.

"I know you think you're fine," Nic interrupted. "But you will need stitches and a tetanus shot, just in case." He kept hold of her and addressed Dr. Robertson, "But thanks for the offer."

"OK, I'll leave you to it, then. It is nice to meet you, Raey," said the doctor, nodding at Raey.

Raey shrugged her shoulders and smiled back at Dr. Robertson. "What are we going to do with him? He's such a good guy," she praised.

Nic turned back to Raey and apologized, "I'm so sorry for putting you in that situation. Thanks for going along with the girlfriend part. Seeing you hurt, well, it just…" he paused, "unsettled me."

"Well, I sure hope you don't kiss all the girls that need a tetanus shot and stitches."

"Careful, I might give you one in your bum if you get cheeky."

While Nic cared for her injuries, the nurses roamed past her door, wanting a glimpse of Dr. MacNicol tending to his 'girlfriend.'

Something inside of her was proud to pretend that she was.

ELEVEN

Nic's public display of affection made being away from the Isle for a couple of days more difficult. She had booked a B&B for her and Isobel in her favorite lazy village of Plockton prior to landing on Skye. But Isobel's baby had her own timetable and arrived earlier than expected, so instead of girl talk, she roomed with her thoughts for two days, thoughts of her attraction to Nic that insisted on intruding on the peace of reading and basking in the sunshine.

Raey sat alone on the shore of Loch Caroon, her head propped in her hands and her arms still seared by Nic's hold on her, his lips and embrace clinging to her memory longer than the pain of the stitches in her arm. They both downplayed his actions, but the tension sparked throughout the room even after he pulled away and tamed his attention.

Dr. MacNicol's girlfriend? Is that what Nic is thinking? This is ridiculous–I can't let Josh go!

Isobel insisted Raey visit her and Isla again before going back to the States, so on her drive back from Plockton, Raey bought a take-away lunch for them from Isobel's favorite café–the corner of the world where they had often met for curriculum planning and chats about life. The prospect of relaxing and sharing freely with Isobel, her closest friend on the island, buoyed her spirits, like sinking into a comfortable seaside garden chair under the sun and shelter of a cherry tree.

When Raey protected her arm from Isobel's long hug, Isobel pulled back in alarm, "What happened to your arm?"

Raey nonchalantly responded, lifting her arm, "This wrap makes it look worse than it is. I slipped on the mud while hiking and needed to get twelve stitches. You should see the size of the bruise on my bum, though," she added with a giggle.

"Okay, bare it, girl." Isobel teased.

"I'll pass on that for your sake," Raey said as they both laughed.

Raey directed the conversation to avoid talk of Nic. "It could have been much worse. It definitely caused me to count my blessings." She watched Isla sleeping with her hands covering her eyes. "You," Raey squeezed Isobel's arm, "and you, sweet Isla, are two of my biggest blessings." Raey lightly caressed Isla's chubby cheek.

"Aww, I love you, too." Isobel's smile made Raey feel at home.

Raey removed her shoes and settled on the couch, hugging both knees to her chest. "Oh, I almost forgot. Thank you again for sending me your dad's book. I bet he was thrilled that a publisher picked it up. He's such an expert. Our students loved the hiking field trip he led. I know more about the birds on Skye than in North Carolina now."

Isobel leaned over her tiny newborn bundle. "You are so welcome. I remember seeing the delight in your eyes, too, as he guided us." Isobel explored Raey's face.

"He made it all so exciting."

"He loved seeing you and the kids all jazzed up." Isobel

paused again and intently searched Raey's large, brown eyes. "How are you doing, really?"

"It's hard not having him. Every day I want to scream at life. Nights are the worst. Work has helped keep me busy, but it's like life has just become a series of motions that I'm really good at going through."

"You'll get there. It takes time. Sometimes, a lot of time. You don't have to rush yourself."

"Yeah, some days, I make a step forward, and some days it feels like I take two steps backwards."

"I'm so sorry. But be gentle with yourself."

"I'm tired of feeling numb. Skye is such a magical place, so I thought coming here might spark a change, some awakening. It's not easy, but I'm fighting for that each day."

"I hope being here isn't too hard, being in all the places you and Josh were together."

"It's hard but also strangely cathartic."

Raey switched to a simpler subject. "How is my favorite professor?"

"Isla is Dad's greatest study."

"I bet he can't take his eyes off her."

"She is his new hobby. That and mothing." Isobel lifted her eyebrows and laughed as she said, "He attracts them at night on a cloth."

"Moths? All I know is that if I'm attracting something at night, I hope it's not moths."

"Right?!" Isobel kissed Isla's cheek and beamed, "But this is the absolute best thing to cuddle in your hands at night. Would you like to hold her?"

Raey snuggled Isla close, kissing her fingers and inhaling her new baby smell. She marveled at how Isla had changed since her first visit to the hospital.

"She was worth every moment of the twenty-four hours of birthing pain." Isobel glowed with pride over Isla. Her face turned to worry as she continued, "At first, it alarmed us that the doctor on call was a pediatrician, but he was great. He had this easy, calming nature. It was reassuring, though, when the midwife arrived just in time for the actual birthing part."

"I bet! I'm so glad everything went well."

"I have to admit that during my estrogen overload, I did almost want to slap the pediatrician's syrupy sweetness right out of him. He kept saying, 'Just let me ken what you need.'" She flailed her hands and smacked them on her lap in exasperation. "Heck, I didn't ken what I needed. He was supposed to ken that for me!" Isobel ranted.

"Was he just trying to comfort you?"

"Yeah, he was. His looks comfortably distracted me, too. They kept the urge to rant at him at bay."

"Oh, I remember you saying he was a looker. Well, don't you have all the luck? And I can't believe you just said that." Raey leaned in to talk to Isla, who stretched in her sleep. "Isla, don't listen to that silly mommy of yours. You know your daddy is the handsomest man on Earth."

"Luck, yeah right. I looked the crappiest I've ever looked in my life, and I was in the most pain I've ever been in my life, and I had hormones splashing through my body, and Dr. Gorgeous MacNicol kept asking me how I'm feeling. That's the kind of luck I had!"

"Does Dr. MacNicol have gorgeous blue eyes?"

"You know him?" Isobel inched closer to Raey.

"Yeah, he's the grandson of the owners of the B&B I'm staying at."

"Well, do tell! I can see from the flush on your face that there's some interest there."

Raey mockingly slapped Isobel's leg. "No, it's nothing." She raised one eyebrow and teased, "But he is a very patient tour guide. Coached me through the Bad Step hike."

"Uh-huh," Isobel prompted, "Is that all he coached you through?"

Raey smacked Isobel's leg again. "Stop! You are right, though. He is gentle and genuine."

"Oh, and just how gentle, Raey?" Isobel teased as she shuffled closer to Raey and examined her face for an answer. Then she promptly scooped Isla from Raey's arms. "This little girl is going to sleep in her crib while you get down to business spilling all the details."

Raey nervously organized the parameters of her story before Isobel returned. Pulling a throw cover over her legs, Isobel dove right in. "Okay, go! Don't leave anything out."

Raey pared down the details to keep Isobel's eager mind from misinterpreting the time she and Nic spent together. Isobel interrupted her short retellings with questions, searching for connections Raey was unwilling to share. She harrumphed at Raey's clinical renditions. Raey remained vigilant to keep Isobel from sniffing around emotions she didn't really want to reveal, even to herself. Isobel scrutinized her words and body language for the slightest cracks, the smallest opportunity to pry her open, to nudge Raey into clarifying her thoughts and feelings.

Raey shared her two-date secret but not his kisses. She held that close while she nurtured the melody behind its gentle rhythm, her senses still alert to the tender touch his lips branded on her skin. Knowledge of his kisses would have Isobel waxing on about the destiny of their meeting as a fateful cosmic alignment.

"I bet Dr. MacNicol is eager to do a follow-up check on

you when you get back to the B&B," Isobel teased, covering her laugh with her hand when she continued, "Oh, sorry! Did I say *you*? I meant your arm."

"He said I didn't need one unless a problem arose," Raey boasted pretentiously.

"Oh, you definitely have a problem, and it's not your arm."

"Stop!" Raey laughed. Her wrenching gut agreed with Isobel.

Isobel threatened with glee, "You had better keep me in the loop on the developments with your hiking coach, girl."

"There won't be 'developments.'"

"Uh-huh, no further comment." Isobel stifled a laugh.

Chatting the entire afternoon whittled the day away. The babe floated in a land of dreams, no cares, no worries. There was no faster path to peace than witnessing Isobel relax into being a mom, cradling her daughter cocooned in her lap.

On the drive back to the Shelter Hill Guest House, thoughts of Nic wandered through Raey's mind. *Why hadn't he reached out in the past couple of days?* She squashed any expectations of his connecting, but they came roaring back.

I could simply text. Sitting two seconds with that thought, it registered as not-so-simple in her head. Her fingers couldn't do it. She wondered what a few days of no communication from him indicated. She ventured guesses which side the weight of the pendulum swung toward; friendship or desire. *Which do I want it to be?*

Despite her reservations, she sat in her car in the B&B parking lot, debating with her phone. She would judge how things stood between them from his response to her text. She coached herself through her dilemma. Whatever he texted, she would be grace under pressure when she faced him.

Then she initiated a text.

Raey: Haven't heard from you.

Nic: How'd you get this number?

Well, that's awkward. Is that his idea of a warm first response? Really?

Raey: You texted me.

Nic: ☺ I'm teasing you. Remember when you asked me the same thing? I'm sleep deprived.

Oh good, teasing from him was a good sign.

Raey: Oh, sorry. I didn't realize you are at the hospital.

Nic: I'm not. I just got home. How's your arm?

Raey: Good as new…thanks to you.

Nic: I want to check it out. I'm going to get some sleep first. Connect later tonight?

Raey: Sounds good.

* * *

But Nic didn't text her back that evening. She both feared the space he occupied in her mind and wanted to foster the closeness they created. The idea of meandering to the welcome desk for a chance chat with Finlay or Maisrie or a drink in the lounge in hopes of seeing Nic flitted through her mind, but she stayed on her seaside balcony. Experience with his kind of schedule told her he had probably been called in for an emergency. But nerves told her something different. She fell asleep watching a movie and woke to an 8 a.m. text.

Nic: Let's chat.

Raey: Okay, go!

Nic: In person. Want to catch dinner together?

Raey: Sure

Nic: Great. Meet at the counter at 7.

* * *

Raey uttered a quiet "Hi" as she approached the reception desk that evening. Reserved upon seeing him, she stuffed her hands in her pockets.

Heeding her cues, he leaned in, held her softly at the elbow, and smiled as he said, "I'm sorry I didn't text you. The hospital called me in for an emergency. An eight-year-old ended up needing an appendectomy. This is an exhausting week. Keeping my shift and covering for another doctor makes for a full week of kids' crises."

"Um, then why are you smiling?" she asked with scrunched eyebrows.

"Because you are upset."

She arched her eyebrows, cocked her head, and curtly responded, "I think you better explain that one."

With a lopsided grin, he teased, "Seems someone might miss spending time with me. That's worth smiling about, wouldn't you think?"

She had missed his low timbre, their give and take, his subtle challenges, and his overt humor. Her insides churned at how quickly the pleasantries of conversing with him dismantled her defenses.

"I'm not a fan of communicating via texting. I like hearing your voice and seeing your face," he responded, as if repeating the same thoughts swirling in her mind.

"Definitely a benefit seeing my face," she joked, outlining her face with her hands.

"Definitely," he said, letting his words linger in the air between them before adding, "and your arm. Let me get a quick peek."

Their third Not-a-Date was different–no distractions, phones tucked away, dining in a secluded corner of a restaurant full of people they paid no mind to. He leaned across the table, focused solely on her, close enough that she resisted the urge to caress his stubbled chin and muscled arms that moved with the same easy, fluid motions of his stories, lulling her to forget her reservations.

When the dinner dishes were cleared and replaced by dessert and Irish coffee, the conversation turned more direct. She considered his willingness to approach difficult discussions a by-product of his medical training.

Nic's eyes captured hers, and she clutched her coffee cup. After choking back his initial words, he started again, "Raey, I've wanted to tell you that Josh shared his cancer concerns with me when you two lived here."

Stunned silent, Raey swallowed hard as Josh's name intruded upon their evening. When her heart rate descended, she responded with the only words she could find at that moment, "Oh, wow."

"He told me he knew he wouldn't beat the cancer."

Raey sucked in her breath at hearing Josh's thoughts coming from Nic's mouth, but Nic's connection with Josh oddly comforted her.

"He worried that once you guys returned to the States that you'd get lost in your pain and his family couldn't be much help."

Raey cleared her throat and looked up from the swirl in her cup. "Why did he confide in you?" Raey asked. "It's weird because I never met you when we lived here."

"I don't know. Maybe knowing that I'd lost my parents, he considered me a good ear to bounce ideas around about recovering from the pain of losing someone."

"Hmm," Raey's eyes searched Nic for answers he couldn't provide.

"One night, when I teased him in the locker room for being slower on the court than normal, he shared his diagnosis. He had just gotten the dire news. He rambled about making it through the treatments."

"So very much Josh," Raey reminisced. "I wonder when that was because he knew for a couple weeks before telling me."

After a long swallow, Nic's voice faltered as he finished explaining, "I could tell he was in anguish, so I didn't question his thoughts. I just let him talk it out."

Swirling the diamond on her finger, Raey explained, "He knew I didn't like spending time while he was alive talking to him about what my life would be like after he died. His family is my family, so he worried that my best friend, his sister–they were close–would be caught up in her own grief and wouldn't be the best person for me to process things with."

"When I saw the name Raey Davenport on our books that day you asked for trail information, it was quite an awkward surprise."

She didn't utter a sound, expecting him to elaborate on his explanation. She recalled Isobel raved about him as her doctor. "So, this," she pointed between them, "is you helping me with my grief?"

"No! Well, yes. Wait, absolutely not. I assured Josh that you would find your way."

"How would you know?"

"From his description of you, it was obvious that you were a woman of strength and independence. You'd find your path through the grief of losing him, in your own way, and at your own pace."

She smiled at hearing who she was to Josh and mumbled under her breath, "Hmm, he probably said stubborn."

"Huh?"

"So, how would you assess where I am with my grief, Dr. MacNicol?" she questioned defensively.

"Honestly, I'm not sure where you are, but I know this," Nic paused to pace a reverent response and pulled her hand into his, "you don't need me to tell you where you are or to tell you where I think you should be."

"Your response is very unlike Josh's. He thinks I need to get on with things and tells me not to waste my days." She concentrated on his thumb gently rubbing across her fingers.

"He *tells* you?" Nic's grip on her hand tightened. Astonishment crept into his eyes as his focus moved from their hands to her face.

She hesitated a couple of seconds, pulled her hands from his into her lap, and fixed her eyes on the table as she proceeded, "I know you'll use your Doctorese or psychological analysis when I tell you this." Raey swallowed hard and stopped speaking. After seconds that ticked like hours, she pushed herself up straighter in her chair and looked him directly in the eye. "I've spoken with him several times on this trip."

Without flinching, Nic waited for her to continue. "And?"

"He showed up at several treks I've taken. I literally see him. I feel him, physically and emotionally. We talk with one another. He pushes me to move on." Her frankness shocked her.

Nic's double take delayed his response. "See, there are plenty of voices in your head. I still think it would have been a bad step to add my advice into the mix."

"Bad step, very funny." She lifted a smile to him.

"Sometimes, people want to climb out of their mental trenches at their own pace," Nic clarified.

"But sometimes they need help, too," Raey confessed.

He studied her face and then softly asked, "Do you need help, Raey?" His empathy brought a quick mist to the edge of her eyes.

"No, well, I don't know," she whispered, bowing her head, afraid to blink.

"Well, I'm offering my hand, Raey, but you'll have to reach out and take it." He laid his palm open on the table.

Raey leaned back into the oversized chair and contemplated the creases in Nic's palm, an extended lifeline. Paralyzing anxiety kept her hand lifeless in her lap.

Nic's palm lay still atop the table like an unanswered

question. His eyebrows drew together as he surveyed his hand, and his jaw tightened as he observed her concentration.

With no words, she leaned toward him and rested her open palm on his, threading each finger one at a time between his. Serenity flowed through her as they both focused on the answer they held in their entwined hands. Gently pulling his hand toward her, and unknowingly his heart, Raey responded, "Come on, time to go."

They finished the evening on Shelter Hill's terrace under the stars, watching the sun's ambient light fall below the horizon, unwilling to let the night go. Their clasped hands hung between them under the moon's shimmering path across Portree Bay. Words between them slowed as they searched for a way to say goodnight to the day, to one another, to her choice to place her hand in his. His palm abandoned hers and a chill shiver rippled over her skin. His warm hands tilted her head back, and he stared into her face, bathed in the moonlight. When he pressed his lips gently to hers and kissed her deeply, he overwhelmed every one of her senses.

TWELVE

R aey groaned, regretting not setting her phone on silent before her head hit the pillow. Sharing an apartment for years meant Brenda would overlook her bed head on the Facetime chat, so she swiped to accept the call and endure Brenda's chastising for not updating her on Nic.

Conversation about both men felt perplexingly taboo. She couldn't explain the visits from Josh. If she hadn't physically touched him, she could be convinced she conjured him as a coping mechanism.

Raey never kept things from Brenda, but she was reluctant to share her affection for Nic more deeply, wanting to hold it closely. Raey bolstered herself against Brenda's pleadings for information.

"Hi. How are you? I'm keeping things exciting over here." Raey lifted her arm to the screen to reveal her bandage. "I slipped on a hike and got twelve stitches."

"Oh, you poor thing. Did Nic take you on that hike?"

"No, I went alone. That's what I get for gawking too long over the black-faced lambs, I guess," Raey laughed, omitting the part about Nic administering her care.

"Keep an eye on that. Go back to the doctor if it gets redder or oozes."

Thankful that she didn't reveal Nic's profession, Raey said, "No worries. I spent two days relaxing in Plockton right after, so I'm on the mend."

Raey directed the conversation to spend a good amount of time talking about her sight-seeing adventures and her visit with Isobel and her baby. Then she steered their conversation to Brenda's love life. "I'm seeing quite a few pictures of you and your handsome man on social media."

Brenda sang Brian's praises, relaying their recent happenings.

"Raey, he's the one," she said with high-pitched glee.

"Well, if you're admitting it, then he is. I'm so happy for you. Here comes the bride, aye?"

"That just may be," Brenda furtively responded.

"Ahhhhh," Raey squealed. "I'm so happy for you."

"We're talking September. I wanted to ask you this in person, but I can't wait," Brenda shrieked. "Will you be my matron of honor?"

"Yes, yes, absolutely yes! I had better be!"

Raey joked about changing her plans and taking up Ainsley's offer to stay and teach in lovely Skye. Like a deflating balloon, Brenda's enthusiasm in the conversation waned. "Brenda, I'm sorry I said that. I'm not moving to Skye. She offered me free cranachan cake for a year, though."

"I know. It just reminded me of Josh, and then if you…" Brenda's voice trailed off.

When Raey and Josh moved to Scotland after getting married, it placed an emotional strain on her and Brenda's relationship. By quickly navigating beyond that comment, Raey hoped Brenda would see that she gave the job no real consideration.

A doorbell rang and Brenda's phone fumbled in her hands

when she moved to pick up a package from her stoop. Raey yelled, "You're making me dizzy, flopping me all around while you're opening that package."

"Woot, woot!" Brenda cheered. Her mood lightened as she showed off her newly purchased black and white polka dot bikini. Suddenly, Brenda spouted enthusiastic words, and Raey knew life back home was heating up.

"Something special going on?" Raey asked. Hearing Brenda's excitement over the purchase of a swimsuit, Raey yearned for one of their long and lazy beach days, but time with Brian would eclipse their beach time together from now on.

"A four-day trip with my man to the Keys," Brenda squealed.

"Engagement party for two?" Raey asked.

"Yes, ma'am. Living our best life."

"I'm so happy for you. When are you going?"

"Leaving in two days."

Brenda would never agree to a trip with a man if she didn't also see "forever" in her future. In their ten years of friendship, Raey had never seen Brenda invest deeply in a guy until Brian. She dated men, even a couple who hinted at more, but Brenda skirted their inclinations.

Raey felt conflicted over this changing season in their relationship. Even though Brenda's happy news thrilled her, her thoughts selfishly circled around how this affected her. In her head, she favored the change, even cherished it. But gnawing pangs of loneliness merged with her joy. When she married Josh, Brenda struggled to adjust to choices that left her out, especially their move to Skye. Raey hadn't intended to neglect their relationship, but the physical separation rippled into an emotional distance. Her love for Brenda never faltered.

It wasn't replaced but took a natural back seat to the impracticality of keeping close while living on another continent. Brenda had remained steady as her wingman. Understanding all this didn't comfort her now.

Raey had depended on Brenda as a constant confidante since Josh died. Brenda's growing intimacy with Brian had altered their bond. Once married, Raey wouldn't be Brenda's go-to person, and Brenda couldn't be hers. Facing that chasmic gap created a real ache in her chest. Visions of beachside vows and a wedding dress danced in her head, but so did waves of dread at the changes ahead. Walking the beach or winding down with a glass of wine in the evening would become Brian's privilege. A bittersweet exchange.

"So, you've avoided talking about Nic. What's going on there?"

"Well, since we last spoke, I've been gone, and he's been busy. We went to dinner once." Raey omitted any details. Brenda would read too much into Nic's care of her arm and their happenings at dinner.

"Hmm. Sounds like you found balance. Still unnerved?" Brenda asked.

"Finding our friendship. Spending time with any man besides Josh terrifies me."

"Change is difficult."

The friendship developing with Nic would be easier to explain when she returned to North Carolina. Brenda would consider it progress. Face-to-face would be the only way she would dare try to explain Josh's visits in the mist. No matter how many hours of concentrated effort, she wouldn't be able to solidify an explanation about his visits that didn't make her sound stark raving mad. Honestly, she coveted her moments with Josh and didn't need anyone's commentary dampening the sweet memories of their encounters that lingered in her head.

After hanging up, Raey checked her phone for the time. Breakfast hours wouldn't begin for a half hour, but Raey dressed in comfortable jeans and a sweatshirt to head downstairs. Maisrie would certainly offer coffee, as she provided free beverages for the guests to enjoy in the solarium at all hours of the day–flavored waters, teas, fruit juices, and sometimes even whisky.

Maisrie did a double take as she entered from the kitchen's swinging door and spotted Raey bounding down the stairs, her earliest arrival yet to breakfast. She filled more tea bags and greeted her, "Good morning, child. Ye must have another big day planned to be at it so early."

"Actually, today I have no set plans." Raey splayed empty palms wide as she scanned the room and said, "I get first table choice for your delicious breakfast. While I enjoy the best seat in this house and take in your serene view of the water and gardens, I'll decide what my last days will hold."

"Oh, my, lass! What happened to yer arm?" Maisrie surveyed Raey's bandaged arm.

"I'm just fine," Raey assured her. "It's a small hiking mishap. In fact, Nic ended up being the one to stitch me up."

"Oh, aye. I'm glad he mended ye," Maisrie said with a note of optimism in her voice as she patted Raey's hand.

"Me, too," Raey smiled, knowing Maisrie would not understand the depth of her agreement.

"Please sit and relax. The fog will rise soon to give you a lovely Skye day. I must finish just a few more tasks before bringing it all out. Is there anything special ye might want?" Maisrie enquired, handing her a cup of black coffee.

"Not a thing," said Raey. She added creamer until it turned

light caramel, then stepped outside the solarium to stand at the edge of the garden, inhaling the smell of damp earth. She hoped the moist, brisk morning would transform into absolute perfection with a wee bit of sunshine.

The screen door hinge squeaked behind her, breaking her solitude. "It's all set out for ye, lass. I'll be right here tending to the garden and feeding the birds. If ye need anything, just get me."

Maisrie's generosity of spirit and comforting words took Raey back twenty years, to the day she and her mom had prepared a special anniversary dinner for her dad. She had hindered more than helped, but her mom had still found ways for her to be a big part of the gift for her dad. At eight years old, she had proclaimed that she made the mashed potatoes all by herself, never mind that she hadn't peeled or cut them and had only flicked the switch for the KitchenAid to mash them. Toasting the bread in the toaster, crumbling each piece in her hands, and spreading ketchup on top of the meat had her thinking she made the meatloaf for Dad's favorite meal. Her mom trusted her to choose the tablecloth, set the table, and fold the napkins all by herself. They both wore their favorite dresses and jewelry. Her mom blotted red lipstick on Raey and allowed her to light two tall white candles for the table and choose the music on the stereo. It seemed such a grand affair. The brownies with caramel running through them didn't seem ordinary. Dad teased Mom that both she and the brownies looked "simply elegant" as he twirled her in the kitchen. When Raey asked what that meant, Mom smiled down at her and said, "He likes his elegance simple, and apparently, I'm just his style." That didn't clarify things, but she sensed her dad's meaning when he winked at her, leaned down, swept her off her feet in one fell swoop, and the three of them circled in dance together in the kitchen, while her dad belted out "Truly."

As lavish a hostess as her mom, Maisrie provided a decorative, plentiful, and sumptuous affair. She genuinely enjoyed greeting her guests each morning. *What was Maisrie's life story?* Raey noted Finlay's absence the last few days, and she missed his usual rambunctious cheer at the morning gatherings.

Raey ate more than she intended and ambled toward the patio overlooking the bay with her second cup of coffee, encountering Maisrie plotting her garden aloud.

"Speaking to a ghost?" Raey joked.

"I'd give orders to the entire royal house of Stuart if that would move this earth," she joked in mock exasperation.

"I'm up for that," Raey offered with a skip in her voice.

"So, ye have those kinds of connections?" Maisrie turned toward her and smiled, wringing her hands in a tea towel.

"Of course!" she winked and then added, "Seriously, I'd love to help you get this done. Just tell me what you need. My day is yours."

"Oh, that's very sweet of ye, but guests can't be performing chores for me."

"Please, put me to work. I'm used to keeping busy and today is a lovely day to be outside."

"I'm not sure I can complete my plans for today. Finlay is not feeling well enough to help pick up our order from the garden center, and they can't deliver it for another two days. So much for taking advantage of this lovely day." Raey caught Maisrie's faraway pondering as she puffed up her cheeks, blew air out slowly in release, and then pursed her lips side to side.

"I'd be happy to pick it up for you. Is it just down the road there at Shrubs Garden Center?"

"Are you certain?"

"I'd love to help. I'm sure."

"Thank you so much. It's quite a load. Let me see if Nic left the truck. He said he'd try to get it picked up today if his schedule didn't change. I don't know if he took his car or our truck."

The unexpected mention of Nic's name sent a tingle of anticipation up Raey's spine. When Maisrie left, Raey walked to better view the water and shake off her nerves. She didn't want to appear flustered around Maisrie, but the mention of Nic triggered her heart to pound faster and spilled spontaneous warmth throughout her body.

"The truck's still here. Here's the print-out of the order and the keys. They should load it all if ye ask. I'll make ye dinner in exchange for doing this. Call if there are any complications, but it's all paid for. And thank ye so much again."

"Deal! I'll get a move on."

"Oh, they don't open until 10 o'clock, so no hurry. I hate to add this, but could ye look over the petunias, geraniums, and daisies before loading to be sure they don't look sickly. If Paul or Frances filled the order, it will be fine, but if one of those young pups did, they might not care."

"Sure, no worries. I'll suggest an exchange if they don't look good," Raey assured her, glad she recognized the names of those annuals. "Would you like some help here before I need to go?"

"Oh, you're a true keeper," Maisrie's voice beamed. "Yer welcome to help me get this flower bed ready," she added, pointing to demonstrate where to pull weeds.

Later that morning, when Raey returned with the order, she took off her sweatshirt due to the beating sun and worked side by side in single purpose under Maisrie's gentle direction. She understood where Nic's quiet strength and assuring nature originated. She hesitated to ask questions but too many sat on the tip of her tongue. Why did Nic live with them at the B&B and not talk about his parents much? She waited until they established a working rhythm before detouring into questions about her and Finlay, "So how did you decide to run a B&B?"

"Once the kids moved out, it seemed a good way to earn money with such a big house and excellent location. We're our busiest about half of the year."

"It sure seems like quite a lot of work," Raey probed.

"It wasn't our plan to still be running it full time, but maybe it is keeping us young," Maisrie smiled. With a bit more reservation, she added, "Although, it might be getting away from us as of late. We're fortunate Nic is around to help."

"I haven't seen Finlay out front the past couple days," Raey remarked.

"He's not feeling his best lately. He's looking right peely-wally. I'm forcing him to rest, which makes him cranky as a bear. It's best he stays away from the guests," she joked in her dry-voiced humor. Raey couldn't imagine Finlay, the jovial king of extroverts, as grumpy.

"Who will help run the B&B when you retire?"

Maisrie remained silent but kept digging and loosening soil, purposefully reserved with this family information. Raey chastised herself for being nosy. The ease of relating with Maisrie made her forget to keep an acceptable distance of a guest.

"Once upon a time, we planned to continue on here only as part-time assistants when my daughter and her husband took over full time." Maisrie frowned and looked Raey in the eye. "But it's been nineteen years since I lost my only angel, and my sweet boys, Nic and Alasdair, lost their parents." Maisrie stabbed her trowel into the earth, stood up, stretched her back, and wiped a solo tear from her cheek. "I'm sorry. Sometimes when I talk about her, the sadness overwhelms me."

Willingly taking off her emotional suit of armor, Maisrie braved being so open. So honest. So vulnerable. And so like Nic. That's what scared her about him. He gave the same open and honest answers.

Raey surprised herself and wrapped her arms around Maisrie. "I completely understand." She released Maisrie when both of their emotions stopped see-sawing and relaxed. "I'm sorry to bring that up."

Maisrie slid her hands down Raey's arms to hold her still at the elbows, warmly searching her eyes. "Baby girl, you are truly a bonnie lass," she rolled her *r* slowly and long. "Dinna fash. It's fine to bring up. Hear me, now. Our lives should share all of who we are, all our past steps, good and bad. Whit's fur ye'll no go past ye. God will give ye the stamina to carry-on. Digging out of the hole her death plunged us in brought the greatest challenge of my life, but I couldn't let it defeat us, especially for Nic and Alasdair. We're all well on a path forward, but worries pop up now and again."

Blanketed by the security of Maisrie's grip and words, Raey fell vulnerable to the pain welling up of losing her parents and Josh. Maisrie empathized with Raey's pain. Had Nic shared her life's story with his grandma? *Baby girl.* The memory of the rise and fall of her mom's voice washed over her. Maisrie's cadence triggered a ripple of belonging.

Maisrie left her reflective moment to check on Finlay. Raey planted red and white geraniums, hearing her dad's voice in her ear as she hummed the words he sang so often to her mom.

"Must be a great song in your head you're humming." Nic's intrusion into her daydream startled Raey, and she fell back on her bum. She whipped her focus toward him. "It knocked you on your arse," Nic laughed.

Raey stared up at his strong cheekbones, embarrassed. "Oh," she paused, 'Truly.'"

"Yes, truly."

"No, that's the name of the song."

Nic shook his head and offered his hand in assistance. "I should listen to that song if you find it so mesmerizing." He winked and pulled her up with more force than she expected, landing them face-to-face, chest-to-chest, and putting Raey in the immediate predicament of deciding to take a step back or stay planted. Her stillness revealed which side of her mind had won the war. The simmering questions that kindled dither and doubt vanished in his presence. How easily his mere proximity smoothed her frustrations but also confounded her. She stared at her hand still clasped within his as if it struck a traitor's pose. *Josh, forgive me.*

Nic adjusted his palm as if intending to dance, and then shocked her when he did exactly that. He raised their entwined hands above their heads, challenging her eyes to see the dare in his. His unapologetic admiration invited her to linger there. Whether from the spell he cast or from her need to belong to him in this moment, she remained locked in time and space. He spun her like a ballerina, softly grabbing her hip, and pulling her off-balance. Her backside pressed against the length of his body. He swung her around to face him and then dipped her backward, her smile evidence of her acquiescence to his bold move.

"Lass," he whispered. She held still, longing to hear the rest of his beckoning. He drew closer, within inches of her, and she found herself momentarily speechless. Her heart could barely contain her anticipation. Nic searched her face before continuing, "You're getting a wee bit dirty."

Before Raey could jerk away from him in denial, he pulled her onto her own two feet and let a grin slide slowly over his face. His hands brushed her hips before moving them to point at the belly of her shirt where she had absentmindedly wiped her sweat and dirty hands. His smile revealed a jokester's glee. Rose-tinged cheeks and a bashful half-smile betrayed the desire coursing through her body. She stared open-mouthed, thoroughly dazed, and thoroughly perplexed.

Maisrie's cheerful entrance interrupted their suspended lingering, "A pretty face suits the dish-cloot." In pretense of trying to wipe the dirt from her shirt, Raey lowered her head to smooth the scowl brewing between her furrowed brows. Maisrie and Nic both chuckled at her confusion. Raey found little consolation when she discovered Maisrie misinterpreted her scowl as ignorance of her expression rather than knowledge of an intensely intimate embrace with her grandson.

Nic sidled up to comfort her by wrapping his hand around her shoulder and explaining his grandma's phrase, "She's giving you a compliment, lass. She means that with your lovely face, it won't matter that you're wearing dirt on your shirt." She moved away from his grasp, hoping Maisrie interpreted it as her moving quickly to wipe her shirt.

Maisrie rescued her from her discomfort by directing the conversation at Nic. "I'm so glad you're home from the hospital a wee bit early. There's more time to celebrate together."

Raey gleaned no answers from her questioning glance at

Nic. He overlooked the bay, discomfort displayed in the squint of his eye.

"It's been a long day of getting the garden in, so I invited Raey to our dinner for her hard work." Maisrie stretched her aching back, winked at Raey, and then hinted to Nic, "I've got everything ready in the fridge for dinner. Can I possibly persuade my dear birthday boy to grill us some delicious burgers again while we get cleaned up?"

Nic rubbed his neck and his charm faded to monotone as he retorted, "Brilliant maneuvering, Gram."

"Birthday?" Raey blurted, her eyes volleying between Nic and Maisrie.

"Yep, the big thirty-one." He responded with no fanfare. "I'll change my clothes and fire up the grill. Eat in an hour?" Nic exited without saying goodbye. Maisrie followed his quick paces into the atrium.

A shower and change of clothes provided time to clear her quandary over Nic's dance move and his apparent reluctance to celebrate his birthday. She wished she had a card or small present for him, but enjoying the evening with him would have to serve as her present.

Raey had only applied mineral powder with an SPF to her face while in Scotland, but tonight she added mascara, blush, and a light pink lipgloss. She exchanged her first choice of long sleeve t-shirt for a teal Aran cardigan she had bought on this trip. She arranged her hair in a messy bun and then smoothed her hands down her sides as if straightening her sweater. Giving her introverted self a pep talk in the mirror, she exhaled a laissez-faire calm.

Maisrie relished putting her obedient grandson on the spot, asking him to spread the white linen tablecloth, light taper candles, and offer a toast before their meal. With each flamboyant task, Nic raised his eyebrows. She responded with similar good-natured fun by whipping a couple swats at his bum with the tea towel ready on her shoulder.

"You're never too old for a swat, ye ken," she teased.

He stole the towel off her shoulder and gently returned a swat. "And neither are you, Gram," he playfully responded.

Once they settled down to eat, Nic rose with his glass to speak. "A toast to the hard labor of our earth workers today. We truly dig them. It's fun sowing and growing, but even better enjoying the fruits of the harvest. May this wine and company cure their ills and aching backs." Maisrie shook her head in silent amusement at Nic's witty tribute, and Raey grinned at his light-hearted humor. He raised his glass, and all joined in with a, "Slàinte mhath."

"Iain, my boy, cheers to yer right clever toast," Finlay said, slapping Nic on the back.

"Yes, Iain, very clever," Raey quietly emphasized his name as she leaned into Nic, flashing him a knowing smile. The last time she spoke his birth name, he dared to kiss her.

"It's Iain Stewart MacNicol," Nic boasted as he squeezed her knee under the table. "After my father."

"God rest their souls," Maisrie added, making the sign of the cross.

Finlay moved to stand behind Nic, gripping Nic's shoulders as he said, "Ye know, son, your grandma and I have been blessed to watch ye grow through the years. It's an honor to celebrate ye tonight. We know this is a tough day for ye, for all of us, but ye handle yerself well. I'm very proud of ye. Happy birthday."

Raey searched Nic's face for clues about Finlay's somber tone. Nic mischievously flashed an eyebrow at her but provided no hints of the difficulty Finlay alluded to. She lowered her head and muffled her laugh at Nic, who was clearly uncomfortable with Finlay's lavish praise.

Maisrie added, "Ye gave us so many lovely moments through yer growing years." Maisrie's eyes glistened with adoration as she continued, "Such a clever boy. I loue ye very much. Let's eat, everyone."

Finlay added, "Raey, he's always been a clever lad. We had to watch out for the mischief-maker in him, though."

"Only a time or two," Nic claimed with a wink.

"Trying to prove yourself as capable as your older brother didn't help," Maisrie inserted.

"Remember the motorbike race?" Finlay burst into a jovial recollection of Nic's youthful antics. "I still consider ye the winner just for the scheme."

"The means do count, Finlay," Maisrie corrected.

"Alasdair saved money to buy a motorbike. At fourteen, Nic thought up a get-rich-quick scheme to get himself one."

"Well, his dirty room got him caught." Maisrie folded her arms and gave Nic a glare. "That's the only time I'm admitting to yer dirty room being a good thing."

"Maisrie found two large dice and a bunch of money under his dirty laundry."

"Talk about money laundering!" Nic said as laughter erupted among them.

"He invited his buddies to play street craps on Friday nights. They all paid him a fee to play." Finlay laughed and shook his head as he pounded the table in excitement. "Pure barry! Just pure barry!"

"I lent the barn wall to shoot the dice against and my eyes as the look-out," Nic explained.

"That is not brilliant, Finlay," Maisrie argued.

"Lass," Finlay directed his words to her and pointed at Nic, "he's got the brains."

"I'm not even sure what to say about that story," Raey giggled.

"Um, I've learned that saying nothing is best," Nic said, pointing toward Maisrie.

"Sorry to say, it would have taken ye a long time to catch up to yer brother's money from working on the docks. But ye win for your efforts!" Finlay said.

"Well, I'll admit that I advanced a wee bit in my schemes from changing the spelling grade on my report card."

"Well, ye were too young to ken changing yer teacher's D to a B with blue ink would be quite noticeable," Maisrie said.

Finlay chuckled and asked, "Who's giving him the excuses now?"

"Well, I think I've turned out just fine." Nic paused. When no one responded to his comment, he held his hands out expectantly and added, "And now is where we all agree to that."

Maisrie and Finlay pretended to lock their lips, but Raey said, "I agree."

"And that's why I like you best," Nic jested and clasped her hand.

Maisrie encouraged Finlay to drink more water and slow his ebullient speech as he entertained with stories of Nic throughout the evening. Maisrie strategically imparted her comments and corrections between clearing dishes and serving dessert, allowing Finlay time to catch up with his breathing and regroup to further dramatize his stories.

Raey caught Maisrie's occasional attentive glances toward Nic. The dram of whisky warmed her insides as much as the animated blather between Finlay and Nic. The evening flew by. Raey was engrossed in the magic of being a part of a family that teased and laughed so easily at themselves and protected and cherished one another.

Finlay rose to close his yarn of exploits as the sun faded behind the horizon. "Thanks for quite a tidy burger, Nic. Ye certainly could have been a chef if ye hadn't chosen doctoring." He rubbed his belly and said, "Now's a good time to take the cat and my sweater and fall asleep in front of the telly. Very nice to have ye, lass."

"You tell wonderful stories, Finlay." Raey flashed both eyebrows at Nic, as if she were savvy to his secrets.

Finlay squeezed both Nic's and Raey's shoulders. "Night all. Happy birthday, Iain."

After Finlay left, Raey rose to leave and said, "Oh, Maisrie, what a heavenly dessert. Will you share the recipe?"

"Oh, it's baked raspberry and bramble trifle with Drambuie. It's Nic's favorite and an easy one. I'll write the directions out for ye. I make it every year to celebrate his birthday."

"Thank you so much for a lovely dinner and evening," Raey said to Maisrie.

Nic closed his eyes as Maisrie continued, "It was also my daughter's favorite. I made it for her every year on her birthday. Celebrating Nic's birthday is hard for him, so having ye for dinner made it a bit of a party tonight."

Nic tilted his head toward Maisrie and gazed at the ceiling as if examining the delicate design as the spider wove her web. He razzed his grandma, unraveling the crafty web she was weaving to lure Raey. "She needs no excuse to bake a cake, but it's very cute to watch her hide behind having you for dinner since she promised me she planned nothing special for my birthday."

"Well, I limited the celebration to one special guest. He might have chopped off my head if we'd sung 'Happy Birthday,' so I'll consider myself lucky."

Nic plotted his next move as intentionally as his grandma maneuvered the evening. He leaped from his chair, leaving it wobbling back and forth, and planted a zealous kiss on Maisrie's cheek. He whispered in her ear, "And I love you too, Gram. I see what you did there. Thanks for a special birthday dinner party. Even though I cooked my own burger." Maisrie understood Nic's dismissal, but her smile revealed she fully cherished his technique.

"You two scoot. I'll clean the rest of this mess."

Nic grabbed Raey's hand and teased Maisrie. "Hurry, Raey. Let's go before she changes her mind."

As they walked away, Raey squeezed Nic's hand and hit him on the shoulder with her other hand. "Why didn't you mention your birthday?"

"Now why would I do that when it's way more fun being hit by you?" Nic rubbed his arm, pretending it hurt.

Raey apologized and rubbed his shoulder where she hit him. "Why don't you like to celebrate your birthday? Thirty-one is not old, you know."

Nic stopped in midstride, closed his eyes, and moaned, "Mmm, could you rub that again? That felt good."

"Stop," she insisted, yanking on his hand.

"My parents died on my twelfth birthday. It's hard to celebrate that day."

Stopped in her tracks, Raey said, "Oh, wow. I'm so sorry." Raey wrapped Nic in a tight hug. "Today would be a tough day. I know it's hard, but I love that Maisrie still celebrated you."

Nic tilted his head back. "Well, it turns out I spent it exactly like I wanted."

She released his ardent gaze as they climbed the steps to her room.

"I'm glad you got your birthday wish." Raey opened her door and stood in the doorway.

Nic stepped closer to her door and clarified, "Well, not all of my birthday wishes."

"No?" Raey dared to add, "Then what shall I grant you?"

"A sunset hike to Neist Point and–"

Raey interrupted, "You recall I promised that in exchange for you wearing a kilt?" She leaned into his chest and wrapped her arms low around his waist. Nic's eyes searched hers for permission. When he spoke, she softly set her finger over his lips to quiet him. "I'm granting you a goodnight kiss."

Parting her lips to brush his lightly with hers, she pulled back slightly to slow his eagerness from taking control. He froze in place, his confused and pleading eyes drawing her in. She pressed into the softness of his lips, molding her lips around his. She found courage in the strength of his arms. The pressure of his mouth begged for an answer, so she clung to him with the intensity of one falling. Content with losing control, she kissed him long and desperately, as if running out of time. When she released him from their rushing tandem dance, she opened her dizzy eyes to meet the fire in his. He pulled her back to his lips, lingering until their passion simmered.

Resting their foreheads on one another, their skipping heartbeats slowed to a steady rhythm and the heat of their bodies cooled. The sensation of his lips on hers might soon fade, but his kiss had seared a lasting imprint on her memory.

Caressing a path down his arms, she clasped his hands and tenderly said, "Happy Thirty-First, Nic."

"Thanks for my gift, mo chailin alanine, beautiful girl." Nic brushed a kiss on her forehead before turning to leave.

Raey balanced against the doorjamb as he walked away, exhaling a breath she didn't realize she was holding.

From the end of the hallway, he turned and called, "Raey." Her eyes focused on the way his face lit up with a wide grin and smiling eyes. "I like the way you make birthday wishes come true!"

What have I gotten my heart into?

THIRTEEN

Only four days remained before her return to the States. Raey lay in bed, her trip tunneling to a close, and envisioned a day trip to one of her favorite places on the Isle, the Dunvegan Castle and Gardens.

She followed her inner compass. This clear day with gentle winds was perfect for tromping in view of the Cuillin Mountains or kayaking on Loch Harport near Bracadale–adventuring without an exact agenda, free floating like eagles across the bay. She might even pop in at the Talisker Distillery for a final toast to Scotland, leaving the weekend open for lazy days.

She wished Josh could have witnessed her casual approach, forgoing plotting a well-researched, detailed plan of nearby points of interest and places to eat. His irritation with that aspect of her nature had caused a few arguments, the biggest being after he had accepted the job in Skye. She wanted to return from their honeymoon in Scotland to tie up any loose ends before moving to Skye for good, but he didn't see the need for that. Her brain had organized on overdrive in the face of such a huge change. Residual miffed feelings taunted her even now at the memory. She had argued with him that a smooth move to Skye would benefit them both.

She snickered at the memory, nearly five years ago. Like a petulant child, she had clomped her heels on the hardwood floor and stomped down all eight steps of her seaside cottage, walking the streets of her neighborhood for well over an hour until she planted herself on a park bench. A young girl giggled in pride at letting go of her swing's chains at just the right moment to jump from the top of the arch to the ground without incident. Raey loosened her frown and her clenched fingers from the green slatted wood. She wanted to fly, too. She released her fury at Josh, yielding her unflinching position and her control masquerading as righteousness.

That Josh had been right about a virtually seamless move still annoyed her. She secured a teaching position and found comfortable friends in her co-workers. They rented a cottage on a small loch with the mountains in the distance, a bit too remote for practicality's sake, but the allure of the land had contributed to their decision to move to Skye.

Raey stood before her bedroom window. Puffs of mist rolled past the panes as she arched into a contented sigh. Skye had worked its motivational magic.

She supposed the true test would come when she returned to North Carolina. Contrary to the pure desolation of leaving their dream behind years ago, this time, the return home would be a restoration, a rebuilding. Leaving had been a race against time, crucial for obtaining the best care for Josh, and part of the collateral damage of Josh's cancer.

Did she meet her goal in returning to Skye—to get a firm grip on her life? Raey promised herself to meet future challenges with the same determination she now possessed. Certain that emotional ups and downs would arise, she allowed herself backward steps but determined not to get stuck in her past again.

Continuing to test this reborn Raey back in North Carolina, where the rubber would meet the road, she would seek a new way to frame herself. Simple possibilities piqued her interest. Inspired by Maisrie's beautiful flower bed, Raey would plant petunias and geraniums in the plot in front of her seaside cottage. As an ode to Nic, she might even offer weekend hiking or biking events for young kids in the area. She exhaled, content with her resolution to fill her days with new possibilities and relationships. Visiting Skye, the catalyst for her change, allowed her not only to reimagine her world but also to envision a new beginning.

These last few days, she didn't feel like her old self. She felt more like a new self, more comfortable in her skin again, like a ship moored in a protected harbor, coasting calm waves. Yet, her chemistry with Nic stirred a strong wind to blow across those placid waters. Her insides jumped when the phone rang.

"Good morning, Earth Woman. What's in store for you today?" Nic greeted her like an upbeat tour guide.

"I'm headed to the lovely Dunvegan Castle."

"Ah, visiting the old fortress of Clan MacLeod, are ye?" Hearing his jocular voice cheered her.

"I love that grand staircase at the entrance. It reminds me of one of our Victorian plantation homes in North Carolina."

"Better not compare the eight-hundred-year-old home of MacLeods to the youngster of a house in North Carolina aloud, lass. If you're not nice to the MacLeods, they might put you in the dungeon to die."

"Legends and lies," she smarted back and then said, "but on one of our visits, I read about that happening to one of the wives. Kind of gave me the creeps."

"Well, you may get rained on a wee bit later today. They're saying the blue sky might not last."

"I hope it doesn't rain, but I'm geared up just in case. My plan is to spend the day there, meandering through the garden oasis and touring the loch to see the seals. I've never done that."

"What? You're not doing the fishing boat tour?"

"If there's time."

"Or save your fishing for this weekend."

"Yeah, that could work."

"I can suggest the perfect spot."

"Where?"

"Okay, I want you to sit when I tell you." Nic waited while she obeyed. "Otherwise, from what I know about you, after I explain, you will wear a wee path in the rug at my Gram's, and then we'll need to replace it."

"Auspicious, Nic. But I'll play along," she said as she plopped on the bed, springing up and down as she talked. "Okay, I'm sitting down. What would you like to tell me?"

He spat out his offer as quickly as possible and spared taking too many breaths to avoid her interjecting questions or concerns, "A buddy just offered me a week at the Rothes Glen House in Moray, east of Inverness. I'm on call starting Monday, but I'm thinking of making it a long weekend. Are you game?"

Raey was struck speechless. The idea of being alone with Nic all day and all night drew a mix of shock and interest.

"It's a nine-acre baronial mansion. His parents own it and are traveling for a month. He's getting ready to put it up for sale for them. He said I'm welcome to get lost in it. The caretakers are a married couple who live in a cottage on the property if we need anything.

"I don't know what your fancy is, but we can do some sea fishing at Spey Bay, which has some braw sandy beaches, or on the Spey River. If you'd like to watch dolphins, we can find them there, too. And if a pheasant shoot or roe deer stalking are your cup of tea, you can try your hand at those. It could be an epic finish to your trip."

"Hmm. I'd say stalking is out. And I'm not a fan of guns, so that's out too," she purposefully teased him, acting as if she struggled to decide, but truthfully, it sounded absolutely delightful.

"And no strings attached," he assured her. "It could be a great way to expand your Scotland experience in your last few days." After waiting for her answer, he added, "Maybe pretending you're a damsel in distress in one of its towers is to your liking."

"So, you're thinking of causing me distress or locking me away?" she yelped in mock alarm. "I think you definitely need to work on your art of persuasion, Nic." She prolonged her answer, in spite of Nic's eagerness for her 'yes.'

"Not at all! I'm your vacation rescuer. It's a no-distress trip."

"Now you're talking. No-distress is to my liking." Raey fell silent and then added, "Hmm." She pondered aloud, "Umm." Continuing her ruse, she let her voice trail off in hesitation.

"And to help you with that no-distress trip—it's only forty miles from the airport, so there's the bonus that I can drop you at the airport Sunday on my way back."

"Oh wow, now that is convenient!" she responded, disguising her dismay. The airport meant leaving Nic forever, and she wanted more time with him.

"Yeah?" The eagerness in his voice grew.

Encouraged to find the freedom to accept without overthinking his offer, she stared at the rug pattern her feet traced, relaxed her shoulders, and projected in a serious tone, "You are free the entire weekend?"

"I'll take it off if you decide to go with me. A mate will cover my shifts since I covered for him the last few times he needed it. We could leave tomorrow morning. No pressure, really. How about we leave your answer as a 'yes' and plan to leave tomorrow morning by 9:30, knowing there's a possibility of a 'no' if your brain runs ahead of you?"

"Very funny. I'm good with the 'yes.'" He had certainly learned the nuances of her personality in their short time together.

"Seriously, back out if you get a better offer, but it sounds like a great place to hike, fish, golf, drink whisky, get lost, or whatever else you imagine."

"I love the offer," she interjected.

He continued with his persuasion as if she were still undecided. "Now that Pops looks like he's on the mend, I don't feel like I need to stay close by. An eight-bedroom house seems like a waste for one person. And you don't know this about me, but I don't like to be wasteful. I'm environmentally friendly."

"Hmm. You're environmentally friendly, all right. I do like that about you," she ruminated. *Certainly easy on the eyes, if not the earth.* She feigned deep contemplation and added, "I do like that I would be closer to the airport."

"Ouch, I'm wounded. The lass says 'yes' because she likes that she'd be closer to the airport."

"Well, this trip could certainly give you time to share more about you," she proposed.

"Okay, I'll be ready for you. Ask away."

"I plan to! See you tomorrow morning. Don't forget your toothbrush. We want you to remain environmentally friendly." She teased him with one last comment.

As soon as she clicked off the call, her brain orchestrated the questions she wanted answered. She needed to dive deeper into the heart of him, to soak up the closeness he offered. There was so much of him she wanted to get to know. Leaving Scotland in three days meant leaving Isobel, Maisrie, and Finlay, but most of all, it meant saying goodbye to Nic. Three days with him wouldn't be enough.

She dreaded their goodbye. Spending her last three days enjoying Scotland with him would make the pain of leaving him worse. How would she say goodbye to someone she wanted to say a lot more hellos to?

Their connection was more than friendship. Three thousand miles and an ocean apart was a daunting long-distance from him. She couldn't cope with not being able to see his smile in person or hold his hand or kiss him goodnight. Phone calls would not be enough for her. How long would that suffice? Would Nic consider a long-distance relationship?

Her insides jumbled with nervous energy as she readied to visit Dunvegan Castle, her favorite spot. Her thoughts pinged from *What am I doing?* to *What-ifs?* like balls in a pinball machine. Verbalizing a "Yes" to his offer energized her, and she looked forward to this weekend adventure with him more than any other she'd had in the last month.

I want Nic in my life, but how?

FOURTEEN

R aey prayed for Dunvegan Castle to work its magic and distract her from obsessing about spending an entire weekend alone with Nic, only to then say goodbye to him. Venturing the less familiar route south and then along the west coast of the island demanded her attention. If it weren't so early, she would follow the signs that directed tourists to the famed Talisker Distillery, an enticing remedy for taking the edge off her nerves. Every good Scot agreed that anytime is a suitable time for a wee dram of whisky, but she was more comfortable reserving that right for later in the day. Instead, she veered into the parking lot across from it at Caora Dhubh Coffee Company. When she opened the door, the aroma of freshly baked cakes assaulted her. After friendly banter with the barista, she ordered a smooth, flat white coffee and a chocolate coconut flapjack.

After overhearing the couple ahead of her in line for coffee, Raey vetoed her plans for the castle in favor of a six-hour boat tour of the Isles of Canna and Rum. She laughed that sprites must have conspired such a swift change of her mind. Sipping the smooth warmth insulating her insides, she headed in the unexpected direction, excited for what lay ahead.

Just in time for the departing tour, she paid and joined the small group. Skipper Colin, clad in a black skullcap and cream Aran sweater, prepared the group with guidelines and information for their journey. A young, humorous fellow, he mimicked tourists' blunders of putting their lifejackets on backwards and upside down, which made her chuckle. When two ladies struggled to secure their lifejackets, he emphasized while assisting them, "Now lasses, trust no others more braw than me while on the water." He winked and froze in place, statuesquely staring across the horizon. In his best pirate rendition, he gave his final instructions, "Any unruly tourists will find yer thumbs wedged in the isle's Punishment Stone. Ye'll be left to ponder yer misdeed, just as offending islanders were once punished."

Choosing a seat at the stern of the boat, Raey relaxed into the steady hum of the pontoon motoring through the blue loch. A gray wash of clouds skirted across the Cuillin Hills. Skipper Colin pointed out gray seals, dolphin pods, and basking sharks along the western coastline of Skye. They arrived an hour and a half later at their first destination, the remote Isle of Canna.

Tourists stepped ashore after a facetious warning from the captain, "Beware the shape-shifting kelpies or those horses will lure ye to a watery grave."

Raey struck out alone during their allotted time to explore the isle, intent on seeing the remains of a four-hundred-year-old castle, An Coroghan. The refuge atop the eighty-foot-high stack, was later used as a prison. Upon reaching its base, a tiny marker staked in the ground warned of its dangerous condition and steered visitors clear of the structure. Taken aback momentarily by this rustic sign's caution, Raey spun her ponytail through her fingers, fielding both agitation and contemplation as she determined who might witness her transgression. *This place deserves to be seen. I can't leave here without chancing it.* She imagined charging the steep trail to the top like a warrior defending this neglected outpost from those who disregarded its unique beauty. *It could be dangerous. I should follow the rules, but this time, I'm doing what I want.* Overcome by the temptation, she scrambled up loose gravel to the tower, mindful of crumbling stone. A lintelled entrance survived in the mortared wall.

Crawling the steep incline to the fortress outlook, she peered across the top of the prison toward Canna Harbor, a carving of watery inlets through a magnificent green blanket. Bathed in the peace that the valleys and heights bestowed, Raey's heart slowed to a normal rhythm as her mind wandered across the landscape, remembering God's long ago promise to walk beside her through life. Her next intruding thought jolted her peace for a moment—how fortunate she was to find a friend in Nic, a man that didn't avoid her crumbling but provided a stabilizing force. She didn't make becoming her friend easy and doubted she'd have his patience if the tables were turned. She didn't want to let him go.

As she trekked back to the group's meeting place at Café Canna, she marveled at the parallels between the condition of her heart and this land—such fierce landscape bore such tranquil beauty.

After only a light breakfast before a boat ride, a steep climb, and then exploring the Isle of Canna for an hour, she savored a mug of soup and a cheese, tomato, and red onion chutney sandwich from the cafe as if they were delicacies.

Their scenic ride continued past Canna's Prison Rock and Black Beach and the Puffin Stack on their way to Rum Island, unveiling sheer cliffs, an abundance of dolphins, basking sharks, and minke whales feeding in the tidal streams. Before anyone called the black and white birds nesting in the burrows of the mountain summits pigeons, Skipper Colin boasted that Rum's colony of 60,000 Manx Shearwaters was one of the largest in the world. When he pointed out the soaring golden eagles overhead and the perched white-tailed eagles that Scotland successfully reintroduced, she quietly clapped her hands as if presented with a gift. She hoped to follow up this jeweled experience by spotting sunning gray seals.

Raey squinted through the sun as Skipper Colin pointed out a shipwrecked trawler, grounded at the base of a rock buttress. He joked, "Don't worry about the swells and wreckage. I haven't imbibed quite the amount of rum as that skipper, yet!" Its skipper had fallen asleep and failed to make course alterations. Upon closer approach to this whale of a vessel, the *Jack Abry II,* stranded to float eternally on its side since 2011, she spied rust bleeding from its entrails.

Observing this vessel, built to weather ocean-sized storms, in its wrecked condition disturbed her. Raey lamented her life's course, but she determined her wrecked vessel of a heart, too long moored in place by a running knot, was not beyond being salvaged. She crafted this course to Skye as part of that rescue.

Finishing the boat tour just before four o'clock, she considered her first solo sea adventure a clear success and proudly headed toward that wee dram she had promised herself that morning, especially since the Talisker Distillery was less than a minute down the road.

On the way to her car, she glanced back and waved when Skipper Colin summoned her, "Did the Kelpies get ye, lass?"

She gave him a conciliatory chuckle when he dangled her car keys in his hand. Holding her wild curls that the wind kept whipping in front of her eyes, she extended her hand to reclaim her forgotten keys.

"I got lost in my reveries of the lovely day, Skipper. Thank you so much!" she said, embarrassed by her oversight in front of this outgoing, brawny man, standing over six feet tall and a mere two feet from her.

"It's Colin," he corrected her and shook her hand in greeting before releasing the keys in her palm. He smiled in welcome, as if he took personal responsibility for her joy. "Nothing like a wee dram of whisky to top off that kind of day. Would ye like to join me at the distillery?"

She skimmed the gravel with her foot, stalling to read the situation while other passengers thanked him for such an entertaining tour. "Okay, sure," she graciously, yet cautiously, accepted. "I considered making that my next stop anyway. I can't stay long, though, because I need to get packed."

"Great, I'll meet ye there. I need to wrap up here, first. I'll be five minutes behind ye." As he pivoted back toward the office, she surveyed his easy saunter in tight jeans and the Sea Skye Boat Tours emblem stretched taut over his shoulder blades. As he pulled the door open, his gaze flicked to her, and he waved with a knowing grin when he caught her looking at him. Nonchalantly, she waved back and quickly looked away, swinging her keychain lanyard as she hurried to her car.

Colin took longer than five minutes, which gave her time to restore her equilibrium. Standing at the table across from him, Raey's whisky and water reminded her of the disaster of her first swallow of whisky. A small laugh emitted at that memory to which Colin raised inquiring eyebrows. She relayed the story of her novice move. She had gulped and immediately discovered why whisky was the national drink. It was as fiery as a resilient, red-headed Highland warrior wielding a sword. She had barely kept the drink from spewing across the table as she clasped her hand over her mouth, freezing until she could recover from the cauterized hairs in her nose. From then on, Josh often teased her by asking if she wanted a *sniffer*. She learned to savor the drip of the spicy, woody, honeyed bacon bite down her throat. Every whisky she imbibed since then reminded her of him.

"Enjoying whisky is like a journey, not a destination, aye?" Colin swirled the amber liquid in his Glencairn whisky glass. "Just take yer time. Open yer mind to new ones, ye ken." He raised his eyebrows and tilted his glass toward her in acknowledgment of her first try.

"Mm-hmm." Raey took a sip of whisky, captivated by his eloquent exuberance.

He continued his tour guide recitation as he sipped from his glass, "Being new to the drink can be like a minefield. The range is as vast as the variety of tastes. It can be all too easy to select something that is way outside yer comfort zone and put yerself off drinking it."

"What would you suggest, Skipper Colin?"

"Ye cannae go wrong with the single malt whisky, but much depends on yer palate." Was it his outgoing, affable nature that gave her the distinct impression his whisky lesson was a disguised hint at how to select a partner? "Start gently and break yerself in. Whisky is for the adventurer, and ye seem to be one," he claimed, saluting her with his raised glass.

"Wow, an adventurer?" she mused, set off kilter by the final words of his whisky monologue. She must have successfully hid her nervous energy. "Must be my wild, wind-blown hair. And you sound like an advertisement for Talisker," she teased as she joined him by raising her snifter.

"History in the making. Slàinte mhath!" he bellowed and enjoyed a dram.

"Slàinte!" She raised her glass to toast. "How's that?" she asked.

"My great, great grandfather helped start the Talisker Distillery," he said, nodding to the sign over the bar, "so I've been sweet on whisky for quite some time."

Suddenly intimidated, as if in the presence of royalty, or as she preferred to imagine him, the rebel son of royalty, Raey's natural curiosity surfaced. *Why did he run tours if his family once owned the oldest and most famous whisky distillery on Skye?*

Across from her stood the quintessential laid-back Scot–a very muscular, handsome, and wealthy man, no doubt–but still just a gorgeous specimen of a man. His gregarious charm drew her into innocent flirting, something she no longer feared after her visits from Josh and chats with Nic. She raised her chin a little higher, having fun with being reunited with this side of herself.

"Your Majesty," she teased.

A crooked grin slid from the corner of his mouth as he glanced down briefly at the glass clutched in his hand. Staring at her for a second too long, he played his hand. He set his elbow on the pub table, leaning inches from her face, and professed in a voice syrupy as the liquid at the bottom of his glass, "Bonnie lass, the proper title from ye would be 'Your Royal Highness.'" He ended his corrective gesture by arching back for a long final swig, slapping his glass down to the wood, and readying to receive her next barb's volley.

She met his challenge, for she, too, considered herself a force to be reckoned with when it came to witty repartee. He gave as good as he got, but his confidence with a pleasantly unpredictable script emboldened hers. She intentionally mimicked his moves and quipped, "A most impressive display of wit, Lord Talisker. Where might your kilt be? And along those lines, if I may ask what a Scot wears un…"

Colin's loud combination of cough and grunt rendered her speechless. She froze, as if facing imminent danger. He stealthily peeked both ways, like he was searching for nearby spies. "My lady, ye are not permitted to ask that question."

Like a damsel relieved of the ogre's distress, Raey batted her eyelashes, crossed her arms, and reprimanded him in a high-pitched plea, "You scared me!"

"I'm letting ye in on vital information, lass," he retorted in warning. "Asking a kilted Scotsman that question, well, that might get ye forty lashes or maybe even kilt!"

Over the next forty-five minutes, Colin told fanciful stories of his family's history.

On their way to their cars, Colin stopped in the middle of the parking lot. "I'm obliged to entertain yer original question and provide you with the knowledge you sought."

"Okay?" she said, not recalling an unanswered question.

"For the record, I'm a true Scotsman," he proudly proclaimed.

Unsure of his reference, she figured she'd kindly bolster his claim. "You certainly are, Lord Talisker!"

"But it's my duty to warn ye." He paired his grin with a raised eyebrow as he cautioned, "A true Scotsman might not tell ye what he wears under his kilt, but he might just drop his kilt to show ye. Best ye be careful asking that question, lass."

Raey's eyes bulged, and she slapped her palm over her mouth. Through her giggles, she said, "Oh, goodness me!" After taking a moment to contemplate Colin's advice, a devious smile covered her face. "That's good counsel, Lord Talisker."

Colin shook his head in disbelief and pulled Raey into his

side for a quick goodbye hug. "Naughty, naughty, American lass."

Raey released him with a pat on his back. "Thank you for a great tour today and the whisky."

She grinned at their flirting as she stepped into her car, understanding their banter for what it was. Fluffy and light. No desire, no fear, no pull, no guilt. Not like her attraction to Nic. From their first moments alone together in his car, their connection was risky. He was beautiful to the core and touched her where others couldn't reach. The stakes felt high from the start.

* * *

Since it was too late in the day to travel to Dunvegan Castle, Raey continued her venture with a trek to Talisker Bay. A wide trail wound around a farmhouse, through a couple of metal gates, and past grazing sheep on the hillside who stared as if befuddled by her presence. Stopping to take a selfie at a stone wall, she hiked down the trail as it opened to an inlet surrounded by volcanic cliffs and a waterfall. She bobbled like a flitting butterfly through a pile of large, smooth, black rocks and meandered along a trickle of water that snaked into the spilling waves.

Raey scrambled along the shoreline until she found a smooth rock for a seat and listened to the harmony of the sea roll along the water's edge. A rugged sea stack jutted from the calm bay and guarded the seas and sky like a sentinel. She pulled up her hood and propped back on her arms to allow the little remaining sun peeking through the approaching clouds to shine on her face. The advancing veil of mist nearly hid the islands and the steep column of rock on the horizon.

The beautifully fierce landscape and changeable weather were essential influences on the resolute strength of the Scots. Veined through the generations, perhaps they worked on her, too.

Raey sensed Josh's presence, his still contemplation beside her like a quiet wind in her ears. She greeted him without looking, "Hi there, stranger. I'm glad you're here."

In the suspended spray, Josh focused on her as if committing the lines of her face to memory. "I'm glad I'm here with you, too. I never know when the last time will be."

The realization that this might be the last time she sat with this man eroded any attempt to build defenses against the pain his coming and going caused her. With her trip ending, she dared not squander the precious moments she had with him.

"I know it's difficult, me showing up and leaving like this. I don't like the turmoil it causes you." Josh settled next to her, digging his heels into the charcoal sand.

Can he read my mind? "How does this keep happening?" She pushed her hoodie back to see the wind brush his wavy tresses across his brow and resisted the urge to brush her lips across it, too. "Can we control it?"

Josh fidgeted on the rock and straightened his loose locks, losing the battle. "Those are questions I can't answer. What's happening? It's, well, it's…." He locked his hands in his pockets, and asserted, "It's temporary."

"It's frustrating, wanting something but not understanding how to make it happen." She tossed a small rock into the sea's backwash.

"Nic is a good guy." Josh paused and copied Raey, tossing a pebble into the water.

"Talking about Nic with you is uncomfortable," Raey said.

"But we need to talk about him." He garnered her gaze as

if collecting evidence. Unsure of his words' reception, he took care. "You're leaving in a few days. What do you want?"

She walked to the water's edge. *What do I want?* Frustration washed over her like the waves on the beach. Josh's departure from her life was imminent. Her days in Nic's presence were coming to a close. Confusion teetered on a ledge of control, and her self-conscious indecision about what to do frustrated her. She steadied her voice and released it with the roll of the water over the sand. "We've known each other for a month, and I'm going back home in a few days. How can a relationship between us work?" Raey stared at the horizon, contemplating Josh's question.

What do I want? The answer wasn't as easy as his simple question. It wove a web of complexity too difficult to unravel.

"So timing, a month, is the disqualifier for the next right thing in a relationship with Nic?" Josh closed the space between them and lifted her chin to him, not letting her off the hook on his line of thinking.

"How do you know Nic is my next right thing?" she asked, wanting his thoughts.

He rested his hands upon her shoulders, as if trying to steady her. "The question is how will *you* know?"

She gripped his hands. To hold him or push him away, she wasn't sure. "I don't know. And I don't enjoy talking about a relationship with another man with you," she recoiled.

"I can barely fathom it." He stopped speaking. With a heavy sigh, he said, "You, in another man's arms, is maddening." Leaning into her, he added, "But how often does a dead husband help his wife move on, to find love again?" His breath kissed her forehead.

She squeezed her eyes closed to absorb the touch of his lips lingering against her skin and tears rolled warm tracks over her cheeks to her chin. "I don't know," Raey sniffled. She contemplated his rhetorical question and his presence and added, "Maybe more than we think." A wave of chilly wind filled the void from the heat of his body when she leaned back to take in his boyishly innocent eyes. A worried crease deepened between her brows.

"You will find the answers to your confusion." He tilted her face to place a tender kiss on her lips.

His lips released her, but his gaze held her eyes, and she clung to him. "You are invested already."

She loosened her hold on his waist and asked, "How can you tell?"

"Your heart is involved." His finger circled her heart with each syllable.

"How is it you know that, and I don't?"

"You know it." Josh backed up and paced in front of her, footprints in the sand weaving an overlapping pattern in both directions. When he stopped, he looked her intently in the eyes. "This is how I know. I was on the receiving end of your apprehension when we began a relationship. But I also received your deep love. Something takes over your entire presence when you invest your heart. You want to know everything. There's a certain determination, like stars finally aligning."

"The stars, really? Who are you? Romeo?" Raey brushed off his comment. "Well, I know this much," Raey confessed, trying at clarity even for herself. "Since being here, I'm more ready to move on. I don't have that constant numb, stuck in quicksand feeling." Raey's voice grew with conviction as she confessed, "But with the distance between us and the little we know about one another, I can't be for sure that Nic is my next right thing."

"So, kissing Prince Charming didn't give you your answer?" His poked fun released a hard stare from her, and his smirk revealed he knew the truth. He froze with a tilted head and raised his eyebrows, waiting for her to contest his allusion.

"Moving on is not easy. I sure hope you wouldn't find it simple," she accused.

"Near impossible," he answered her straightaway.

"I hate being vulnerable. It's scary as hell." She jerked her arms down to her side.

"You do not invest more than a few kisses without keen interest."

"Maybe I need to kiss quite a few frogs first." She joked, not liking the direction of their conversation.

"I'm running out of time." He pushed his hands through his hair and froze them clasped behind his head. The same mannerisms that he displayed in their lifetime together when he sped ahead through a difficult discussion. "Speaking as the guy blessed to have married you, there are guys worthy of your love."

"Thank you, I think," she ribbed.

"My words will sound tough, Babe, but I want you to find that bold courage of yours."

She sighed in concession and slumped her shoulders. Nothing she said would deter him from continuing to investigate her feelings for Nic.

"Nic's good for you. He challenges you. He wants a lot from life, like I know you do." Josh moved inches from her. His breath kissed her cheek as he emphasized his last point. "And he really likes you."

Raey rubbed off goosebumps from the shiver that ran through her as she absorbed Josh's words.

"Give love a chance," Josh pleaded, watching her eyes roam the bay. "Give Nic a chance to capture your heart."

"I will try," she whispered, paralyzed in place. Like the mist rolling over the bay, this new commitment spoken out loud to Josh carried the heaviness of an ending. Yet, it brought the lightness of a beginning.

She closed her eyes when his soft lips landed on hers. When a cool, caressing breeze replaced the warmth of him, her heavy eyelids refused to unfold to the horizon. She covered her exposed lips with her fingers, slowly surrendering to the cold reality of his loss once again.

She traipsed unconsciously across the remains of her footprints on the trail and toward her last days in Skye. The loneliness from his parting, once shadowed by a tormenting grief, left her dizzy, but not emotionally wrecked.

His courageous, out-of-this-world love recharged her spirit. She walked each step along the trail back to her car and away from Josh, lost more in contemplating the possibility of opening her heart again than the ache of holding on to a life gone by.

FIFTEEN

Raey stretched languidly to her side, silencing her phone alarm. She stayed awake way too late, committing Josh's face and the lilt of his voice to memory to subdue the never-ending fear that time would fade her ability to conjure his image. She stared at Josh's photo on her phone that she had fallen asleep to, turned the 6:30 a.m. screen face down on her chest, and dozed off until a persistent knock at her door forced her feet to the hardwood floor. Jumping up from the bed too quickly, the room spun around her as she stumbled to the door.

"Good morning." Nic greeted her and nervously shuffled his feet.

"Oh my, please tell me I didn't oversleep," Raey pleaded.

"Not at all. The departure time has now been comfortably delayed to whatever time you are ready," he good-humoredly offered, taking in her pajamas.

"Oh, Nic, I'm so sorry. I'll hurry!" Her feet pattered in place against the floor.

"It's plenty fine. There's no plan that can't be rearranged over these next few days. Just come to the desk when you're ready."

"Thanks, Nic, I'll be right there. Long night," she added as she closed the door.

"Can't wait to hear about it," he called as he walked away.

Her heart rate increased as she recalled her dream. In her dream, she and Nic agreed to meet the next morning for coffee. She struggled to arrive at a place that she couldn't remember and a time she couldn't recall. Her watch's minute hand ticked away as she ran from unrecognizable room to unrecognizable room to find the front door of a strangely familiar house. One crisis after another usurped her time and impeded her leaving. Everything was so irritatingly vague, and then she woke to the reality of missing their meeting in real life.

Relief suffused her body at hearing Nic's assurance to take her time. She wanted to shower and let the hot water erase any hint of the night's toll. Fortunately, she wouldn't need to take the time to pack. Being a planner by nature, she had already packed everything except her outfit and the necessary toiletries.

An easy forty-five minutes later, Finlay greeted her with a chipper "Guid mornin', Chick-a-dee. It's good to see ye." She returned his greeting with a warm smile, wondering what he thought of his grandson and her going on a three-day trip together.

"It was great having ye here, lass. I got all yer paperwork ready." He held her printed bill still on the counter and pointed for her to sign on the line. "Have a great last few days of yer trip. I just dropped the fees and taxes for the days you're leaving early. I appreciate ye giving Maisrie a hand in the garden when I wasn't feeling myself."

Raey handed his pen back and said, "Really, it was all my—"

He waved off her unfinished words. "Yer help was worth gold to me. The next time you're in town, yer stay is free. And, of course, yer first wee dram."

"That's so nice of you. Take care of yourself."

Maisrie hurried from the breakfast area with her arms wide open and wrapped her in a strong hug. "You're a dear. Ye've been a gift to me these past few weeks." She squeezed her tighter and said, "Come back and visit us soon." She pulled back and stared as if waiting for Raey to plan the date right then. "I hope Nic and ye have a wonderful time. I'm happy he's taking a few days off. He needs it. Be sure to keep him in line," she warned, giggling at the impossibility.

"That won't be easy," Raey agreed. Not sure how to address her deeper feelings toward Maisrie, she chose a safe route, "I'm sure I will be back to visit sometime. You all take care of yourselves, especially you," she emphasized, pointing at Finlay. "Listen to what Maisrie tells you to do. You two have a lovely place here. Thanks for everything and for including me in your family dinners."

"Well, yer family now, lass," Maisrie pointed out.

Finlay stood tall, wrapped his arms in front of him, and chimed in with a toothy smile, "When ye endure an entire evening with our clan, we consider ye family." She laughed, and then returned his fond smile as he offered more seriously, "There will always be a chair at our table for ye."

As the kitchen door swung open, Nic's presence commanded everyone's attention. For Raey, he consumed all the space and air. "I'm glad you've arrived," he said. "I see your brain didn't run away with you." Both Maisrie and Finlay stilled and awkwardly stared between the two, waiting for someone to break the spell with an explanation.

"Very funny. But it appears you're the late one," she teased, pointing at her watch as if she'd been waiting a long time for him. "How in the world do you ever get to an appointment on time?"

"Hmm. Interesting. Me, late? Babies and kids make their parents late, so I'm usually right on time," he pronounced, imitating a haughty pediatrician's confidence.

His grandma greeted him with a hug and whispered into his ear. He hugged her back with a kiss to her cheek and a double pat on her back. Raey wished she were privy to their private exchange.

"So, you're pretty excited to be hanging with the doc on his days off," he teased Raey for all to hear as he stepped beyond Maisrie to grab Raey's biggest piece of luggage. He slyly grinned as he leaned down, knowing she would teasingly punch him for saying that, but wouldn't dare to lose decorum in front of his grandparents. His exuberance ramped up her apprehension.

Maisrie swatted his arm and jumped in to defend her against Nic's disconcerting humor. "Now, Nic, don't give her reasons to be anxious around ye."

When they stepped outside, Raey sensed his watchful eye, so she stuck her tongue out at him.

Once alone together on the drive, their teasing tension subsided.

She bounced sideways in her seat and announced, "It's time to play twenty questions."

"Well, I said you could ask away, but if you run out of things to ask, I have some questions of my own."

"Okay, but me first. So, you live with your grandma and grandpa," she paused, anticipating his response.

He taunted her, "Is there a question in there somewhere?"

"Tell me more about your family?"

"Well, you met Alasdair, who's two years older than me. Mind you, you noticed he wasn't nearly as brawny as me, right?" Nic tapped her on the shoulder.

"Oh, absolutely, you're obviously way more muscular," she lavishly praised, squeezing his bicep.

"Oh yeah, do that again." He shook his arm to encourage her touch.

Raey obliged his request to massage his bicep again but finished by pinching him.

He grabbed his arm at the sting, surprised by her antics. "Ow, violence is not becoming, young lady," he snickered and lightly pinched her back.

"Um, your brother?"

"I dinna get to spend as much time with him as I'd like since he's an advocate in Edinburgh. I always thought I'd follow him off the isle. Laurel owns her own boutique, so they're quite busy with their work and their clever wee lass, Clarice. We were thick as thieves and caused a bit of trouble for Gram and Pops in our teens."

Raey joked, "Did he become an attorney to hide all your secret deeds?" They both laughed and Raey inserted, "I can't wait to hear those stories."

"But if I get on to those stories, it will take more time than we have in this car." She found it endearing that his lilt and accent thickened when he spoke about his family, but the finality in his tone suggested a reticence to travel down memory lane.

She quieted her voice as she asked, "And your mom and dad?"

After a pregnant pause, he answered in a sober tone, "Well, you know I was twelve when a car accident killed my parents, but no one ever figured out what caused it. The police inspector thinks their car left the road trying to negotiate a bend and struck a tree going down an embankment."

"That's awful," she said, hoping for more about them.

"My mom was beautiful. Tall and graceful with wavy brown hair. Very loving like Gram. I remember the feeling of her coming into my room to wake me up for school in the morning. She would lie next to me, rub my back, snuggle her face into mine, and talk smooth and low to me until my eyes opened."

"Oh, that's such a great feeling to cherish." Raey caught Nic's glance at her.

"Every day when I came home from school, we'd chat while I ate a snack or did homework. When she asked about my day, if I didn't answer, she would stop what she was doing, lean across the counter close to me, and stare at me, awaiting my response. She waited as if nothing in the world was more important. Of course, sometimes, I ignored her as long as I could until we both giggled."

"I can imagine you doing that on purpose."

"I can still smell her perfume."

"I know what you mean," Raey said, understanding more clearly than he could fathom after she traveled through those kinds of triggers this past month on Skye.

"My dad was my idol. I worked hard in school because I wanted to be smart like him. I didn't really understand what an engineer did, but I knew he had an important job. My brother and I would often tackle him to the carpet when he arrived home from work. My dad got quite animated when he wrestled us. And believe me, Alasdair and I wrestled to win, so we laughed and tumbled and tackled hard."

Raey placed her hand gently on his shoulder, unsure if the gesture comforted him or her more. She sat frozen in déjà vu, seeing a police officer explain the nightmare of her own parents' death at the hands of a drunk driver just weeks after her high school graduation. While she wasn't a child when it happened, she empathized with the void created by losing one's parents. Her hand rested on his arm as they drove in silence, calming the exposed edges of their emotions.

Nic interrupted the quiet. "Those first few years were rough for Gram and Pops and us. We were all trying to survive the same pain under the same roof, and I didn't always manage my sadness well. We mended together into a tight-knit family. Their death, and Gram and Pops' direction, strongly influenced who I am."

"I'm sorry Nic. Such a huge loss changes you forever." She watched his hands adjust their hold on the wheel as he stared at the road ahead.

"I hold many wonderful memories of my mom and dad, but not as many as I'd like." He glanced her way before adding, "I'm sorry, too."

She gave him a questioning glance.

"I'm sorry that I didn't relay my pain when you exposed your grief about your parents and Josh to me. Thinking about that now, I guess I took the easy way out, but I was really trying to let you share. I hope that makes sense."

"I appreciate your thoughtfulness in listening. I was uncharacteristically vulnerable with you then. Truthfully, shifting the focus to you would have been a relief."

"Yeah, I recognize the move." Nic paused before admitting, "I've done it a lot. Even if I hesitate, it helps to share the pain. It makes it easier to carry."

"Is that why you still live with your grandparents–to help with their pain?"

"Actually, I don't live with them. I own a house in Upper Ollach, less than fifteen minutes away, with a beautiful view of the Sound of Raasay."

Her jaw dropped and she turned fast in her seat, her crest-fallen eyes full on him. "Oh, wow! I didn't even get to see it."

"Maybe next time." He stirred uneasily in his seat and flexed his fingers, grasping the steering wheel. His gaze bounced between the windshield and her.

"Sure," Raey murmured, trying to hide feeling cheated.

"I stay at the B&B when Pops struggles with his health, which occurs more frequently these days. I check in and help when I'm not working. It gives me a closer view of how serious things are if I can see how Gram is coping. It was a bonus that it created more opportunities for us to hang out."

"I just assumed you were working when you weren't there." Raey sounded like a spy, prodding for connections. "You have this whole other life that I didn't get to discover. I met the adventurer that likes to be outdoors, but not the doctor that goes home after treating the masses."

Nic bit on his lower lip, and then studied her as he asked, "Would you have wanted to see it?"

"Definitely," she said, stating the obvious with a quick glance his way.

"Hmm." Nic stared ahead at the road.

"Why hmm?"

"Interested–or just nosy?"

She avoided his question with a question, "Why haven't you told me more about yourself in our conversations?"

"I was waiting for you to want to know."

The glimmer in her eyes went flat as she shook her head and muttered, "Ouch. A test?"

When he heard her heavy sigh, he jerked to the side of the road. Leaving the car engine running, he turned to her and begged, "Oh, I'm sorry." He looked her deep in the eyes. "I didn't intend for that to sound mean." Nic wrapped his hands around hers and promised, "I'm more than willing to talk about me when someone wants to invest in knowing me."

"In for a penny, in for a pound, I guess?" she accepted his offer, leaving her hand comfortably in his.

"What?"

"Oh, just a phrase Americans got from the Brits. It just means if you owe a penny, you might as well owe a pound."

"A braw one, to be sure. You're saying you're totally into me, aye?"

Raey blushed at not fully thinking that phrase through before spouting it. Her eyes narrowed into a glare, and she insisted, "It means, 'Whatever you want to offer up, I'm happy to hear all of it.'"

Nic set her hand back on her leg. "Okay, I'm in." He started down the road again.

"Great," she said and settled more comfortably into her seat.

"For a pound," he whispered, glancing her way with a big grin.

She teased an animated grin back at him and let his words hang between them. She stared at his Henley; the haphazard sleeves pushed to his elbows, revealing his muscular and tanned forearms. She reconciled the man beside her with what she knew of his past. Commiserating with his resilient heart that transcended the pain and grief of losing parents, she pictured him as a young boy finding his path to becoming a man. Under his casual, flexible nature, she was certain she would find evidence of a stubborn determination that drove him to the success he had mastered.

Closer to Inverness, Nic detailed the sights as she navigated their final twenty miles to the chateau's estate. Her enthusiasm over the sights and inattention to the map cost them a few awkward turns on narrow roads and a small loss of time, but Nic took her poor instructions in stride.

When periods of relative silence fragmented their conversation, they exchanged quick, sidelong glances, checking in on one another, comfortable to linger in silence. Raey wondered what thoughts he held close.

Nic turned onto the mansion's long, tree-lined entrance. He parked beside a large pond, and they climbed out to get their first view. She joined Nic and leaned shoulder to shoulder against his car door. The Highlands captivated her, but the splendor and tranquility of this countryside manor overpowered her.

"Oh, my!" she said, exhaling an expansive breath and feeling unworthy to claim this as her residence for the next few days. "I feel like a princess," she spouted.

"Which one?"

"Maybe an impetuous Scottish princess."

Nic rolled his eyes.

She slapped his arm and admonished, "You, sir, must get some culture. Maybe we should watch a good movie tonight with a strong princess as the lead."

"So, you're one of those fantasyland fanatics?"

"No, I'm one of those teachers that needs to keep up with what my students are interested in."

"I'm game, but while I might agree you are a fiery lass, impetuous is not how I would describe you, Princess Raey. Your mind churns things over quite thoroughly."

Laughing, Raey facetiously curtsied like a princess with her hands clasped to her heart, signaling that she could not deny his observation. "True, but I possess other admirable princess traits."

Nic clasped his hands formally behind his back, fixed his

eyes on Raey, and bowed his head as he acknowledged, "But of course, and I look forward to learning more of them this trip."

Raey flashed him an *I'm sure you would* smile and skipped back to her side of the car, eager to explore the grounds.

Cherry trees lined the tarmac driveway as Nic steered past extensive gardens and an idyllic fountain surrounded by a rose garden at the entrance to the majestic castle. Dominated by a square central tower that was four-stories-high and two angle drum towers, it rivaled any estate she had ever toured.

Leaving their luggage to retrieve later, they hurried into the castle and wandered from the reception hall, commenting on the Italian mosaic tile floor and magnificent staircase with its continuous, decorative cast and wrought iron balustrade. Raey mentally noted the places she wanted to return to during their stay. She imagined enjoying a dram of whisky in front of the drawing room's white marble fireplace after a dance on the ballroom's Victorian tiling. Maybe one night before bed, she would explore the extensive library and then cozy into a chair in the reading room. She hoped Nic would agree that the formal dining room was too impressive and that they would feel more at home eating in front of the wood-burning stove in the informal dining room. She looked forward to Nic's challenge of a tourney in the snooker room, though she hadn't played billiards in quite a while.

As they meandered down a long hall, peeking into one magnificently decorated bedroom after another, Nic held her hand to guide her into one with a beautiful view of the grounds. As they crossed the large room to stand before the expansive window, Nic asked, "Can you imagine being able to afford the upkeep on this place?"

"I cannot even fathom ever needing, let alone cleaning,

eleven bedrooms and bathrooms and sitting rooms," Raey said, taking in the glow surrounding him at the expansive window as he absorbed the majestic view of the lake.

"Do you think they consider this the master bedroom?" Nic wondered aloud.

"This is the perfect room for you. The chocolate brown and denim blues are so cozy." She smoothed her hand along the large river rock fireplace and rested it on the mantel.

"I think you would love star gazing from that loft," Nic suggested.

"I bet it's a glorious spot to watch sunsets," Raey added.

"This is your room. I'll place your luggage in here, so don't argue," he insisted.

"It's so lovely. Thank you!" Raey said as they left the room to continue their tour. At the end of the long hallway, she turned back to peek and her smile dropped. "Where will your bedroom be?"

"Not far," he assured her. "I'll be just a couple doors away," he said, pointing at the room he spoke about. "I'll take that first bedroom on this wing with the blue and green tartan bedspread and that thick log mantle."

Comforted by his nearness in such expansive surroundings, Raey said, "Oh, that's great. I think you will love the natural feel of that room."

Raey's excitement over the lavish house plummeted when she stepped into the nursery. She halted at the rails of a French white baby crib, smoothing her hand across the blue and green tartan comforter. At the entrance to the playroom, she glanced in and quickly moved on without a comment. As they explored the housekeepers' storerooms, Nic observed her introspective face. The confusion in his furrowed brows echoed her veiled struggle.

"What's wrong, Raey?"

His voice suddenly pulled her from her daydream. "I just thought I would be further along in life by now. That's all."

"Life moves at its own pace. That's for sure." When his finger brushed against her palm, she sought his hand, holding it secure within hers.

They walked in the peace and tranquility of the extensive grounds. Upon seeing the game larder, she reminded him they would find no use for it or the gun room. Drawn to the spray of color along the back of the grounds, she stopped at the large masses of green punctuated by bronze, yellow, and brick-red foliage.

Nic bent down to touch the bright green, low growing stems. "Ah, you would love this garden in bloom. In late July, this heather will be a lovely sight."

"There's nothing that reminds me more of Scotland than hill after hill of heather in bloom. It's magnificent!"

He pointed to one area in particular. "Do you know any of the legends around the white heather?"

She shook her head, her wide eyes encouraging him to explain. "Wild Scottish heather is usually some kind of purple, but white heather is much rarer. Legend has it that Malvina, daughter of a third century Scottish poet, Ossian, was betrothed to a Celtic warrior named Oscar. He died in battle, not an uncommon death back then, ye ken. A messenger delivered the sad news to the heartbroken maiden with a spray of purple heather that Oscar had sent as his final token of undying love. When Malvina's tears fell onto the flowers, they immediately turned white. It's said that upon this magical happening, she uttered, 'Although it is the symbol of my sorrow, may the white heather bring good fortune to all who find it.' So, today white heather is considered lucky, and it's added to table decorations and wedding bouquets. It's considered a Scottish tradition, a way of welcoming you to the family."

She studied him as a slow, *you're so adorable* smile spread across her face.

"Oh, honey!" he proclaimed, hitting his thigh.

"Huh?" Raey's mouth fell open at his use of that term of endearment.

"Scottish heather honey. Divine stuff! And this is not legend. Each year around August and into September, when heather floods the mountains with its lush lavender hue, Scottish beekeepers take their beehives north to the heather fields. There's a brief window when the purple-colored blooms peak. It's the only time to produce heather honey–a true delicacy."

Relieved to understand his use of the word honey, Raey sighed, "Oh, I can't believe I didn't learn that when I lived here."

"It's nicknamed the champagne of all honey," he boasted.

"Well, surprise, surprise, whisky isn't the only thing you Scots do well," she teased him.

"Oh, I can show you a lot we Scots do well if you truly want to know," he quipped back as he stepped a little closer, purposefully bumping her shoulder.

"Er, back to the honey, which sounds idyllic. I imagine being lulled to sleep by the humming of bees and the call of a skylark," Raey said, adjusting his suggestive banter. He watched her face search for her words as she added, "Um, and lying on a rock on an August afternoon with the heather in full bloom and that unmistakable sweet scent drifting up in the heat of the day."

"Wow, you silenced me. That was poetic," Nic mused with

meditative eyes. "Just one question," he added with a grin. "Can I lie beside you?"

"Stop." She gently slapped his arm.

"What?" he innocently appealed with a sloped grin. He grasped his arm. "That stung."

Raey challenged, "Oh, stop."

"I'm being serious," he said with high-pitched, unconvincing incredulity. "I want to go smell the heather, too." He pouted like a child being left home.

"Sure." She drew out that pronunciation, pursed her lips, and stepped beyond him, heading for the house.

"Is that sure I can go or...?" he asked, following close behind. She smiled back at him but said nothing more to qualify her answer.

SIXTEEN

After unpacking her Osprey backpack, Raey arranged toiletries on the bathroom counter and hung her clothes in the attached dressing room closet, which rivaled the size of her entire bedroom growing up. She may be out of place, the pauper and peasant masquerading among the fancy and formal, but she could stitch together an imaginary tale of a predestined shimmering princess and a charming prince inhabiting a castle until the last toll of the clock returned her to reality.

She mocked her fairy-tale imagination. Grabbing a blanket from the ottoman, she wrapped it around her shoulders to shake off the chill of the room and looked out the window at the lush foliage and thickset tapestry of trees that she and Nic would wander through after a hearty lunch. The high king-sized bed reflected in the window, begging her to test its coziness. She impulsively dropped the blanket to the floor and took a running leap onto the bed. Plopping backwards, arms spread wide, she released an audible, "Ahhhh." Resting her eyes, she soon sailed over the misty sea to the land of Wynken, Blynken, and Nod.

A quiet knock at the door interrupted her rest. Nic needed food, having warned her upon arrival that he turned into a bear when he was hungry. Her growling stomach compelled her to join the hunt in the kitchen.

The caretakers sourced a couple of days of basic breakfast and lunch provisions, so they ventured to the fridge to keep his wild animal instinct at bay, finding a quick and easy solution of bacon and egg sandwiches. Raey stalled to watch the doctor at work—assessing his surroundings, and, with his instruments at hand, Nic set to work frying the eggs, humming a tune she didn't recognize.

Flipping his spatula to point at her, he asked, "How do you like your fried eggs?"

"No runny yolk, please," she requested. Raey's nose scrunched up as she gritted her teeth and shook her head in fierce repulsion.

Nic laughed and then mumbled, "That's disturbing. One not snotty, fully dried-out egg coming right up."

"Eww." Raey recoiled and shook her head and muttered, "Runny is disturbing!"

"Don't know what you're missing."

Raey acted like she was choking, and then asked about the bacon, "Crispy?"

"Definitely," he said, imitating her scrunched up nose.

She assembled the toasted bread with the fixings, mayo and ketchup for her and brown sauce for him. In her estimation, Scots ate brown sauce on everything.

Nic's concentration volleyed between their dressings. "How can you pass up this tangy wonderfulness?"

"This American lass has no idea! It's an absolute true wonder." Lifting her spatula high in triumph, she heralded, "Like maybe one of the seven wonders of the world." Mirth spilled from her eyes along with a sardonic grin.

Both spontaneously laughed at her drama and agreed that sharp cheddar cheese was a serious must atop their eggs.

They comfortably moved around the cooking area as if they had shared the space a thousand times. The mouth-watering aroma of the bacon wafted through the room and drew them closer to the oven.

Raey grabbed an oven mitt to pull out the bacon. As she sprinkled sugar onto each strip, Nic's alarm stopped her. "Um, what are you doing to the bacon?"

"You just wait. It will be the absolute EIGHTH wonder of the world."

"Uh huh," he doubted.

"It's like bacon candy. The sugar melts around it and forms a sweet crust."

"Definitely different." His brows drew closer as he watched her work.

"I promise it will be a perfect, crispy, salty-sweet combo when it cools." She borrowed his phrase and said, "It will make your sandwich pure wonderfulness."

"I'll hold you to that promise." Pointing his finger at Raey, he feigned a threat, "Cause if you mess up the bacon, that's not gonna go well, you ken?"

They shared their cider, cherries, and sandwiches on the terrace, serenaded by birds' singing. Butterflies do-si-doed, mingling with the bees skipping from waves of yellow to orange to pink to red. Sweeping her eyes across the private rose garden, she imagined Monet's Giverny. They basked under the blue sky, relaxed by the sun's warmth and the wind's sighing breezes. Curiosity broke their serenity, beckoning them to a closer exploration.

Wiping her last bite before it dribbled down her chin, Raey offered Nic a smile and said, "Yum, delicious."

Nic winked and said, "Well, thank you." He let the subtle suggestive overtone hang between them as he returned her unwitting allusion with his own suggestion. "You're right. I have found the eighth wonder of the world."

Raey posed her best thank-you smile at his intimation but didn't address it.

Nic stood and helped her from her seat. "Let's go wander, Dimples."

The warmth of his hand drew her to cuddle into him as they strolled.

They crossed the expansive lawn to the edge of a canopy of trees and followed a wide, well-maintained trail. Sun filtered through the rustling leaves and wove a tapestry of moving light, making Raey slightly dizzy as she studied her surroundings along the path. When Nic tightened his hold on her hand, she breathed in heavily, inhaling the musky-sweet smell of decaying leaves. He pulled her hand to hold against his chest and gave it a squeeze and soft release. Steadying herself with a slow exhale of the warm air from her lungs, Raey stretched her walk to a near skip, a sense of freedom bursting in her. Hopping aboard an empty gazebo, she waved Nic to hurry, as if he might miss the boarding of a departing ship leaving for a blessed land. He smiled from the corner of his mouth, delighting in her eagerness.

When he landed on the first step, she leaned over and grabbed his hand with the innocent joy of a young girl, positioning him closer to her. The breeze strummed through the leaves, and they swayed to a slower rhythm than her ardor initiated. Her breath stopped when he pressed his lips to her temple. Fortune smiled on her as she lingered in the security of his hold on her in this moment. With her eyes still closed, he interlocked their fingers and gently pulled her back onto the path.

A bridge led to a small island in the middle of the lake. They stopped at its railing to peer into the water, warming their backs in the sun, and pointing out each newfound treasure to one another on this seek-and-find hunt. They spied trout, whose presence was of greater interest to two ospreys hovering overhead. Strolling to the other side of the bridge, they shared a large rock at the water's edge to observe the ospreys. The ambushing hunters surveyed the water, and with their impeccable eyesight, they spotted ripples. They covered the loch with fast-flapping wings, soaring until one finally plunged feet first into the loch. A quick, submerged fight ensued. Due to incredible timing, the osprey emerged with the plucked fish in his talons, but rising proved more difficult. Raey and Nic cheered for success from the sidelines. Water-logged, he rose heavily, carrying his prize fish headfirst like a hood-ornament. He stalled for a length, barely above the water, but his in-flight "dog-shake" dry off helped him to lift and soar to the nest, now obvious in a pine tree in the foreground of the Cairngorm Mountain. They stayed to witness the second osprey hunt with a bit more difficulty. Being privy to nature's primal majesty rendered them both silent.

Once out of the woods, they followed the rock wall surrounding the grounds to the front of the mansion. Raey unexpectedly stopped and ensconced herself on the stone wall. She conspicuously flopped her hands to fold upon her lap and waited with a smile but no words. Nic's furrowed brows prominent, he cocked his head in question. At her prolonged silence, he placed his hands in his jean pockets, glanced at the ground as he shifted his weight to his left foot, leaned his hip against the wall, and waited for whatever was on the tip of her tongue.

"You became obviously quiet on the walk back. What's up?" Raey asked.

"It's probably not good timing, but I'm running out of time. I need you to know how I feel about you." He shrugged and stepped away from the wall.

After a long silence, Nic spoke. "I'm attracted to you, lass. And I don't want you to leave without me saying that I want this relationship. You and me," Nic said, pointing between the two of them. He measured his words. "And if we do this, it will be a tap on a domino. Are you ready to explore what this could become between us?"

He was vulnerable, but she could not be. Clarity could mark the end or the beginning of their relationship. And she feared both.

Am I ready? How will I ever know the answer?

"Are *you* ready?" She avoided his question by posing it back at him. Is he ready for a long-distance relationship? He was too astute not to recognize her ploy, but would he let it go or push her to respond? She berated herself for avoiding the genuine conversation about their relationship. Her jumbled thoughts made working through her feelings nearly impossible. She asked the question in all seriousness, but he jested.

"I'm always ready." As if in stealth mode, he inched closer and placed his hands on her knees.

Curious about his maneuvering, she straddled him and joked along. "You are quite insufferable." *Why is he letting me off the hook by reverting to flirty banter?* Raey played along but didn't dare trust herself to move her hands near his body.

"Dimples, I am suffering." Nic squeezed her knees to his hips.

Ready to offer him my entire mind and body and soul?

An instantaneous burst of laughter from them both released the tension. Mock seduction was not his style. He rubbed his hands across the top of her thighs. Determined not to laugh, but muster a semblance of earnestness, Raey perused his face and asked, "Are you a wraith that has possessed my friend— mind, body, and soul?"

"Because we both know I am the irresistible figure of your fantasy," posed Nic.

Ready to one day call Nic 'my husband'?

The perfection of his sinewy body flustered her. She wanted to lay her cheek at the base of his throat, inhale his cologne, and feel his blood pulse through his neck.

Shaking her finger at him, Raey said, "You are quite cheeky. I must be wary of you."

He pulled her from the wall, sliding her down the front of him. Raey shivered when his lips brushed her neck. Their eyes locked in longing until he chuckled and tugged their entwined fingers. "Come on, lass."

Movement in the nearby brush broke their repartee. Raey clung to Nic, blaming the electricity between them for holding her on edge. How typical of a damsel-in-distress, and she didn't want to appear typical or distressed to him. She hid slightly behind him, concentrating on the sloppy movement in the brush when two white-spotted, rusty red, roe deer fawns tiptoed out of the thicket. The fawns romped through the clearing with innocent folly in a private game of tag.

Raey sank close to Nic and rested her head on his shoulder. Wrapping her arms around his arm, they witnessed the fawns' frolic. He clasped her hands and rested his head on hers, both savoring the unique beauty of the moment.

When their mom sauntered from the brush to their sides,

three sets of large black eyes and tall triangular ears and three black button noses stood at attention. With a quick stamp of her hoof and a snort, the doe alerted her fawns to depart.

Ready to run to Nic to share every exciting new first?

When they could no longer trace their delicate shapes within the brush, the magic of the moment faded. Nic released her hands and turned around to hold her close so that she understood what he meant when he said, "Och aye, that was nice."

"Almost as pleasant as watching those fawns," Raey agreed, staring into his eyes as she ran her hand down his stubbled cheek.

Ready to love him as deeply as Josh?

They traipsed hand-in-hand back to the mansion. Nic's lilt mesmerized her as he shared more about the roe deer. Even though they mutually let his earlier query fade, she heard the echoes repeating.

"Are you ready?"

His question still affected her, a gentle request flitting in and out of her heart and mind.

Ready to be a traitor to Josh?

SEVENTEEN

W hen the credits began rolling, Raey slapped her hand to his thigh, and asked, "Well, what do you think of the fiery lass?"

He rested his legs atop hers on the ottoman and wrestled the popcorn bowl from her lap. "So, this is your heroine, aye?" He tossed a piece of popcorn into the air and caught it in his mouth. Pinching his chin as he chewed, he prolonged his verdict.

"Yes, don't you think a girl who defied outdated customs without compromising her values or integrity is an excellent role model? Who does Dr. Nic declare as his hero?"

Nic contemplated as he chewed, looking at the ceiling as if pulling inspiration from it, and projected decidedly, "I'm thinking of a different Scot."

Raey curled into a laugh and then glanced at him in disbelief to determine if he was joking. "No, say it isn't so."

"The lass laughs? I haven't named anyone yet." Nic pretended offense.

"Sorry, I assumed your answer based on Brenda's TV obsession. I'm listening. Go ahead." She couldn't keep a straight face and hamper the giggles.

"Wait, what Scot were you thinking of?" Nic asked.

Raey encouraged him to expound, "No, you go ahead. Give me a few reasons your hero is worthy."

"I'd venture to guess you'd find him equally impressive. Maybe not for the same reasons I do."

She rubbed her hands together. "I'm eager to hear what you think will impress me."

"He's got cat-like blue eyes framed by an impressive, wavy head of auburn hair."

She elbowed him, eager for better insight into what he held in high regard. "Ugh, I thought you were being serious. You have a nice thick head of brown hair yourself, and while your eyes aren't cat-like, they're frozen lake blue."

"Thanks. Frozen lake blue, huh? I'm thinking about that color. You might make me blush." He fished for more compliments by continuing in jest, "Anything else you admire about me? Feel free to speak of my many other admirable features."

"Was there anything of a more noble nature that you revere about this man?"

He acquiesced, "I'd say that I admire his unpretentious intelligence and leadership. I've followed his sense of adventure. He's loyal to his word. He's fiercely dedicated and will sacrifice for his friends and family."

Rattling those traits off so readily signified that he had obviously given this prior contemplation and that nugget of information was the window into his soul she had hoped for.

"Those are outstanding, righteous, noble qualities. And mind you," she emphasized those words, pointing at him, "they're not unlike those that you possess." In the time they shared together, she had seen him embody those very traits. "Who is this man? He sounds larger than life."

Nic lifted his chin and said with certainty, "Finlay. Pops is the hero in my life." Nic enacted brandishing an invisible sword, a little shy in the face of her praise. "Did I mention he used to wield a claymore like Robert the Bruce?"

"That's sweet. Finlay is adorable. Hold on. I don't get involved with swords!"

"Um, if you're not getting involved with swords, then I'm willing to lay mine down for you." He laughed and switched his train of thought. "Why frozen-lake blue? What does that mean?"

Through all their interactions, they wove an unspoken covenant of courage and understanding. Honoring this, she remained faithful to sharing her genuine emotions with him. "You listen deeply and really see me. I am safe with you. I won't be falling through the proverbial *ice* when you're present."

She startled when he gently pulled her hands together on her lap, as in prayer. He laid his forehead on them, like a knight in confession to his Lady.

In the intimacy of that moment, she forgot to breathe. It seemed natural to rest her head on his. "It is true, or I would not have said so," she breathed softly into his ear.

"I love that you see that in me and that I make you feel that way." When he lifted his head, his desperate blues begged a kiss, but instead he lipped, "Tell me more about your friend, Brenda."

She chuckled at his abrupt change of topic, but she followed where he led. "She's the best pain-in-the-butt roommate I could ever have, and the one that keeps leaving long voicemails on my phone." She hesitated, then added, "Actually, that sounds much less than what it is. We consider ourselves the best of sisters and the best of friends."

"How's that?"

"She's my sister-in-law, but she's also much more. We're kindred spirits. She scooped me up like a stray cat when my parents passed away and included me as a part of her family. In college, I spent most holidays at her family's house. She didn't want me to be alone at my house during summer break, so she practically lived at my house with me during the summer."

"I'm glad you have her," Nic offered.

Raey paused, recollecting, "Eventually, home became more synonymous with her family's house than the cottage at the beach that I grew up in. Since Josh died, she's lived with me there, though."

"I get that. I adjusted, not too well at first I admit, to living at Gram and Pops."

"We became friends my junior year in high school and roommates our last three years of college." Raey leaned toward Nic, set her elbows to her knees, and propped her head on her fists. "Lately, though," she rolled her eyes and teased, "she's a pest because she's found a great guy, so she keeps trying to set me up. She is super concerned about me being alone on this trip."

"Why?"

"She thought I did it for all the wrong reasons."

"What reasons are those?"

"Well, I told you about feeling numb to life since Josh passed away." She checked Nic's reaction, but he held only concentrated interest. "I needed to stop holding in my anger toward Josh." She winced and waffled through her explanation. "Well, not exactly anger at him, but anger at the loss of him and for having to live with just the memory of him."

"That won't go away, lass."

She focused on her fidgeting fingers. "It's illogical, but I needed to be close to him to let him go. Maybe like a final goodbye? But to do that, I needed to go back to the place we felt most together, where we spent our favorite times together. If I could do that, I could feel less, less…" Raey struggled for the right word.

Nic lifted his hand that he had tenderly set on her knee and softly tipped her chin up. She had no choice but to find the empathy his blue eyes offered as he answered, "Paralyzed?"

"Yes," she whispered back, relieved that he understood her pain.

"So?" He lowered his head to catch her downcast eyes once again.

"So?" she mimicked.

"Have you accomplished that?" he answered, sticking to the question, not letting her off the hook.

Raey didn't meet his eyes but admitted, "Yeah, I'm starting to accept his death and release the grip of the paralysis."

Nic stopped holding his breath. "It's difficult, isn't it?" He swallowed hard and the tightness in his throat softened as he said, "I'm glad this trip did that for you." Nic grabbed both of her knees and lightened the mood. "Tell me more about why you admire this movie princess."

She struggled with encapsulating her ideas and finally arrived at, "Okay, I'm just gonna throw out a bunch of words that describe my heroine." Raey jumped to her feet and spoke with certainty, "Brave, quick-witted, stubborn, free-spirited, kind, loyal, adventurous, daring, bold, defiant, determined, headstrong, rebellious, strong-willed, understanding, courageous, tender, skilled, outgoing, impetuous." As she finished, she splayed her arms in the air and with a slant to her chin dared Nic to refute any of those qualities as unworthy of admiration. "Any of those stand out as reasons to admire her?"

"Wow, I think what I admire more than anything is that you rattled off all those with one breath." He grinned mischievously.

"They're all obviously true!" she defended, descending to the couch as her finale.

"She sounds too good to be true. How do you see rebellious and impetuous as being admirable?"

Without hesitation, Raey proceeded with a firm explanation as if she had rehearsed her speech, slapping a fist to her open palm with each spoken *have to*. "Sometimes you *have to* go against what everyone thinks you should do." She slapped her fist to her palm a second time. "You *have to* even rebel against your own need to feel safe and in control of a situation." Again, she emphasized her point by pounding her fist. "Sometimes, you *have to* act before your own mind's *what ifs* overwhelm you and try to talk you out of something that's risky, but necessary."

Nic patted her leg and asked, "Like you did in coming here?"

Did he mean to Scotland or to the castle with him? Clarifying by asking which one he meant would reveal her hesitation of answering one over the other. She rebelled against the yellow-light caution signals in her brain and said, "Being with you here is definitely a risk."

"I'm sure you mean that in the most admirable way, right?" he teased her to clarify.

"I do," she answered, exposing her eyes to his.

"What do you have to lose, Raey?" His question hung in the air, waiting for her to grab it.

She traced a vein of green thread traveling through the fabric of the arm of the couch. "My sense of balance that I'm just beginning to find."

Nic scooted to her side so their legs firmly touched from knee to hip. "Grief takes time, Raey. Let it take the time it needs."

"Grief has become a clingy friend," she admitted, biting her lip.

"It will change. It will still hurt, but it won't consume every part of you all the time."

"Many moments it still does." The clock's second-hand ticked into the silence between them.

"It's still early."

"I think grief is here to stay." Raey flopped back against the couch as if she were exhausted.

"With deep love, grief never leaves." After a pause, Nic added, "Survival is one step at a time."

"It's like I keep pulling myself from the deep to breathe fresh air." She heaved a sigh of relief to say her thoughts aloud and bravely continued despite her pulse ramping up, "But I fear new memories will replace those of Josh–and I'll lose him, forever."

His voice blanketed her. "You won't lose him, trust me." He caressed her palm with his fingers. "Loss changes us, but look at the strength you developed, the way you trusted your instinct to come to Skye."

"Okay, but when it comes to you, I'm playing tug-of-war to keep my feelings in check right now." She squeezed her hand around his.

"Well, I'd keep trusting them. But a loss at that tug-of-war is a win for us," he beamed.

"Aren't you nervous about this?" She pointed back and forth to the distance between them, touching his shoulder with each flick of her finger.

"Scared as hell," he confessed, pulling her to his chest.

Raey rested her head on his shoulder. His quiet demeanor spoke his thoughts louder than the TV.

Raey whispered, "Ask what you need to."

"Is it that obvious?"

"I'm learning to read your silence," she said.

"Are you ready to heal your heart, lass?"

"I'm trying."

"It's cliché, but life is short."

"Oh, Nic, I know." She sighed, wanting to soothe the anguish he felt as a young boy. She had been wrapped up in her own loss but now tightened her hold on his hand, remembering his pain of the loss of his parents.

"I know, Raey, because one American lass's short visit changed this Scot. I just need her to realize it, too." She didn't miss the heat in his eyes melting her to him. Moving a stray curl from her face, his palms cradled her cheeks. Staring into her brown eyes, he set a searching tilt to his chin. She leaned to meet his lips. Her timid kiss begged for more pressure as she grabbed his neck and pulled him completely to her, a crescendo of longing to be fully known to him.

He kissed her as if caressing her entire body, overpowering her senses. Lost in his need for her, he suddenly lifted her from the couch. Dizzy with desire, her legs instinctively wrapped around his waist, binding him to her.

Wolfishly laying her back down on the couch, he settled himself firmly between her legs. His kisses tantalized her skin, making the world around her dissolve, present only to the meshing of their lips.

Her need for him was so basic that it shook her to the core. With the light of the television glinting off the side of his profile, Raey saw the masculine intensity sculpted on his face.

He broke their consuming kiss and breathed, "Stay?"

She loved his offer, and hated her response. But it was true. "I can't."

"I know," he exhaled and fiercely kissed her before releasing her to a night's sleep. "Sleep well."

"I'm going to step onto the patio and listen to the night before going up to bed. It settles me." She offered him a shy, conciliatory smile.

Nic left her to the stars.

When she entered the quiet of her bedroom, she sensed her space was different. Notes of cherished moments from their day were arranged around the room. The first note she saw on the nightstand next to her journal had only a smiley face and the words *frozen lake blue* written on it. Another note on her vanity top had rocks drawn with words above it. *Rock walls are for climbing, sitting, and wanting to kiss you.* She smiled at the mention of Nic's hero when she read the note on her dresser next to her baseball cap. *Pops would love that bacon. Better share that idea with Gram.* His note on the windowsill read, *Grief isn't a forever friend.* The longest note sat in the middle of the bed with a single piece of heather: *Today was the shortest day I've ever had. I wish it didn't have to end.*

Sitting on the edge of her bed, she reread his notes. She pressed them into the pocket of her pack for a keepsake. The turmoil of leaving Nic spread through her like the glow of her bedside lavender candle on the walls. Nic didn't deserve her holding him so close and living so far away. Her heart couldn't do that, anyway.

Eventually, the crisp caress of cool white sheets, the plushness of the down duvet, and the warmth of a mug of chamomile tea eased her mind. When she finally blew out the candle, Raey pledged to examine her thoughts about endings and beginnings, pasts and futures, security and risk.

EIGHTEEN

Raey awoke before the sun peered over the horizon. Frustration at another ending flowed like a torrent, wrecking her chances of going back to sleep. Facing her last day, she wrestled with losing Nic. Their friendship didn't have to end, but continuing it meant missing him from across the sea. His confidence, patience, listening ear, gentle nature—all freely offered to her. No doubt their connection could become more if they lived in the same place. *Could I relinquish being sad about the little time I have left and be happy–be happy for our meeting, not sad for our parting? Not every connection is meant to last a lifetime, right?*

She resolved right then, despite her need for sleep, to pen him a goodbye letter that reflected her deep gratitude for his friendship. She hoped to lock these thoughts in a vault to quell the descending heaviness and tame her anxious heart.

Nic,

You've figured out that I'm not very good at navigating goodbye, but I want you to know how important you've become to me. My sadness at leaving here is much deeper than I imagined it would be when I embarked on this venture. I thought leaving, after being here a month, would be a relief, something I would be glad to put behind me, a running back home to safety and belonging. You've made it all so vastly different for me than I thought it would be, or even than I honestly want it to be. It's hard to leave you. You've been a true friend to me, gently reawakening me with your compassion and gentle honesty. With you, I've so easily been myself. There's much between us that we haven't said. Maybe someday we'll chance to say it. I will miss you.

Love,
Raey

Raey tucked the page of gray letterpress stationery, adorned with mountains and trees, into its envelope. *Wait, what did I say?* Pulling the letter from the envelope, she slowly reread it, stopping to digest her thoughts at the end. Her breath caught and her pulse raced at the words. She couldn't, or warred that she shouldn't, pen those words to him. It would be unfair. Raey rewrote her entire letter, leaving out the troubling lines: **There's much between us that we haven't said. Maybe someday we'll chance to say it.** Her hand hesitated, nearly finished, and she changed the closing to **Truly**.

She tore the original to pieces and then pocketed her second attempt in her coat. The plan to mail her letter from the airport subdued the panic settling in her throat. The weight of the storm in her chest lifted after she expressed her emotions on the page. She could embark on a day completely arranged by Nic and embrace his surprises and spontaneity.

The scrape of shoes on the corridor tile, where Nic texted her to meet for their final day of adventure, announced his entrance. His clean-shaven, doctor persona morphed into two days' worth of stubble. She tamped down her inner seductress, exposed by the warmth in her eyes and pink of her cheeks.

Stroking his fingers along the subtle whiskers on his chin, he delayed his greeting and surveyed her reaction. "Er, this is just me on vacation. No reason for alarm."

Little did he know! Her arousal certainly alarmed her. She slunk toward him, purposefully immersing herself one last time in his unapologetically masculine scent—a sweet, woody, musky mix. *Oh my!*

"I've quite scared you; I see," he joked with a cheeky grin aimed at her absent-minded staring.

"Nope. Not scared, nope. Wow! Rugged works for you!" She studied him for a couple long seconds, and then they locked eyes. "But I would place bets you know that!" She stuck her tongue out at him.

"So, you like me rough around the edges?" He nuzzled into her shoulder, took her hand, rubbed her palm firmly against his cheek, and cuddled up to her like a purring kitten. "Or is it the raspberry scones I'm holding here?" he added, raising a bag in front of her nose. "They match your cheeks."

His hot ensemble distracted her from an immediate response–black leather, three-quarter hiking boots; worn blue jeans with holes in the knees; charcoal gray Patagonia quarter-zip sweater; a silver cross necklace peeking out from a white Henley; thick, finger combed hair; and a flattering *I knew I could make you flustered* grin plastered on his face. She slapped him jokingly on the shoulder, but that slight touch inclined her to settle her hands on his chest and linger awhile.

"I'll go on record as saying that I adore both the scones *and* the scrub." Turnabout being fair play, she winked at him and drew her hand along his chin, and then easily snatched the bag from under his occupied attention.

When she peeked inside and emitted a squeal, he snatched the bag back and warned in a very thick Scottish accent, "Noo jist haud on. Those will be pure barry with some tea and cream from the café just a jaunt away."

They chatted over scones and tea on the drive to Culloden Moor. Walking a gentle trail, they fell silent at the wide-open field where the clans' uprisings met their final, terrible defeat.

They followed a path to a massive cairn, a marker of the mass graves. Nic detailed the events of the hallowed ground beneath their feet. "Hundreds of years ago on a rain-soaked morn, a wet, cold bite of wind had blown across the final resting place of 1,500 Jacobite musketeers. Brutally defeated in under an hour, their bodies dotted the boggy field with muddied blue flags and crimson blood-stained broadswords, targes, tartans, and pipes."

The heaviness of their defeat weighed on her. Nic pointed toward rock cairns littering the countryside and leaned close to grab Raey's arm and undivided attention as he said, "Those cairns remind weary travelers that while the difficulty in navigating life's path may be a constant, all need not be counted as lost."

"Yes, and amen," Raey responded.

"I like to think that the resilient spirit of those weakened clans, stripped of title and tartan, remains alive and well in each living Scot."

"It's definitely alive in you!" she nudged his side.

Together they stood silent a while longer, surveying the field, haunted by grave markers and burial cairns. Nic's telling of the brutal memory of the Jacobite's dire fight for freedom brought it to life. Having lost the gallant battle to keep her life with Josh alive, she understood the Highlanders' struggle to maintain their way of life.

With a short trek to Moray Firth, the afternoon events lifted the dark mist clouding her mood that Culloden field had unveiled, putting a contented smile on her face for the rest of the day. Giving no heed to a mere smattering of rain, Nic booked a boat tour, during which a group of bottlenose dolphin calves treated them to quite a spectacle, bouncing and dancing around the boat. As the boat trundled along toward Chanonry Point, they spotted more dolphins actively hunting between the channel and the river. One put on a show with his catch, tossing his food ahead before plunging back into the sea after it. When the engine kicked off and they drifted on the water, the dolphins dared to venture closer, playing in the waves. One mother swam at a distance with a hearty salmon mushed up between her jaws, while her calf huddled close.

Raey and Nic stared at the water, enthralled by the whoosh of the minke whales breaching in the distance. As they searched for the next breach, Raey noticed that they, too, had spectators. Only meters away, two mischievous seals rested noses and soulful eyes on the water, observing them with a *what's going on here?* query. She glanced at Nic to point them out and found herself the object of his captivated attention.

"What's going on in there, Mischief-maker?" Raey combed her fingers through his hair, swiping it across his forehead to tap his temple.

"Just this," Nic said before he kissed her. Throwing her off balance, he pulled her into his arms, prolonging their connection.

"Mmm. Thank you." His kiss warmed her body and heart. She didn't want the feeling to subside. A dangerous longing rose within her.

After their time on the water, Nic parked at Rose's Café, but when Raey walked toward the door, he grabbed her hand

and pulled her in the opposite direction. He firmly tugged her to his side, spinning behind her to cover her eyes, guiding her steps. He fell into rhythm with her paces, leaned into her right ear, and slowed his speech to a deep, sultry voice as he teased, "You'll continue with your eyes tightly closed if you know what's best for you."

"And if I don't?"

"You risk missing out on further surprises." She heard the smile in his voice.

"So, repeat after me. I pledge not to peek."

"I pledge not to peek."

Nic added as seriously as he could without laughing, "Even though the best specimen of a man is holding his hand over my eyes."

She giggled at his antics and barely repeated the words sufficiently for his feigned governance.

Trying to keep her eyes covered as she bent over laughing, he directed her to repeat, "I will follow…all instructions Nic gives…at the risk of being tickled." If they weren't obviously gamboling, Raey suspected that people witnessing their behavior might think she was being abducted.

Nic guided her around the road sign announcing Fairy Glen Falls. He uncovered her eyes once they traveled well into the cool glen. They dodged puddles and mud by crossing a stream several times by wooden footbridges. Along this musty walk, serenaded by chirping birds and croaking frogs, she suspected her first surprise when a loud splashing shower replaced the burbling burn. Between fallen moss-covered branches, she spied sun-soaked white falls plunging over a black rock face into a gentle pool.

She leaned against his shoulder and entwined their arms.

"Thanks for this treat. This place is the perfect antidote to the heaviness of Culloden."

"Its twin is further up the path. We've got to work just a wee bit harder for it, though, as it's uphill."

On the path to the second fall, she stalled to glance back once more at the first waterfall, committing to memory the magic of discovering it with Nic. Nic filled the space behind her. His hand covered hers on the weather-worn banister. Standing before the water throne together, time stood still. The bog moss splashed a rainbow of color below her feet, and the majesty of the land further captivated her.

Pulling themselves up an incline with the help of a rope lodged in the rock, they climbed the blackened earth to the second fall. Lured by the close roar of the falls, they found their way to a fallen tree trunk edging the pool of the waterfall. They sat on the tree and absorbed the bewitching beauty surrounding them. Raey struggled to find a smooth spot for a seat as conks loaded the base of the trunk. Upon closer inspection, the protrusions she touched were coins hammered into the trunk. A fellow hiker later explained the tradition of gifting the fairies with money for good luck and to keep the water running clear. From the appearance of the trunk, the fairies were very well pleased.

The woodlands darkened as bracken ferns ornamented the green rocks along the waterfall slope, looking as if the blanket of moss sprouted hair. Fronds, lightly swaying in the breeze of this green-laced world, honored the timeless damp, magical air. Mushrooms sprouted from the dark humus and decaying leaves. New life emerged from death. Spongy moss clung to banks and boulders and covered fallen branches and tree trunks. She commiserated with the land's necessity to regenerate for survival. Struggling through the harsh elements of this trip remolded her and instigated her change. A quiet reverence for this mystical land marked their walk back to the car.

Raey grabbed Nic's arm, motioning him toward Rose's Café for a second take-away cup of tea with cream before departing for Inverness and their last meal together. When her shoe rolled across loose pebbles and nearly slung her to the ground, she recovered her balance by grabbing his arm even tighter. In that moment, she clung to the tenderness she saw in his eyes. It disoriented her. Unsettled about her desire to hold on to him, she made light of her clumsiness by splaying her arms out wide to show she regained balance and said, "I'm all good. I just tripped. I'm glad I was holding onto you."

"It's okay. No need to be embarrassed. We all get tripped up. Well, everyone but me." He stuck out his tongue, making her laugh, and ran off to hold the door for her.

How does he do that? Rescue me with humor and allow me to keep my dignified independence.

He trusted her to lean on him to steady herself when she needed. That made her stronger. She wanted to offer him the same. Truthfully, she wanted to be known more to him, but she was out of time. Losing him was inevitable and so was the sadness.

* * *

She hoped for something simple, not elaborate. A full day outdoors called for sharing a warm hearth, a hearty dinner, and a drink, and Nic delivered exactly that, without her hinting. Dinner at the quintessentially Scottish Glenway Inn, on the shore of Loch Ness, couldn't be more perfect. This family-run

Highland pub served his choice of haggis and hers of breaded fish and chips.

They chit-chatted over a dram of whisky.

"Have you traveled much outside of Scotland?" Raey asked.

"Not much. I had to work to earn money for school. I traveled to France with a buddy's family right after secondary school."

"Paris? Ooh la la. The city of love."

"We spent three days there. We holidayed near Tours in the Loire Valley."

"So why aren't you married?" she asked in a freestyle moment.

Nic uncrossed his legs and adjusted to lean across the table toward her. After a dramatic pause, he drawled in his best imitation of Sean Connery suavity, "Because I haven't found anyone that scares the hell out of me, yet," emphasizing the yet with raised eyebrows.

They both laughed. She patted his hand resting next to his malt whisky and added, "Okay, 'Sean,' but could you be less mysterious?"

Quickly grabbing her retreating hand, he held her still with a tilt of his chin and sure blue eyes. "There might have been someone."

The jealous side of her wanted to stake her claim. Raey hoped it was a distant someone. Who was this woman to Nic now?

Satisfied that he stuck with the serious side of this conversation, her curiosity about this woman ramped up. Taming her eagerness, she offered a quick reply, "Care to elaborate?"

"Five years ago, I, no doubt, had imagined getting married."

"What happened?" She tamped down her jealousy to earnest consideration.

Unconsciously, Nic rubbed his chin stubble and pinched his lips. After a sip of his whisky, he summed up concisely, "She moved, but I didn't."

Far, far away, Raey hoped. Her spirit fell at the thought that, by this time tomorrow, she'd be thousands of miles away from him.

"I'd like to hear that story while we take a short stroll on the beach, if you're willing to tell it?" she said.

"Sure, I'm keen for a stroll." He gulped his last two drinks in one swallow and stood, moving to help her from her chair.

She was tempted to remain soaking up the heat near the wood burning stove, but walking the pebble beach might put him at ease to relate more of his story.

Pretending to search for the Loch Ness Monster, the fog and chill settled in under the moon. Nic commented, "It's been about five years since I last sighted Nessie."

Raey reciprocated with a similar legend, deferring to him until he was ready to broach the topic that brought them to the beach, "That's coincidental because that's about when I last saw Big Foot."

Intrigued by her reference, he stopped walking and faced her. "What? Who is Big Foot?"

Nessie was obviously more infamous than Big Foot, so she explained, "You know how people get caught up in these hoaxes and tales? Well, in the States, Big Foot sightings are our legend. He is a big, hairy, ape-like, Neanderthal creature who dwells in the North American wilderness and leaves huge footprints."

"Well, you can update your sightings!" he said as he slouched over, swinging his arms like a primate.

Focused on getting back to the conversations about his close call with marriage, she remained noticeably serious, not laughing at his humor. Compelled by their shrinking time together, she said, "I guess my need to know isn't syncing with your keeping chill on the subject right now."

Hanging his head, he admitted, "So, you caught that retreat, did ye?"

She admired his quick honesty. "It's fine. You don't have to tell me," she begrudgingly offered.

"No, here it is," he spit out. "She is a lovely lass. We dated for about a year and talked about a future together. I thought we were both headed in the same direction. Then she took a job in Edinburgh while I was interning in Skye. I couldn't move. I was proud of her achievements and commitment to her career—and I wanted to be supportive. We kept the long-distance thing going, but it had a slow leak until, well, it went flat."

Relief washed through her that their relationship didn't work out. Then a pang of regret gripped her at her joy over his misfortune.

"Your choice or hers?"

"Mostly mine. The easiest explanation is that I wasn't scared to death of letting her go. She wanted easy, wanting me to be nice, neat, and undemanding."

"And you're not those things?" Raey was confused.

He shook his head and explained, "I wanted someone who chose me every day, who longed to wake up next to me every morning, who couldn't sleep without saying goodnight to me."

"She wasn't that person?" Raey nudged him to continue, and her face went white knowing she wasn't that person either.

221

Raey saw determination in his set jaw. "I wanted a woman engaged in life with me. One who debated dinner menus with me, who needed my opinion even if she didn't plan to use it, who turned to me with her joy and didn't hide her sadness."

"It's good you're sure about what you want."

"And I refuse to give up on that. I don't want half-measures. I saw passion between my parents and grandparents. They were all in, and sometimes all in for the fight too," he said and raised his eyebrows and grinned before continuing, "but still, they were all in."

"Maisrie and Finlay are a precious couple."

"Raey, I know what great looks like. I'm holding out for creating that with someone. With her, I wanted us both to be all in. We weren't both fighting for that kind of, of..." Nic searched for the best word.

"Married life." Raey filled in for him.

"No," he paused and looked her in the eyes, "more like—holy water immersion."

"Intense."

"Yes, every single day, intense," he said.

She grabbed him into a tight hug, laying her ear to his chest.

When her squeeze loosened, he lifted her to peer into pink-rimmed eyes. "What's going on?"

She could barely get the words out. "I'm memorizing you —your heartbeat."

NINETEEN

O n the drive to the airport, Raey and Nic exchanged long glances. They interspersed superficial conversations about wool socks and the weather among the heaviness of their suspended sadness, of feelings denied a voice. She dreaded the final, curbside goodbye, a clinging "please don't go" hug. They wanted what could not be, to change the reality of what was happening. Fear choked her throat closed and the shallow, panicked breaths refused to release her to ask the questions. Was the distance between them widening even before her feet left Skye? Will the sheer weight of her departure fray their friendship?

Will this be my last moment with Nic?

When they arrived, Nic grabbed an envelope and a gift wrapped in his family's tartan fabric from the backseat and placed it in her hands. As if bequeathing a fragile antiquity, Nic rested his hand atop hers, skin against skin.

"Promise to open this when you are sky high in the air," Nic said.

"I will. I don't have anything for you."

"You were the gift. I don't need anything else. I've loved our time together."

Bit by bit, Nic slid his hand away from hers, each slow

inch a thousand miles of missing him. The tear in her heart ached.

After pulling her luggage from the trunk of his car, he stepped back, sank his hands in his pockets, and stood reading her. Void of the ability to speak, she stared at the two feet of roadway separating them at the edge of the curb, soon to be an immeasurable chasm. If she had a train of thought, she lost it. She willed her mind or her feet to move.

Raey stepped into his space and wrapped her arms fully around the back of his neck, pulling him as close as she could get him. His warm breath and firm hands momentarily stilled the loneliness that covered her like a heavy, suffocating blanket. She whispered, "I will miss you very much," and released him from her long embrace.

"I will miss you more." He looked into her eyes. She looked into his. And they were out of time.

He gave a half-hearted smile and wave before turning to leave and disappearing into his car, and she offered a small wave and smile in return. A tear dropped on her cheek as he drove away from her.

She stood alone on the curb, surrounded by the whirl of honking cars, closing doors, rushing feet, rolling luggage, and chatting travelers. Minutes ticked away and travelers moved along. A familiar, overwhelming sensation of loss swept through her.

Solo in a crowd of people, she toted her luggage and her heavy heart to the check-in line and through the security gate. Leaving Nic didn't feel safe at all, more like panic. She sought a place against the wall to exhale the desperation in her chest. A hot cappuccino with heavy cream became a miserable substitute. Sipping its warmth, she was glad she endured the long line for a drink before boarding the plane. It would be the perfect companion for the cranachan cake in her carry-on that Nic had presented to her that morning.

She huddled into her seat and leaned against the window, wishing the middle seat would remain unoccupied. Before settling her bag under the seat in front of her, Raey pulled out her book and the package Nic had handed her at their parting and tucked them alongside her hip.

Outside her window, planes took off and landed to taxi to their terminals. Crews transferred baggage and loaded supplies on planes. The world busied like worker ants scouting for food. She glanced up the middle aisle toward the front of the plane, assessing the boarding process. Seeing the flight attendant still greeting people, she imagined herself racing to exit the plane and falling into Nic's waiting arms. She chastised herself for that incredulously romantic thought and retrieved the package that Nic had given her.

Recalling his reverence upon presenting it to her, she carefully unraveled the black and white checked fabric she recognized as the MacNicol tartan from Finlay's explanation. She unwrapped a burgundy leather-bound book with a gilt facsimile of Robert Burns' signature on the cover. The gilt lettering and decoration on the spine read *The Poetical Works of Robert Burns.* An envelope fell to her lap when she opened the cover. Not yet courageous enough to read it in public, she tucked it inside a page marked by pressed heather.

She read an inscription on the inside cover:

Lena, you are my treasure. Always. All my love, Stewart.

She clutched the cherished keepsake from Nic's mother's collection to her chest–the heirloom a palpable bond to his heartbeat. His dearest memories, his strongest love, his deepest heartache as precious as her to him.

Purple heather bookmarked a familiar poem, "Auld Lang Syne," sung by revelers at the stroke of midnight every New Year's Eve. After imbibing several whiskys that had carried them late into one evening, Nic had recited the entire poem from Scotland's beloved bard proudly and flamboyantly, just as he had for a competition in school. She only knew the first four lines. Seeing his handwriting beside the print brought a visceral sadness and longing. She couldn't readily tell if those notes penned on the page were from days gone by or had recently been written for her.

The last time that song reverberated in her ear, she had been in front of her television, watching hugs and kisses in the streets of New York as the ball dropped and wondering why she had bothered sacrificing sleep to watch the joy of strangers. Alone on her couch, she had been bereft of the hope it represented—beginning another year with your loved one. Thankfully, her mood had passed by the next morning with the purchase of a plane ticket to Skye. She had emerged from her slumber determined to shake herself awake.

Seeing Nic's uniquely masculine writing evoked the attachment she'd formed with him. As if unconsciously caressing his arm, she softly traced the lines of script with her finger. He wrote the translation of "auld lang syne" as "days gone by" and added a note along the margin:

I'd be happy if the days gone by are also the days ahead.

Was she his boldly written wish?
She read his script beside the poem's next lines. He had

indeed written his notes with her in mind. She gasped for air, her eyes drawn to his words, needing to be read twice.

"But seas between us broad have roared
Since auld lang syne."
She read his hopes.

This distance now from you to me is heavy and great, but I pray it won't be a long time till we touch again. Every day, you crowd my mind.

Along the bottom of the page, he had scrawled further sentiments.

Burn's creative embellishments to an old man's song will keep us singing in celebration of one another this year. I'm certain sweet verses will adjoin your life's ballad. Yet, I pray the best of memories become our memories.—Nic

Tears pricked her eyes and blurred her vision like the moon eclipses the sun, casting shadows on her heart. Becoming lightheaded, she reached overhead to increase the airflow to her face. She could hear the beat of her heart in her ears. When she turned to a sprig of white heather that bookmarked Burns' famed "A Red, Red Rose," she tried to slow her breathing, but to no avail.

"...And fare thee weel, My only Luve,
And fare thee weel awhile!
And I will come again, my Luve,
Tho' it ware ten thousand mile."

She read the last four lines twice because he had circled them and then turned the book sideways to read his plea written vertically along the page.

Raey Rose,

Your head is, no doubt, spinning from my words. I walk with two feet on the ground and don't tend toward hyperbole like Burns, but the metaphor here is clear and true. A very fresh thing grew for both of us this June. The weeks pass by as smoothly as the rhythm of this poem. We'll be 4,000 miles apart, not 10,000, but I hope our separation will be a short while.

Come again!

She stared at the tray table, found her breath, and willed her insides to calm before emerging tears turned to sobs that she couldn't quiet. With his bold words on the page before her to read and reread, a visceral surrender arose. His words deeply touched her. Grasping unmistakably what he desired, she braved the letter.

Nic strove to be intentional with his words, so while she didn't understand his greeting, *Jo*, she recognized his attempt at affection in his Gaelic. She would translate his words when she had Wi-Fi.

Jo,

As you know, I would much prefer to be saying this in person. But I want you to see my words, this letter, so you can hold them before you through the days ahead to read again and again. Don't doubt my words. They are simple and true. When you are unsure, read them again.

You weren't ever planning to stay in Skye. You

embarked on a plan to say goodbye and move on with life. But you also found a hello in me. It wasn't easy just standing by as you outmaneuvered your demons, each one wanting to drag you down with anger, doubt, and regret, but I was proud to watch as you fought for victory. I'm grateful you found them much too heavy to bear and laid them down here in Skye. You accepted the challenge of choosing love over war when I walked into the middle of your battle to pursue a future, and I'd like to continue forward at your side.

Having just said hello, I don't want to say goodbye. I'm crazy about you. I think you know, but in case you doubt it, there it is. And in case you want to spend a lifetime together, I've been so daring as to include a return ticket back to me. Time won't stand still for us. My life will go on. Your life will go on. But I want our lives to go on together.

So, choose us, choose me. Pleading or begging aren't the ways I'd want to convince you. You must choose on your own to place your heart in my hands.

I am scared to death to let you go!

Hoping to hear from you before the heather is all gone.

mar sin leibh an dràsda

Goodbye for now,

Nic

Before stepping on the plane, she had known his heart's desire. If she admitted the truth, she'd known their natural rhythm together unfolded the day they trekked to Bad Step, but throwing caution to the wind was not part of the plan she had envisioned. Her gut told her she needed to go home before choosing him. The need to be home and the desire to be with

Nic dizzied her, like her mind was on a merry-go-round, an incongruity too staggering to hold together.

Agitated that he knew her so well in such a short amount of time, she panicked at how to respond in the face of his bared honesty. He was right. Her certainty of their circumstances wavered. How could the circumstances of a month bring them together for a lifetime? She doubted her ability to even make such a rash decision.

He pledged a promise in writing for her to cling to, if she so chose. Her life hung in the balance on her terms. She waged a war between head and heart. If her head didn't resist, her heart would easily win the battle.

A quiet voice broke through her musing, jolting her attention, "Are you all right, ma'am? Is there something I can get you?" She pulled the letter to her chest and blinked into the faces of the two gentlemen in her row and the flight attendant, her struggle revealed in the tears rolling down her face.

TWENTY

Racey scrolled through her phone contacts and found Nic. Her finger hovered over the green call button. Three days since saying her goodbye, and she couldn't postpone her call any longer. It would be cruel. Words are hard. Jumbled or not, she owed him the truth.

His calm hello set her at ease, and she jumped right in.

"Thank you for the gift. I'll cherish reading your mom's copy of Robert Burns. I can't believe you gave such a precious heirloom to me."

"It's yours now. A little Scotland for you to keep by your side. There's no one else I'd rather have read it."

"Your words are the best."

"I'm glad you have them. I meant every one of them."

"The fog has lifted. It's like the sun shines brighter. The very first day back I potted some of the same plants I did with Maisrie."

"That's what you were hoping your trip would do, right? A new view?"

"I signed up for a training class to run a half-marathon in September."

"That will definitely take a wee bit of your time."

"My principal is sending my new list of students that will

be in my class this upcoming school year. I'm going to organize a picnic and team building activity for the kids before school begins."

"The kids will love that."

"This is the first time in a long time that I have looked at life this way."

"I'm glad for you. You're doing it. Getting the life back you wanted."

"I don't want my motivation to dwindle. I'm unsteady in embracing this new normal. As normal as life can be while planning Brenda's wedding."

"Enjoy every part of it. Asking you to stay was unfair. I didn't want to lose you."

"Not unfair, but unexpected."

"What are you thinking?"

"I need time. I've spent the last couple years clinging to the past. Now, I'm determined to look my life square in the face and see possibility. It's a shaky feeling."

"I like possibilities."

"Were we living a fantasy? Was our time together real?"

"It was."

"I still have something to prove to myself. I no longer passively sit out my days here. It's like forging a day of my own design in Scotland. Now I'm crafting an entire future. Running and planting don't create a future. But I wake each day excited to nurture growth so that one day I will enjoy flowers and the finish line. I haven't faced my days like that for years. I grasped the reins of desire and gumption in Skye, but this can't be some waning charge now that I'm home."

"There's no timetable for an answer. I'm just praying you'll come back one day."

"Nic," she stalled, "I hate that being home means being

without you. Figuring out who I am without Josh doesn't mean I don't want to be with you. It doesn't mean I don't miss you."

"When you're ready."

* * *

At the end of the first week back home under the sunny skies of North Carolina, she rode her bike to the cemetery for an overdue heart-to-heart with her parents. She took the long route to glide under the dappled shade of giant oaks draped in Spanish moss.

Leaning against their headstone, she confessed it all. Josh's showing up in Skye to help her move on from the melancholy his death spun her into. Nic's offer of a new life. She left a chunk of her heart in Scotland, and she didn't want it back. But she wasn't sure if she could give the rest of it away, either. So much of it had been Josh's. She grasped, once again, the independence they'd birthed in her. *Don't worry, Mom and Dad, I'll be okay. Promise.*

On the way home, she detoured to Britt's Donuts, stocking up on treats for her and Brenda. In elementary school, lazy Saturday morning bicycle rides with her mom and dad to Britt's Donuts on the boardwalk were her favorite. When her pigtails gave way to a ball cap and ponytail, her parents challenged her to work a little harder for her glazed goodies. First, they pedaled to the state park, walked the three-mile Sugarloaf Trail, and then cruised to the donut shop. Sometimes, they reversed the trek and took a dozen to Sugarloaf Dunes, overlooking Cape Fear River. On those days, she knew she could coax her dad to find and feed the Venus Fly Traps. *Nic would love doing that.*

Scotland worked its magic on her—giving her a new

outlook on embracing life. Her despondence over Josh faded, but memories of Nic sneaked into her head all summer long.

Settling into her North Carolina beach summer rhythm didn't take long—waking without an agenda of immediate responsibilities and slowly relaxing into the day, free of expectations. July summer days flew by quickly when she scrapped an alarm, savored long strolls or runs across the soft surface of the sand, perched for entire days at the shoreline with books, music, and podcasts, and sought out local evening concerts.

She wondered how Nic spent his July days. She easily pictured him working, hiking, helping guests from the front desk of the Shelter Guest House, and making Maisrie smile. But at night, when she was alone with her thoughts, she envisioned him relaxing under the same moon as her. On the deck of a whitewashed cottage, whisky in hand, he searched the Sound of Raasay for dolphins and watched eagles soar.

After the final fitting for her matron of honor dress in mid-August, she hosted a meet and greet picnic for her class of upcoming fifth graders, a new venture for her. They trekked through Carolina Beach State Park and played cooperative games, accomplishing goals as a team. She pictured Nic discovering this place steeped in Civil War history, its forests, sand trails, wetlands, osprey, and white-tailed deer. It wasn't Culloden or Fairy Glen Falls, but he would find the majesty in it just the same.

Spending the first part of summer break in the land of the mist proved some things remained the same no matter what sky she healed under. The sun and moon rose and set over the ocean waves; the tide waxed and waned; and her heart still constricted and released. These days, void of numbness, held an unusual arrhythmia, uneven and erratic. The whirl of activities to prepare for Brenda's wedding kept her occupied, but with that hectic busyness came an unsettling. Living with new possibilities was an unstable rocky terrain, thrilling and unsteady.

Amid wedding preparations, she and Brenda took a rare moment to unwind together. They cycled on a heat-of-the-South night through the back roads to the corners of the world they grew up in. Then, they grabbed a bite to eat on the pier, soaking up the restoratively slow pace of a late August evening in view of fishermen hauling in their catch and cruising sailboats. *Was Nic watching different sailboats on a different bay from a different patio, miles across the world?*

"This wedding brings up a lot for all of us. How are you doing?" Brenda asked.

"I'm cherishing the memories. Barefoot in the sand, rustling sea waves, a setting sun. Unforgettable. I'm so happy you have Brian to share that with, too."

"It's a dream come true. You and my mom have been such a big help. All the big things are done, and we have less than three weeks until the big day."

"Cheers to you and Brian." Raey raised her Diet Coke. She considered saying Slàinte, but it didn't fit. "You and your mom created a beautiful wedding day memory for me. I want you to have the wedding of your dreams. We're going to dance the night away under the stars."

"I might be a little embarrassed by Brian's dancing moves, but he sure has fun." Brenda imitated a goggle-eyed gulp.

"Did I tell you how Nic twirled me after I planted flowers for Maisrie?" With a red face, she relayed the story and his comment about being dirty. They laughed at her embarrassment and his antics.

"He seems like a guy that helps you have fun."

"Sometimes, he's a challenge."

Brenda listened as she relayed Nic helping her through the Bad Step trek.

"Doesn't sound like he's a challenge at all. Sounds rather like he challenges you. That's a good thing for you, if you ask me."

The moon rippled across the water and she blurted, "These last couple months, I've realized that I don't need Nic. But I want him."

Brenda examined her wide-eyed. "Well, it is nice to see you attack life with your old vim and vigor."

"I miss him."

"I noticed. You share more about him than Josh these days."

"I'm so sorry. Sharing stories of him keeps him close."

"No. Don't be at all. I understand."

"What am I thinking? Am I living in fantasyland?"

"Why would you think that?"

"I meet a guy, an ocean away, and how many days did I even know him?"

"It's not how many days or how many miles between you. It's simply how you feel about him."

"I miss him, but I can't commit to him. I feel like I just got *me* back. And I'm trying to live in that truth."

"Why not talk it through some more with him?"

"Wouldn't calling him be giving him false hope?"

"You don't have to have your entire future laid out to talk to him. What do you want to give him?"

"Give him? I'm living my life again, facing the future."

"And he's not in it? Are you afraid to give yourself to someone besides Josh?"

"That's a big give, don't you think?"

"Yes, I do. But as difficult as it is, we want you to be happy."

"I want him, but I can't see a clear path to having him in my life. I feel good about who I am right now, but I miss him. For us to have a chance would mean a move. That's a huge change to see *if* a relationship would work out."

"You know as well as I that it works out because you work at it."

"How can I call him when I can't give him a promise?"

"Do you need to make promises to him?"

"Texts, phone calls, and letters across the ocean aren't enough for a relationship."

"With the determination that I've witnessed in you this summer, I think you'll figure out a way."

"But Brenda," she stalled as worry lines creased her forehead, "Josh will always move with me in my heart. Do you think Nic can handle that?"

"Oh, I see." Brenda hugged her and said, "There's only one way to know."

* * *

Summer vacation ending meant a bittersweet slide from barefoot days and flip-flop nights into socks and sneakers and backpacks filled with books and homework. Long cicada serenades from high in the treetops replaced the rumble of crashing waves. Cool velvet-blanket breezes replaced the thrum of the porch fan on lazy summer nights. Sleepy bees haphazardly moseying through the garden clover left the night to the magic-making fireflies.

The demands of the new school year usurped her nightly leisure of a binge-worthy television series. With the September sea breezes, she settled into her school schedule and thought of Nic tending to patients. She wrapped herself in her teal cardigan she had bought on Skye to draw closer to him. Scrolling through the pictures of him on her phone only deepened her longing.

Many evenings, Brenda and Brian cozied on the screened-in porch with a glass of wine, watching the oranges and pinks of sunsets flow into the blues and greens of the sea from the outside sofa. Someone was missing on her couch, and she knew who it was. The weight of Nic's body suspended over her the night before she left Skye, his eyes begging her to stay, melted her insides.

The night before the rehearsal dinner, Raey hunkered down in her comfortable, oversized patio lounger with a novel. She searched the skies for a falling star, before the forecasted, patchy fog rolled in. No longer that antsy young girl lying in the tickling grass, arms stretched wide below the heavens in search of constellations, she had the patience to wait on the spinning of the Earth. She had once sat right here and begged for the spin to slow down through her last days with Josh. A gray moon backlit the glistening intricacies of a spider's arduous efforts among the deck railings, weaving a web of survival.

The slide of arms across her skin didn't alarm Raey, as she instinctively recognized how Josh enveloped her quiet spaces. His breath caressed her cheek as he whispered, "I just want to hold you." They lingered in this position, sharing the moonlight rippling over the waves, watching the mist crawling across the evening sunset. Raey didn't talk but grasped his hands, afraid this spell would break, and Josh would once again disappear.

"Let's walk the beach," he suggested and entwined their

fingers. Her breath caught when she pressed her fingers against the silver band on his finger. She habitually glanced at the silver rings on her hand, the weight of them on her finger forgotten until this moment. Passed down from his mother, he said the set matched her beauty and strength.

He stared intently as she studied her rings, and reassuringly squeezed her right hand three times, their unspoken sign for *I love you*. "Showing up like this, it might seem like I'm a man out of his mind," he sighed. "I just need to say some things before I'm out of time."

Stopping at the water's edge, he released her hand and bent to grab two smooth rocks embedded in the warm sand. He turned to her and said, "You're a stone's throw away from a new beginning in your life. I want to leave you with something." He placed the rocks in her palm and cupped her hands closed, examining her face with a silent question in his eyes.

"Rocks?"

Josh peered at the weathered rocks in her hand and then up at her. "They still glisten. They're infused with color. Just like you. They are my gift to you." He tugged the square diamond on her finger, and her head raised at his gesture. "Can you take *this* rock off now, Princess?"

"No, I can't." Her words, like red sparks, spurted from her mouth. "And I can't believe you are asking me to."

His words mixed in her head, a confused spinning. Her brain struggled to register her position on the sand for a split second. She fought for balance as his soft lips sunk into hers. Pulling her to him, he moaned in relief and finality, as if arriving home after a long journey.

"Remember when we lived on Skye and, to your delight, you found a morning rain and mist rarely hung around for long? Early on, you got frustrated that our plans were ruined, but later, you smiled at the miracle of a beautiful day hidden behind dark clouds. Your life is like that. It's rough at times, but never lose faith that it is going to be a jewel of a story."

His deep, rich voice in her ear soothed her the way a cool, gentle breeze comforts on a humid day. She sunk her weight into him and balanced against his chest, his stubble grazing her cheek as she embraced his warmth and strength. All too soon, he would be gone.

"Is this the last time?" she asked.

Josh didn't speak, just shrugged and rested his head on hers. He strayed his gaze to the moon's misty reflection that glistened a straight path to the horizon. She clung to him in case this moment was her last with him, his last words, his last smile.

He took a step back, holding her hands, and with a tremor in his voice vowed, "If I could keep holding you, keep kissing you, keep hanging on to you, it wouldn't matter what those clouds blew in." His somber gaze met her eyes as he released his hold on her. "This may be the last time, so I need to say, 'I'll love you, always.'"

Goosebumps rippled up her arms as suddenly her hands alone held the rocks. Chilled, she placed the stones in her denim shorts' pocket and wrapped her arms around herself, staring at the mist floating across the water. She trudged along the shoreline to the lit boardwalk railing that signaled her beachside cottage.

The steady roar of waves and an oversized pillowed couch sedated her sorrow as Raey fell asleep on the screened-in porch until a muffled summons schlepped through her brain fog.

Brenda hunkered to her side on the couch and shook her

fully awake. "Hey, hon, what are you doing out here? You're going to catch a cold."

She winced upon recalling Josh's arms enveloping her in a warm embrace. "I saw him, B. Josh held me," she said, rubbing the slick edges of the fleece blanket wrapped around her legs. After taking a couple deep breaths, she shared the rest, "We walked the beach, and he whispered how much he loved me. Then, he disappeared." She couldn't voice his proposition to take off her ring.

"Aww. Those are special dreams." Brenda's voice lifted with relief. She hugged her and said, "You're lucky. I wish I could see him. I miss him so much."

Raey feared explaining the visit, so she held onto Brenda's neck and promised, "I'll pray for a dream like that for you to treasure."

"I'm still hoping." Brenda raised crossed fingers.

"But after seeing Josh, I had the most disturbing dream."

"Oh, I'm so sorry. That's a terrible way to ruin a good dream. What happened?"

After awakening to the urgency in the dream, Raey's mood took a nosedive. In her dream, she lounged near breaking waves with Josh, the cool froth nibbling at her bare toes. Entertained by a flock of sandpipers speckling the shoreline with their wagtail manner, she smiled at their bobbing heads, teetering tails, and crouching to dine on coastal delicacies. One diner teetered toward her and perched on her chair, expelling a quiet wheet-wheet-wheet.

Afraid to stir the brown-eyed piper from its curiosity, she listened as its high-pitched whistle sped to a beckoning alarm. It hopped onto her hand and pecked at it as if poking the sand. With a flick of her wrist, she shooed it away, but after a quick jump flight, it obstinately landed back on her hand. Then it hopped into her lap, staring at her through its white eye-rings. She searched for help from Josh, but his chair was empty. Again, it pecked her hand and then stilled, checking for a reaction from her. It pecked and checked and pecked and checked until her skin broke. Unruffled by the pain or blood, she refused to bid it goodbye or abandon her seat.

True to the warped narrative of dreams, she suddenly found herself in a doctor's office with Nic as Dr. Mac. He gave her a diagnosis, sadly informing her that she experienced sepsis of the heart, triggered by the sandpiper digging into her hand. She relayed her symptoms while he stood over her, shaking his head but unalarmed by the sandpiper's actions or the fact that she couldn't move her hand.

Strangely, she remained mute, able to convey her ailments to him in silence. Besides the obvious hole seeping blood into her open palm, she reported a fever, racing heart, and trouble breathing. Nic then perfunctorily enumerated other symptoms that she hadn't noted. She screamed, "Hurry! Do something. If you have a diagnosis, then fix it!"

When Raey finished the retelling of her nightmare, she blankly stared at Brenda.

Brenda asked, "So what needs to be fixed? The sandpiper is telling you something. I think he's afraid you're not listening."

"You think this is about Nic? Don't you?" Raey slapped her palms on her lap and waited in agony.

Brenda held Raey's hand as she counseled, "In Celtic mythology, sandpipers are symbols of transition and change They're always on the move, so Celts believed they offer guidance and support as people navigate new paths. You steered your way forward when you went to Scotland! Maybe, it's steering you forward now."

"That's exactly my problem. I don't know how to navigate forward with Nic."

"Your sandpiper might be supporting you and asking you to make changes, maybe to your body or life. Maybe it's asking you to look harder at your struggle over Nic," Brenda said, and then she hesitated and swallowed hard before adding, "or where you might be in denial."

"And that is?" Raey asked.

"*You* have to find that answer. But you might not get any relief until you determine how you will move forward with Nic. Birds in a dream can represent goals, aspirations, and hopes, but they can also reflect joy, harmony, spiritual freedom...psychological liberation...and love."

"Uh-huh?" Raey waited for more from Brenda.

"I was elated to see that the weight you carried to Scotland had fallen from your shoulders when you returned, but what will you do with this restlessness over Nic?"

"I adore watching the sandpipers from my porch night after night, but now they're hacking at my hand." Raey blew out an exasperated breath.

"Maybe you're being pulled apart by your desires or some emotional or spiritual conflict? Don't you think that is about Nic?"

"Yes." Raey contemplated the words Nic had written to her in his letter and the question he had asked her—words on a page she still held too close.

"Sounds like you have an idea of what your dream is telling you. Think about this. That bird doesn't like to plunge deep into the water. He dances between the shore and water. Maybe, you are like him. Are you afraid to dive into this with Nic? What two worlds are you poised between, Raey? North Carolina and Scotland? Josh and Nic? Are you delicately dancing between keeping your feet safely on the ground while wrestling to test the waters of the unfamiliar and risky?"

"As if I haven't been drowning in the waters of the 'unfamiliar and risky.'" Raey flipped the cover from her legs and stretched to break her position. "Wow, all this from a gory sandpiper dream. Could it be that I just fell asleep to sandpipers pecking food from the sand?"

"I guess that's for you to wrestle with. But either way, it's trying to get your attention, get you moving."

"He's ready when I'm ready to be all in."

"And you can't be all in?"

"From this distance?"

"Can you visit him again and see?"

"He had a long-distance relationship that didn't work out because she wasn't all in."

"You aren't giving him enough credit. He's put himself out there for you, and he's willing to wait."

"I am giving him credit. It's me I don't trust."

"If you don't try, then how will you even know?"

"What if we try and it doesn't work out? I don't want to hurt him."

"He's a grown man and knows what he wants. You are a grown woman and you want him."

"How can I carry two men in my heart? And ask Nic to understand that?"

"Ask him."

"But what if I can't ever fully give him my heart? Is he really all in, no matter what?"

Before retreating to her bedroom and a list of wedding to-dos, Brenda said, "Honey, maybe you need to listen to your little friend." She patted Raey's knee twice and stood, leaving Raey alone with her own conclusions.

"What do you mean?" The irritation in her voice showed.

Brenda's shrugged shoulders and raised hands annoyed Raey, although it was her suspicion of the meaning behind the dream that truly ruffled her feathers. From the bedroom, she heard Brenda yell, "Call him, Raey."

Since arriving home, she missed Nic's tender caress and his presence that eased the low-grade ache that swirled through her like ripples across a pond. She stared at her phone. After two months since her last call, what would he think about her reaching out now? He said when she was ready. She still didn't feel settled, but she wanted to hear his voice and know about his days.

She checked the time on her phone. Five hours ahead would be early morning on Skye. She dared her pulse to calm and hurriedly opted to text before she changed her mind: **I miss you.** Staring at her phone, she waited for a response that never came.

Nic, don't give up on me.

TWENTY-ONE

"Well, that didn't take you long to return to being a Southern softie," Brenda teased Raey for wearing a sweatshirt on their convertible ride to meet the wedding coordinator for final arrangements before the rehearsal dinner that evening.

"I got used to wearing sweatshirts and jackets in Scotland, but I'm mostly back to fitting into this weather, too. The September morning breeze is getting cooler." The refrain blaring on the radio became Nic serenading her. Her sandpiper pecked its way into her thoughts, wavering her emotions when she didn't intently bat him away.

"I'm so excited about my matron of honor gift for you. Thanks for going through all this planning and emotional craziness with me. It should be delivered by the time we return home. I hope you love it."

Brenda, Miss Gift-giver Extraordinaire, gleaned joy from seeing people's eyes light up with surprise. With a vault for a mind, she could lock away Raey's comments to produce the perfect gift Raey had forgotten that she said she wanted. After moving in with her, Brenda ribbed her about falling asleep reading with the light on and not exerting a little effort to click it off. Brenda found a touch lamp to fit her décor, so Raey only had to tap the base of the lamp to turn it off. Brenda constantly corrected her for grocery shopping with her bike, worried about her balancing bags on her handlebars, so she bought her a collapsible folding handlebar bag with a quick release button that allowed the bag to be removed easily for collecting her groceries in the store and then transporting them home. Being both practical and extravagant, Raey could never guess what she would come up with next.

One afternoon, staring at the pelicans flying overhead while lying on the beach, Raey mentioned she would like to soar softly through the sky and watch the world below like a bird. That offhand comment turned into a lovely hot air balloon ride for her and Josh to celebrate their engagement. She wracked her brain to figure out what she had said recently that Brenda locked away and transformed into a gift, but she knew better than to spend too much time contemplating Brenda's unpredictable gift giving.

When they arrived back home after a busy day of last-minute wedding preparation and a nice seaside lunch, Brenda moaned that the delivery must be late and immediately headed to take a shower. Raey poured two glasses of Moscato for them to enjoy on the porch before gearing up for the evening rehearsal festivities. With hands full, she stepped around the curtains with the push of her elbow instead of pulling them back, keeping the late afternoon sun from heating the room. Holding both wine glasses in one hand, she clumsily pulled on the sliding door. It wouldn't budge. She lifted the security stick out of the track, a tricky balancing act. As soon as she released the stick, the door slid open.

A ghostlike figure, covered in billowing curtains, walked into the room. Raey squealed and backed into the corner. She held both wine glasses away from her chest as if blocking the intruder. After a double take, her fear and adrenaline abated into shock. Nic stood six feet away from her. He placed his garment bag over the back of her couch, on guard for her next move.

"Wine is a very unique weapon of choice," he said, taking the glasses from her hands she still held out in front of her. "I definitely would be subdued by that," he chuckled while setting the glasses on the coffee table, as if delicately disarming a bomb.

Brenda squealed from the hallway, hands pulled close to her chest, clutching her heart, "Do you just love your gift? Nic's your plus one."

"He definitely got my heart racing," Raey exhaled in a long breath. Her fixed concentration relaxed into a sly smile as she skipped close and wrapped her arms around his waist. "Welcome to my home." They smiled at one another, and then she whispered in his ear, "You are very sneaky."

Sighing in satisfaction, Nic whispered back into her ear, "I aim to please." They shared a happy glance, and Raey figured her face turned pink.

"How long do you get to stay?" Raey asked, hoping for an extended stay.

"Unfortunately, I only get this weekend. I fly back very early Sunday. But we've got an entire thirty-two hours together. I was scheduled to be on call this weekend, but with some maneuvering, I managed to get three days off in a row."

"You two already talked," Raey extended her arm toward Brenda, "but let me introduce you to my best friend, Brenda, in the flesh. As you can see by her wicked grin, she is proud of her fine work." Raey turned, clicked her tongue, and gave Brenda a suspicious glance.

"Nice to meet you in person." When Nic directed his focus

toward Brenda, he caught the tail end of her exaggerated expression and thumbs-up, relaying approval of Raey's handsome date.

"You're a hard one to get a hold of, but apparently worth the trouble." Brenda's flailing hands mocked exasperation but then wrapped him in a hug. "I'm so glad it all worked out so you could come for my special day. It's good to meet you in person. And Raey will certainly enjoy herself more, having you here," she tittered.

"I'm happy to be invited," he politely responded, staring at Raey over Brenda's shoulder, begging with his eyes to be rescued from her long embrace.

"Wow, flirt much?" Raey pulled Brenda from their hug.

"Well, it has been a long time," Nic added after checking his wristwatch. "I mean, it's been nearly two hours since I recovered from the flight attendant's constant attention."

Like sweat drops conform until gravity compels them to fall across the brow, Raey hesitated until her courage tipped the scales of her inhibitions, and she grabbed his palms, swung them low to hold aside her hips, and leaned in to kiss him a long hello right in front of Brenda.

Pulling a few inches apart, she parroted his smile and stared, unsure of his reaction. She whispered, "So, why didn't you text me back?"

Picking up on the tension, Brenda politely exited. "Oh, I better get ready for the rehearsal dinner. Will you both excuse me?" she asked, not waiting for a reply.

"Well, I switched shifts to get this weekend off, so I worked like crazy. But mostly, Brenda swore me to secrecy, so I decided to face your possible wrath when I arrived."

Raey pouted at him in disappointment.

"Plus, honestly," his voice mellowed with caution, "I

wanted you to want me to come. We haven't talked in awhile." His eyes begged the question, "And Brenda invited me without you knowing. I am hoping you are okay with it. Are you?"

"Yes! I'm more than okay with it." She grabbed his head with both hands and pulled his cheek to hers. His cheeks puckered into a smile when she said, "You came all this way for only thirty-two hours?"

"It's not only thirty-two hours, Raey." His husky voice probed her senses as if it were a savored dram of soothing whisky. "I'm here for a lot more than that. Time and space don't fill moments, Raey. People do. And you fill every moment with everything I want." His eyes twinkled with mirth as he winked at her, and a gleam of mingled appreciation and expectation flickered across her face.

"I'm very glad you are here," she asserted, matching his courage. He relaxed his stubbled cheek against hers once more, and a current of energy charged through Raey's body.

If she'd learned anything from her trip to Skye, it was that her life could only expand in proportion to the courage she mustered. Having him here, touching her, taking cues from her, she chastised herself for not reaching out to him sooner. He took a big chance in coming without her knowing, and she vowed to abandon her fear of future heartache.

Wrapping her arms tighter around him, she asked, "Will you forgive me?"

Without hesitation, he responded, "You're forgiven."

She pushed slightly away from him, searching the lines of his face. "You answered mighty quickly. You don't even know what you're forgiving me for."

"I don't need to. I can forgive you for anything. You wouldn't purposely hurt me." He tilted his head in question.

"I don't want to hurt you."

"Hurt me, how?" Nic asked.

Their conversation quickly took a serious turn. Struggling to collect her flustered reflections, she jumped in mid-thought, "Do you understand when I tell you it is not possible to move on from Josh, only to move forward with him?"

"Hmm. Better give me some more." He loosened his hands around her waist to run them through his hair and sit on the ottoman, creating an unexpected space between them.

Raey kneeled before the ottoman, settling herself between his legs. He followed her deliberate movement as she gripped his hands and fumbled through her words, "Ugh, I'm not explaining myself well here. What I mean is…" Raey looked away as she swallowed for more air and then targeted his eyes. "Josh will always be a part of me." She placed their clasped hands over her heart and whispered, "Here." Finding resolve in his attentive, blue eyes, she released one hand from her heart and tapped her temple, adding, "And here."

Nic cradled her hand back in his.

"I can't help that. That's not something I heal from," she pleaded, as if he'd mounted an argument. "And because of that, he will be a part of the next life I create. Can you move forward knowing that? Does this even make sense?"

He released the air in his chest he had been holding. "It makes sense. But I don't need to forgive you for that." His soft lips hovered above hers, and he stammered to breathe his next words, "Yes, I can create a life with you, Raey, all of you." He found permission in her gaze and pulled her to his chest. Their desire united in a long, deep kiss.

Her concerns dissipated like a lingering mist lifted by the sun's rays. His warmth and closeness caused her heart to skip through their hours together.

* * *

Thirty minutes until go-time, Raey tried to control appearing more nervous at the wedding than the bride. Despite waiting in a small, air-conditioned hut for the wedding coordinator to give them the cue to begin the procession, beads of sweat collected on her forehead. On a similarly warm day, not too far in the past and not too far from this stretch of beach, she had donned a white dress, stood hand in hand with Josh, and pledged her entire hereafter. Standing now as Brenda's matron of honor, she said a silent blessing for Brian and Brenda's long life together.

She stretched out her hand and stared at the pale line marking her naked ring finger. That morning, she willed herself to take her rings off to honor her newfound commitment to live her new life. Warring with her decision, she slowly slid them over her knuckle and then back down her finger. She had never taken them off. Since the day he had pledged his love and faith and placed them on her finger, she had worn them faithfully. Cancer tested the strength and courage of her vow *to take him as my husband, to have and to hold, for better or worse, for richer or poorer, in sickness or health, to love and to cherish from this day forward, till death do us part.* She wanted to honor Josh's memory by including him today, so she slipped her wedding rings on a gold chain.

Raey's eyes teared up imagining how Brenda's older brother would have offered his little sister warm words of encouragement and kissed her before she walked down the sandy aisle. Raey drew Brenda into a warm hug as they waited together and then softly opened Brenda's cupped hand, laying her rings in it. She stumbled as she spoke, "This is, um, this is yours today. It was your mom's set. They're the rings Josh put on my finger on our wedding day. Wear it as your something borrowed."

Raey wiped a tear from Brenda's eye and found a confident rhythm for her words. "Josh loves you. He's here today in your heart."

Brenda clutched the set to her heart and wrapped her other arm tightly around Raey. "This is perfect. I love you for doing this."

"He would have wanted to be here to tease you about being a good wife. He would be happy you found love. And sweetie, if you receive half the love Josh gave me, you will be a very blessed woman."

Each minute that ticked by felt like an hour, and she assumed it must also be the same for Nic, sitting alone in the audience, knowing no one. Finally, she clutched hold of her logical big-girl brain. *For goodness' sake, Nic is a grown man and a doctor who has been thrust into many new, uncomfortable situations through the years. He has his own life, owns his own home, and takes care of his grandparents and himself every single day. He flew across the pond to be my surprise plus one, knowing a matron of honor has endless duties, so why do I need to check on him and make sure he is okay? He'll be fine without me by his side for a little while.*

His mild demeanor hid his superpowers—confidence, resolve and strength. Yet, she couldn't help peeking for a glimpse of him when she lined up to walk down the aisle. She spied him sitting alone at the far end of the second row on the bride's side, his arm casually hanging over the chair as if hugging the occupant. Exhaling relief at his relaxed face and posture, she focused on his back, white shirt pulled tight across his broad shoulders, no longer hidden by the gray suit coat hanging behind his white chair. Nic brushed his fingers lightly through his textured hair, messing it enough to create the perfect seductive show and then turned his head. His piercing cobalt eyes changed in intensity when they captured hers. He appeared more commanding with a light shadow of a beard. It caressed his face in a lighter brown haze than his locks, augmenting the effect of his eyes. She contemplated which look she most admired, this formal attire or his casual cut jeans and sweaters. If she were one of his patients, she would have difficulty concentrating on his words because his lab coat would not disguise a physique developed by rugged outdoor hobbies. He scanned her entire body and smiled. She waved and he winked.

Two giggling young teen girls pointing at Nic distracted her. A sense of pride suffused her limbs as a blush heated her cheeks. Josh's parents walked into view, and Nic stood to greet them, shaking their hands. Nic wrapped his loose hand on top of Mrs. Davenport's, holding her hand as they exchanged smiles and easy conversation. Waves of acceptance and relief washed over her.

His undivided attention would be hers shortly.

Josh should be here. Her heart skipped and her breath stopped when she saw the vacant seat Brenda reserved for him next to her parents. His suit coat, complete with a boutonniere and pocket handkerchief, hung over the back of the chair. She stood behind Brenda and stared across the aisle at the men lined up behind Brian. Josh's absence in that line, like the hole in her heart, weakened her knees. She gripped her bouquet to find a tangible strength as her eyes filled with mist. She glanced at Brenda's mom and their eyes met. Raey recognized the emptiness sheltered behind her smiling facade and let a tear trickle its entire lonely path down her cheek without swiping it away.

Brenda and Brian recited their vows. "To have and to hold from this day forward." Raey imagined greeting her own groom at an altar, repeating those vows to Nic, and her body stiffened in panic. She bent her knees before she buckled at her traitorous thought. She couldn't leave Josh behind…the man she vowed would be the love of her life. *Will I be able to surrender my whole heart to Nic, even if I want to?*

The duty of smiling through the ceremony and the pictures completed, she breathed deeply to gear up for the party— celebrating Brenda and Brian's love and dancing cheek to cheek with Nic. A few minutes before the reception officially began, she stole a brief walk to the water's edge to get her bearings. When she watched the couple's first dance, she didn't want tears to flow with Nic beside her.

She stood mesmerized by the sun holding itself just above the water's distant edge. Its reflection rippled like lightning on the water. Goosebumps emerged with the breeze caressing her skin, reminding her of the slow, gentle slide Josh's arms used to envelop her in.

Raey sensed Nic's essence without seeing him. How long had he been standing there?

"Who's winning this staring contest, you or the sun?" Nic asked.

She tucked her chin to her chest, wiped tears off her cheeks, and turned to find him steps away.

"Difficult day without him?"

"This is a hard one," Raey breathed, steadying herself to keep her tears from becoming a deluge. "His sister's wedding…." She wanted to explain more, but nothing came from her but a headshake.

Nic recognized the silent, quick seconds before drowning, and Raey seemed close. Drowning victims couldn't call or look at their rescuer. Nic threw her a lifeline to grab hold of. "Is there more inside there?" Nic said as he took her hand. His sympathetic eyes offered her a rescue if she would grab hold.

His sincerity drew her words slowly to the surface. "I expected this to be hard." Her head bobbed low for her to swipe under her eyes again, cupping them as if the light were too much to bear. "I thought I could manage it. And I am." Her faraway stare gazed north along the beach. "We got married on this beach. Memories of him are everywhere. He's not just Brenda's biggest silent cheerleader. His favorite color is the blue of the bridesmaid's dresses. He's wrapped in his parents' hearts, while they cling to one another for strength. His optimism is embodied in the promise of their wedding vows. I needed a few private moments to let my tears subside."

"Missing loved ones is difficult. I'm sure his entire family is thinking of him today. My words won't ease your pain. But can I hold you right now?" Nic slid his hands low around her waist. They absorbed the final moments of the melting sun in silence while she embraced his calm, laying her head back against his chest. When Nic enveloped her like a shawl, his protection felt like settling into home. The beat of his heart thrummed with the sounds of the surf. A jolt flashed through her—Josh asked that same question. *Can I hold you right now?* His words melded her past with her future.

Without asking, his hands fell and pulled hers in a silent invitation to walk the beach. She sensed this natural, *next right move*, as if she had conjured his thought.

"You look so beautiful. I'm having trouble not staring at

you. I hope you don't mind it for a little while longer because I only have a few hours left with you," Nic said as he squeezed her hand.

She shot him an appreciative, look-all-you-need smile. "So, then you're throwing your hat in the ring to win the staring contest?" she teased as she cuddled into his side.

"I'd throw whatever it takes to win that contest." He adjusted her hips to face him, clasping his hands together at the small of her back.

She smiled at him, hoping to convey the depth of her feelings. "I'm so glad you came." That sounded like a cliché in her ear, but she truly meant it. She didn't want to be with anyone else today. Looking directly in his eyes, she added, "I wish you could stay longer." She understood if he doubted her sentiment after not reaching out for two months.

"I had no choice. I had to come. I'm not letting you sit out a dance," he asserted with a wink.

"Had to?" she asked.

"I figured if it is a mistake, it is a mistake worth making."

"The only mistake is that we haven't done it yet," Raey hinted by pulling at his arm and nodding back up the beach toward the reception dance floor.

"We will. But can we chat first?" Nic asked.

Neither the cool sand burying her feet, nor the purplish-pink skies, nor the soft waves could lift the ominous heaviness that invaded her body. This conversation might require some space, so she turned toward the ocean, breaking his embrace, and bent to pick up a partially buried, broken shell.

"Where are we?" he asked, his voice competing with the roar of the waves crashing along the shore. She expected his directness.

Diverting her eyes from him and flipping the shell back

into the water, Raey ached for a clear and concise answer to give him. "This just isn't simple or easy for me. I don't want to disappoint you or cause you pain."

He interrupted her, "Raey, look at me." She cringed at seeing his imploring face as she struggled to help him. "I love your honesty you gave me when I first arrived. Here's mine. I'm not afraid of work. I don't expect life to always be smooth and uncomplicated." His eyes pitched to the ground. "God knows it hasn't been easy for you or me," he admitted. "But everything about you fazes me. And I'd like a much larger measure of that in my life."

"I faze you?" she asked aloud. "Somehow, you don't make that sound like a good thing."

"Frankly, you scare the hell out of me," his lowered voice, strangely reticent. He ran his fingers through his hair, waiting for her response.

Completely taken aback, she instinctively straightened her back and pulled away until her brain kicked in again. Her breath stopped when she recalled the answer that he had given her for why he hadn't yet married.

"Can we sit?" She motioned toward a lounge chair belonging to a nearby condominium. He reached out to hold her hand as they walked, keeping their connection.

Seated side by side on the same chair, Nic waited for her to gather her thoughts. "All these emotions are waging war in my head. The battlefield is quite bloody and crowded." She tried for a little levity.

He responded in kind, "Good thing I'm fighting for the Queen's side."

His masked vulnerability gave her the boldness to explain. "I don't want to weigh you down with my doom and gloom, but I'm not sure I can be everything you need right now. If I'm brutally honest, as much as I want to be in a relationship with you, I'm scared I won't allow you all the way in. I know you want that. Every relationship needs that."

"I do," he acknowledged with a nod of his head.

Raey paused, pulling at her lower lip. "I'm holding onto Josh's memories while looking toward a future with you. I need to know that I'm ready to love again. It should be easy to just fall in." She flung her hand, holding her sandals out wide in frustration. "But it's a scary fall. Letting go isn't that simple for me."

He used her metaphor to make it easier for her to continue. "We may lose a battle early on, lass, but that doesn't mean we've lost the war."

Worry lines creased between her eyes. "There's a powerful urge to keep my will locked in a vault, hidden even from myself. But I'm promising to stay open and be honest. My head says to be all in, but my heart is afraid that I'm not there, not yet. You're a dream come true, but you're also real. I want you, but I don't want to hurt you."

With the word dream, her thoughts drifted to the sandpiper pecking her hand. Brenda had told her to listen to him.

"And?" Keeping his eyes on her face, his fingers softly traced hers.

Raey's eyes met his, but her shoulder-shrugging resistance didn't deter Nic.

"That figure eight design in the sand that you're concentrating on making with your pretty, pink-painted toes tells me you're creatively avoiding saying something. There's still more you need to say," he said as he nudged her to proceed.

Raey self-consciously stilled her foot and finished, "You are so right for me. But sometimes working toward letting myself be fully known to you seems risky and monumental. I'm sorry. That's why I didn't call or write these last months. I couldn't figure out how to say 'Maybe' with thousands of miles between us without it seeming like a 'No.'"

"Well, most things having to do with me are monumental," he joked and stretched one long leg out over the other, propped back on his long arms, and splashed a dazzling smile at her.

The wind picked up and flipped sand across her legs as if whipping her into action. Scooting closer to grab his arm, she stared at her flexed feet as if checking her pedicure. "I want to give you clear answers before you leave, but today I'm a mess. My emotions are everywhere with the wedding and having you near me for such a short time." She hesitated and searched for the perfect words, drawing fingers to pinch her lips. "My past and future collided. It's overwhelming."

He leaned back on the lounge chair and pulled her on top of him in one fell swoop. Before she could fight back or think, he stilled her with his reply. "I'm standing guard right here until those tumultuous battles in your heart prove that the Queen has victoriously conquered her own heart."

As Raey pushed herself up to look at him, each bicep responded to her weight. She held on as if for dear life. Nic continued his low-toned vow, "And Raey, we will win the war." Like her sentry, he guarded her heart.

They walked arm in arm toward the twinkling lights of the reception floor. He stopped mid-way and locked both arms around her waist, pledging, "In case you need to hear me say it, you don't have to work to be everything I need. You already are."

"Right now you need a dancing partner."

"There's my girl, ready for an adventure."

Nic charmed her throughout the remainder of the evening.

Their twirling and swaying created a surreal magic that made everything sweet, simple, and possible. She relaxed in his arms; the worries that she had splayed out before him vanished for the night. Fireworks bursting color across a moon-shadowed horizon marked the end of an evening that felt like freedom to Raey.

TWENTY-TWO

They fell asleep in one another's arms on the couch in the early morning hours, and at some point, she moved to her room. She slept between nudges from her watch's vibrations. Zzzziiipppp extracted her brain from its fog. *Nic to the airport. 5:30 a.m. Uber.* Jumping up, Raey edged around the corner of her bed, off balance, and caught her little toe. Functioning coherently on three hours of sleep constituted a tall order for a girl that needed at least six. She hobbled, shaking her foot, and found Nic sitting on the kitchen counter, expectantly awaiting her arrival.

Rubbing her eyes, she caught him studying her wedding picture hanging on the wall. He grinned at her disheveled entrance. Her bare feet chilled on the kitchen's ceramic tile as she stepped toward him. She lightly scratched his thighs with her nails. He clasped both arms behind her neck like a delicate necklace, the tips of his fingers lightly caressing her bare skin. His legs wrapped around her, pulling her tightly to him. They greeted one another with their smiles.

She cupped his face, and they stared at one another. The air in the room thickened without words. The clock ticked down their remaining moments as she committed his face to memory

—dark brows framing his deep blue eyes, the slight arch of his lips, the faint shadow along his strong jaw....

Her pulse beat faster when he leaned close. She closed her eyes when soft lips heated the hollow at her throat and dotted their way along her collarbone. When he paused, the sleepy bliss faded from her brown eyes, quickly replaced by deep longing. His lips brushed along the links of her gold chain to the edge of her shirt. His hair teased her neck, and a zingy citrus aroma tantalized her nose. Words were lost to her.

"I more than enjoyed my time with you," he said.

She intended to respond in kind until his breath warmed her ear when he whispered through a controlled exhale, "I'll miss you." Goosebumps shivered her skin.

She wrapped her arms around him, letting them fall against the counter below his belt. "I will miss you more."

"Hmm?"

His lips kissed her skin from jaw to cheek to temple, and then he brushed the roughness of his stubble along her cheek. He cupped her face with warm palms and the softness of his lips settled on hers with a feather light nudge of his tongue. Like a moth drawn to light, her lips relaxed on his without hesitation. Laying his hands firmly on her hips, he pulled her tighter to him. Their lips pressed harder, urgently holding each other. Heat burned up her belly, through her chest, and over her face as her lips fell full over his mouth. The dance of their tongues deepened as their lips matched one another, searching and finding what they needed.

She didn't want to stop, but a few soft kisses to his cheeks returned her breathing to near normal, and she found her words again. "I'm not sure how to do this goodbye. This..."

"Shh," he said, stroking her hair and pushing it behind her ear to settle his lips on her eyelid.

"But you leave in minutes," she murmured.

"Is it goodbye?" he asked.

"I don't want it to be." She nuzzled her head under his chin, against his chest, hearing his strong heartbeat. The ticks of the clock mocked their peace.

He lifted her chin to meet his eyes, and spoke through lips lingering softly on hers, "Then let's not let it be."

"What's the next step then?" Hope rose in her voice.

"You'll know it," Nic confidently professed with the certainty of an old sage.

Raey wrapped her arms around his neck, grabbing his hair. He locked his wrist behind her waist and penetrated her soul with his soft, slow, unwavering words, "You'll know, and I'll be waiting."

"Maybe I just won't let you go." She kissed him with a fierceness that dared the hands on the clock to move, a vow to deny time its victory, and he matched her desire. As timeless as these moments felt, the vibration of his phone signaled their end.

"That's my hope," he continued, holding her hand and pulling her to the door with him as if begging her to come. Before he turned the doorknob, he grabbed her cheeks once more, kissed her quickly, and promised, "I'm banking on us."

When brake lights and blinker no longer lit the driveway, she closed the door to the empty space he left behind. Both hands clung to the doorknob, wishing that pulling it open would reveal him standing on the other side. She eyed Josh's stethoscope hanging on the coat hook next to the door. A pang of loss and remembrance bolted through her chest, and the rhapsody of being in Nic's arms collapsed. Breathing and moving became cumbersome decisions. She curled under a blanket on the sofa and rose much later with the warmth of the sun.

After such a perfect evening together, the door to a life with Nic opened wide. So much for holding her heart close. She handed Nic an IOU on a silver platter, and now hoped that she could find the collateral for it.

Nic reeled through her mind that day as she took a long bike ride. Stopping in Carolina Beach State Park, lemon-yellow butterflies escorted the change of season, skipping across her nose and spiraling through the air like mini tornadoes. She shopped for the week's groceries, prepped for her classes, and read a novel on the porch.

She moved on with the day, but his absence tormented her, a familiar pang that plagued her when she had said goodbye to Josh. Except now, she had a choice. And that choice was her second chance at having a great love in her life again. Having shared a very small glimpse of her world with Nic, her cravings for him flitted throughout every part of her. She wanted to collect new memories with him. The kind you make when you share a life together. Waking up to the hustle of the day…fighting over schedules…planning a family–she didn't care. She wanted to be where he was.

Yearnings wafted through her mind on Monday at school, but at the daily pace of fifth grade, she outran them, and they became shadows. Sweet Adeline bounced into the classroom, excited to see friends after being sick for a week. After lunch, she tugged on Raey's sleeve and begged with tired eyes and a whisper, "Can I go home?" Raey drew her close, rubbed her back in soft circles, and encouraged her to make it through the couple more hours that remained of school, but her pink-rimmed eyes and slumped shoulders begged again, "But Ma'am, the sick isn't over yet." The simplicity and strength of that statement hit Raey's heart, finding solace in one who certainly understood.

Oh, Adeline, the sick isn't over yet for me, either. She thought her heart had recovered and found its place. She, too, inherently understood that it couldn't recover until she allowed it to rest at home. She needed to take it home. She mistakenly thought she had.

After days of assuaging her hunger for Nic, she had to hear his voice. She called him Friday night. When he answered on the second ring, she teased, "Hey, you. You're bloody pecking around in my head."

"Then it's a good thing you called me because I think you are going to need a doctor."

"I do." She held her breath and waited for his response, placing much weight on this phone call.

"Well, lass, tell me your symptoms. I'll recommend the right one for you."

"Repetitive thoughts."

"Hmm. Repetitive thoughts of what? So, you might need a psychologist?"

"Heart…burn." She winced at admitting that so slyly, but outright.

"Oh, you need a GI doctor, then. Sorry ma'am, that's not my specialty."

"What is your specialty? You might treat some of my other symptoms."

"Well, as a pediatrician, I will need to refer you to a specialist."

"I don't want any other doctor. I'll stick with you."

"Well, keep in mind, you get what you asked for."

"That's what I'm counting on." She skipped past the

teasing. "I'm surprised you answered your phone. It's 2 a.m. your time."

"I saw a call from the States and didn't want to miss talking to you. I'm on call this weekend, and it's surprisingly quiet. You called when you thought I wouldn't answer?"

"No, I wanted to hear your voice and didn't want to wait."

"I've been missing you like crazy, too." The compassion imbued in his voice summoned something deep within her. She closed her misty eyes as he spoke, imagining his gentle manner, and let his late-night honeyed tone comfort her.

"But I've kept busy working a lot." Nic struck the core of their predicament, making the next few quiet seconds an eternity. She couldn't tell if work demanded his time, or if he purposefully volunteered to work to fill his time. For the next thirty minutes, they shared about their workdays and their wishes for filling their days ahead with one another, but their call got cut short when a page beckoned him back to work. Fortunate to have garnered this amount of uninterrupted time, she, nevertheless, deflated at their quick goodbye.

She stared at her phone for several seconds before tapping the end call button. They built no bridges toward future promises, and it left her breathing like a collapsed lung gasping for air. She curled her legs under her, rested her head on the arm of the couch, retreated into her thoughts, and fought against a wave of melancholy tinged with regret.

If she had her way, she would have fallen asleep listening to his voice. He hadn't pushed her to commit to anything during their conversation. He patiently listened, responded, and easily shared the monotony of his days without her and the urgency of his work life. His ease with these unstable moments drew her in. His certainty about her bolstered her courage.

She ached without him in her space. Having heard his

voice, her desire for him multiplied. He was waiting for her to step into the boat and be carried away, whether or not waves crashed. The longing for what she could have emboldened her. She dared to slide into the dream of a life with Nic and wrote him a letter to say everything she didn't over the phone.

Dear Nic,

This is my vow to begin anew—with you.

You were so right to put your thoughts on the page for me to have near. I, too, want my words penned as proof for you to read again and again. Know that the word thanks doesn't hold the weight of what my heart bears for you. While I know you don't want to be held reverently at a distance like some idol, I will adore you to my last breath for tackling the distance to come after me, literally. Deeper still is my awe and gratitude for a man that fights demons that are not his own and stands strong and still, praying for me to blink after the blur of battle when inconvenient complications and casualties of a life lost still clutter the horizon. You did not give up in waiting for me to find my way to you, but you moved first toward me. You blanketed me in your calm resolve and your relentlessly stirring faith, which steadied and nudged this wobbly, shaky-legged fawn to move.

I've lived in fear of my past because loss became such an embedded part of who I am. I thought nothing could be good again. After losing Josh, I feared finding a friendship like ours, a bond, a love that Josh and I had spent years building. In all fairness, I wasn't sure I had the strength or desire to search for it or even do the work. I feared drawing anyone into the same web of loss that entangled me.

Ultimately, I fear losing you, too, before I actually have you.

Your visit painfully revealed that my future will be bland and barren without you. Being without you is a persistent ache. I have done much soul searching about moving forward after Josh, but, of late, it is all about moving forward with you, Nic. I've marveled at how wanting to be in your life could happen during our brief time together. I've searched myself to discover if I'm just trying to escape a tormented existence, but finding a future with you helped me face my past with more clarity. You've colored my life, letting my sad memories fade into the background.

Once, my fear of the past overshadowed any desire or compulsion to create a future. I feared I couldn't adapt as you might want me to or as quickly as you needed. But I now know that all my wonderings, my comparisons, and my worries were fear tactics pecking at my brain, keeping me from focusing on you and me.

I need to dispel any looming misconceptions about where Josh fits into our relationship. I worry that this might make you uncomfortable, so I want to be sure you have my thoughts. I searched my soul, and I'm ready to step toward our relationship, offering all of me, holding nothing back. But I can't imagine not keeping Josh alive in spirit because he is part of the fabric of who I am now, just as I hope you will want to be.

I desperately want you to know that we are each other's. You are mine. I am yours (if you still desire that after reading my hopes and wishes). No passage of time can ever change the importance of the life that we will build together. Love is not a consumable commodity. It's resilient

269

and regenerates to create more love. Our friendship is rooted in a genuine love, a love watered by many passing streams.

This is the clearest way to say that I'm ready to move forward with you if you still want me. I want the life together that we've dreamed about. I'm not a half-measure kind of woman once I make up my mind. This is me saying I'm all in and hoping you will take this journey with me.

What say you?

Love,

Raey

Raey read the letter several times after completing it, chewing her nails and biting her lower lip. Reading each line slowly and imagining his reaction to her thoughts, she changed a few lines to better explain herself. She even worried about how to best close the letter. But love is what she held for him, so she wrote it. She prayed he would recognize the sincerity in her words and the fierce dedication they represented. She vowed that being in his orbit was worth facing the many difficult changes of the days ahead. Misting skies, pelting rains, and howling winds would not dampen her desire to be with him. Something had changed in her, monumentally moved her, like the shifting of tectonic plates.

An excruciating week later, express mail delivered his response. Raey's heart raced at the sight of his handwriting on the envelope when she pulled it from her mailbox. She wanted to rip it open like a Christmas present but halted, setting his letter softly on the counter. The prospect of him not wholly wanting her crept into her head, and she lost her breath at the thought of his rejection. She braced both hands on the counter and stared at the envelope. For a second, she readied her mind for a response she feared. Then, reminded of the words Nic had gifted her before she left Skye, she expectantly ripped it open.

Dear Raey,

I will always move toward you because I want you. All of you. I'm searching through the mist for you. Come back to my shore, little sandpiper.
Love and evol,
Nic

P.S. I love having your personal handwriting to read again and again, but I can't wait to hear your voice. Call me as soon as you get this!

She released all her pent-up worry, tears of joy and relief flowing down her face. His short letter so simple, so direct, so witty, so him.

"Okay, what is evol?" she immediately asked him when he answered on the first ring.

In high spirits, Nic replied, "Finally, I get to hear your voice! These were the longest two days of my life. Even harder than waiting for the Nintendo 64 Gram got me for Christmas in junior high."

"Me and a Nintendo 64 are on the same level of your longing?"

His chuckle morphed into a low growl. "Uh, absolutely not, Raey. My longing for you…." He swallowed and shook his head. "Well, mmm, just absolutely not!"

"Oh, thank goodness."

He teased her, "And *those* are the first words out of your

mouth to me? For that, I'm not telling." He waited before adding, "But I need to tell you something else right now."

"Yeah?" She wondered what important news he needed to share. The "wheet-wheet-wheet" of sandpipers called in the background.

His tone switched from silly to serious as he began, "Ye know, I wanted to tell you this in person, but you should hear this now, so I won't wait. I need you to know it."

"You're being very ominous, and it's scaring me. Is everything okay with Finlay?" Raey quieted.

"Raey?" he asked, his heavy voice shook.

"Yes," she implored him to finish telling her the news.

"Just making sure I have your attention."

"And this is torture," she whispered under her breath, not intending for him to hear.

"Raey, I love you. I don't want to live without you."

"Oh, Nic. I love you, too. And I want to be with you as soon as we can make it happen," she promised, relieved to say those three simple words that shaped all her emotions. "But those were the longest seconds of my life."

"So, curiosity is killing the cat, huh?"

"Is it a Gaelic word? I couldn't find it?"

"I'll give you a hint."

She waited eagerly.

"Backwards and forwards," he said.

"Love spelled backward is evol. You are very clever."

"That's what my love for you is. Endless. Not confined by space and time."

TWENTY-THREE

Raey's ticket placed her in the middle of the plane, achingly close to her destination. Sitting near the window, she bounced her leg and harrumphed at passengers' lack of preparedness to depart–crowding the aisles and slowly retrieving bags from the overhead bins. When she finally stood in the aisle, she clicked her phone repeatedly to check the time, minutes passing like hours. She tempered her urge to text Nic, wanting their first words to be spoken face to face.

Hurriedly following the signs for luggage pickup, she scanned the crowd, finally spotting him leaning against a wide pillar. His quirky smile indicated he relished spotting her searching for him.

She froze to take him in—clad in blue jeans and muscled into a black leather jacket offset by a cream cable-knit turtleneck framing a stubble beard. She conferred her approval with a sultry smile and a purposefully slow perusal of his body, head to toe. Before she realized it, he closed half the distance between them. A sudden urgency to be near him compelled her feet to skip along the black and white tiles, like a dancer barely skimming the surface of the floor to hit her mark under the spotlight. Her fingers released her carry-on luggage at his feet, while her eyes remained on his face. She fell hard against his chest, wrapping her arms tightly around him, and synchronized her breathing with his. His body absorbed hers as she melted into him.

Raey broke into the intimacy of their shared bliss. "What took me so long?"

Nic's arms lowered tightly around her waist, squeezing through her down jacket. He matched the same possessive intensity as he placed a strong kiss on her forehead. His warm breath settled near her ear, stirring her hair like curtains in the breeze.

Raey slapped his back and grabbed onto his sweater as if she were a drowning victim holding her head above water. When her eyes welled with tears, his throat tightened into a knot. He inhaled and then slowly shared, "I was waiting for you. I needed you to be ready to choose me, totally on your own."

Raey rushed to insert, "I do. I choose you, totally."

Nic smiled at how she twisted his words and explained, "I didn't want you to be corralled by my emotions or my desires. Everything about us is a big deal to me. I didn't want to give some type of ultimatum and scare you. I wanted all of you to want all of me without pressure from me."

Raey's head bowed, nuzzling into the warmth above his heart as she confessed, "You understand me well."

The tightness in Nic's throat subsided as he laughingly added, "Believe me, I'm not a saint. As much as I have wanted to push you at times, you needed to decide what you wanted in your own time and way. I imagined charming you something fierce on many occasions, but stealing you out from under yourself would only lead you to regrets. The last thing I wanted was to be a regret."

A slow tear spilled down her cheek. Realizing her mistaken

fear of losing him, she admitted, "When we were apart, I'm not sure if I doubted me, or if I doubted you."

With no hint of condemnation in his voice, he comforted her. "That's why I gave you my letter, Raey." She lifted her hand to wipe away a tear, but his soft lips set upon it first, feather kissing it away.

She grabbed each side of his smiling cheeks to force him to focus on her words as she proclaimed, "You can have all my heart and soul. I give them to you." Raey paused in contemplation for a couple seconds before adding, "And all my luggage, too." With a grin and a giggle, she quickly pulled him toward carousel B, but not before he planted a long kiss on her cheek.

An early morning mist suspended over the bay. Cool ocean breezes and the melody of gentle waves provided the perfect backdrop for a pleasant run. When Raey sat on the bed to put on her running shoes, she glimpsed Josh's leather journal sitting on her nightstand. She had warred with herself about leaving it in North Carolina, but bringing it felt right. A cross and the words "Life Is a Journey Best Traveled Together" were embossed on the front.

She traced their names, 'Josh and Raey,' at the bottom above their wedding date. Opening the book on her past once more, she logged the final entry to him and packed it with her keepsakes.

Dear Josh,

It's no surprise to you that I have found great love

again. Both of you are the best of men. Nic has been patient with me and understands me. He realizes the life that I have lived with you will be part of my tomorrow with him. I'm blessed to have found the love of a wonderful man twice in a lifetime. I will always cherish you, my first wild ride through love. I'm excited to begin another adventure with him.

I will love you–always.

Feeling stronger and faster than usual, Raey stretched her stride and finished at the shoreline below the B&B. A sandpiper scurried along the wet sand, probing for food. She laughed at its retreat as the waves rolled in.

His arms embraced her from behind, and she rested in the moment against his chest.

"You found it, Princess." Josh's voice jarred her, making her feel exposed. She turned to his warm smile.

"Oh, you startled me," Raey gasped.

"You look happy."

"I am."

"You were my treasure." He searched her eyes. "I'm glad you're sharing your love again. You deserve Nic. He's genuinely attracted to your soul." He grinned, adding, "Well, and probably attracted to a few other things about you that I can think of…."

"Ahem," she laughed and interrupted the direction of his thoughts.

"I will miss you." His words untethered her heart but not her arms.

She massaged her fingers through his wavy brown locks. "I

thanked God that I found you and chose you to be my always and forever. Living without you was more than I thought I could bear. When I was afraid to risk loving, Nic helped me to trust love again."

He slowly released his breath with his next words. "This is meant to be, Raey."

"I struck gold loving you." She squeezed his hands three times. "And now with Nic, I'm at home again."

"Be happy." Josh searched her eyes and then the skies. "The mist is lifting. Beautiful blue skies will be a perfect start for your new journey."

"I won't say goodbye. I'll carry you with me, always." She rested her face against his chest.

"Thanks for being the love of my life," he said before kissing her with searing tenderness, neither willing to break away. He loosed her hands from his waist and walked into the mist. A tear of gratitude trailed her cheek as he disappeared before her eyes.

Raey walked back to her room and sat with her soul in the sunspot on the carpet. She yearned for this day, a new beginning. She didn't budge at the knock on her door.

Brenda entered and announced, "Lattes to the rescue." She puzzled at Raey's disheveled hair, serene face, and satisfied silence. Squatting next to her, knee to knee, she handed over the latte and silently joined the saturation of peace that the morning's sun beamed through the window. She followed Raey's eyes to a tapestry of a Scottish blessing, hanging above the dresser.

"And may the blessing of the rain be on you, may it beat upon your Spirit and wash it fair and clean…." Raey read aloud. Hugging the latte in her hands, she stared at it as if she weren't sure how it got there. Her first sip ended with a wide smile directed at Brenda.

"You have always stood by me and helped me to find my way. Your understanding has been such a blessing."

Brenda reached out to hold Raey's hand. "I am truly happy for you, Raey."

"I have been doubly blessed to be loved by Josh and now Nic." Raey studied the lid of her latte. "I'll miss you terribly."

"I will miss you so much. But Nic is what is best for you. I'm certain of it," Brenda said.

"And I'm sure Josh approves of me sharing the rest of my life with him."

"He would, and I certainly do." Brenda squeezed Raey's hand in affirmation.

"It will hurt to be so far from one another. Your parents have always supported me. I will always consider them mine. And we will always be sisters."

Brenda raised her latte cup. "Amen and Slàinte!"

* * *

Sitting in the car park that evening, Raey laced her hiking boots.

"Are you ready?" Brenda reached over to secure Raey's last hairpin.

"No," Raey said, searching in the distance.

Brenda's face washed in worry. "What are you waiting for?"

Raey smiled at the question Josh posed the first time he appeared to her. She didn't falter with her answer now and unequivocally responded, "I'm waiting for my kilt-wearing Scot." His Range Rover pulled into the car park minutes later.

Once upon a time, Nic had asked her to share the best sunset ever at Neist Point. And once upon a time, she had added that she would grant that trek if he wore a kilt. Today, they planned to make that dream come true.

Far from the typical wedding aisle, they walked hand in hand, hiking boots to hiking boots, kilt to wedding gown, to the lighthouse at Neist Point for their sunset wedding ceremony. Surrounded by their closest friends and family, they pledged their love to one another at their seaside altar.

A reception at the B&B followed their sunset ceremony and an idyllic moon glistened over the bay. She rested her cheek against Nic's and dedicated their first dance as a continuation of her vows. She softly sang into his ear "I choose you" as an intimate declaration. In a hundred lifetimes, she would choose him again as her forever. His cheeks lifted and his arms grabbed her tighter in agreement.

In the silence after the song ended, she studied his face. "What is that I see in your eyes?" she asked.

"Just a little happy mist," he replied.

She hugged him close and whispered into his ear, "I love you, my man in the mist."

EPILOGUE

From the window of the atrium door of the B&B, Nic followed Raey's deliberate dance through the garden. Like a bee flitting from flower to flower, she carefully bent to pull a stray weed and smell the flowers grouped in her hand. The creak of the door interrupted her reverie, and she smiled back at him.

He opened the door wide for her, steadied her, and kissed her gently on the cheek. "Mmm, good morning, Sunshine," he sighed in contentment. "And to you, too," he added, bowing to lightly rest his lips atop the large rise of her belly.

Nic tugged a sprig of white heather from her bouquet and tucked it behind her ear, explaining, "Just a wee bit of white heather because you are my wish come true."

She tugged at his collar and pecked him on the cheek. "And you are mine."

He pulled a second small sprig and situated it with the first. "And it means protection," he said as he cradled his palms around her pregnant belly.

"Ah lass, you do know, aye, that I love you backwards and forwards for all time?"

"As I do you," Raey said and leaned to kiss him good morning.

WITH GRATITUDE

It would have been impossible to complete this novel without the caravan of family and friends who traveled shotgun on this wild ride. As the reader, you can skip this part of the book, but this is my opportunity to say thank you for their sacrifice of time and energy and their contributions of inspiration and encouragement. Each person, like the piece of a puzzle, contributed toward the completion of my first novel.

My husband, Rick, has been a constant sounding board. You are my beginning. The original idea morphed since chatting it up with you on that Florida beach. One day, the dream of trekking through Scotland will come true! You are the main character in my love story, always, until the end.

Thanks to my mom, Rose McClarren, for being my earliest writing champion. Once upon a time, you asked, "What's something you'd like to do before you die?" Here it is! You planted the seeds of gumption and possibility and watered them with your spirit of belief in me.

Mr. Wonderful, Tom McClarren, is my truest Scottish hero. My dad calls me a romantic. This is your "fault." Thanks for the "check-ins" to see how all was proceeding and for dreaming with me.

My three adult children and grandchildren are God's blessing. You are the weird and wonderful that fill my life with joy, thanksgiving, wonder, and love.

Ricky and Lena, thanks for your candy heart story. Your tech expertise saved me a brain ache.

Ariel and Dustin, the Keurig you purchased for me was a game changer in finishing this novel.

Daniel and Kayla, your retirement wish for me to spend more time doing what I love most—spending time with grandkids, writing, and traveling—is coming true.

While my grandkids waited for Memaw to finish editing, Niah asked the most important question, "Why are you writing a story?" My answer: "So you can read it someday, Sweet Girl."

It was a vulnerable experience letting this raw baby out into the world for the first time. My sister, Chrissy McClarren, received the earliest draft of the manuscript with loving arms and assisted from the wings at every step. Thanks for believing in the story's beauty and helping me to carve and sculpt to better reveal it.

Andy Raego, thanks for being the saint that revived this panicked heart when my hard drive crashed.

Thank you to my brother, Kevin McClarren, who is a rare gem of a man to read a draft of a romance novel and give feedback.

Thanks to Kim Baer, aka "Jade," for dubbing the editing of this manuscript multiple times as "fun" and an "obsession." You helped me find my words and expanded your heart and soul for this project so much that I now see angel wings. I'm as amazed as you that I "put all these words together to make a book."

Thanks to Brenda Childers for your reading feedback and for being a great cheerleader, providing words of encouragement. "Slow pace is still a pace."

Thanks to Teresa Davis for sacrificing vacation time to edit.

I call my editor, Megan Montgomery, a Godsend. She

came along at just the right time and said all the right things to inspire me to develop more depth in the characters. It's better because of you.

My website and book cover by Lena Roberson blow me away. My heart sang from the moment you said, "We totally got this. We'll knock this out of the park together." And she did! The book cover is what I imagined from the beginning.

Thanks to every student I ever taught to write. Getting our words right is hard. Find your voice and write away!

Thanks to Tim McGraw for creating music that keeps me writing.

ABOUT THE AUTHOR

Cherie Roberson writes romance novels for fun. After retiring from teaching, Cherie loaded up on chai tea and fulfilled her dream of writing a novel. A very misty walk on a Florida beach with her husband and a canceled trip to Scotland because of a pandemic inspired her debut novel *Man in the Mist*.

She and her husband of thirty-five years live in a small town in Illinois surrounded by cornfields. Together, they raised three children to be better adults than themselves, their greatest feat.

If she is not traveling to faraway places, a mountain, or a beach, she's planning her next adventure. When Cherie is at home, she plays games with her two grandchildren, tames her extensive garden, or reads other authors' words.

Please leave a review on Amazon or Goodreads. Every review has a tremendous impact for authors. Share a few lines about your favorite parts.

Find out more about Cherie at https://cherieroberson.com/
Follow her on social media.

facebook.com/cherierobersonwrites
twitter.com/crr3bears
instagram.com/cherierobersonwrites

Printed in Great Britain
by Amazon